—— A NOVEL ——

FEW ARE
CHOSEN

GREG MAHER

ISBN: 978-1-4866-2524-6
eBook ISBN: 978-1-4866-2525-3

Word Alive Press
119 De Baets Street Winnipeg, MB R2J 3R9
www.wordalivepress.ca

WORD ALIVE
—P R E S S—

Cataloguing in Publication information can be obtained from Library and Archives Canada.

To my wife—my life, my all, my everything.
It is with her loving encouragement that I move forward with my writing.

PROLOGUE

Sunday

The decision I'm making will change my life forever.

The sky is a shade of blue I've never appreciated before. Thousands of diamonds sparkle as the breeze makes its way across the surface of the lake in which I'm immersed. Quiet surrounds me and nature, feeling the moment, cooperates with a hush that is almost deafening. Peace extends outward from a place deep within me, a place I would like to think is my soul.

The Lord touched me earlier that morning as the church service ended. I took the first step into the aisle that led me to the front, where I professed my belief in Jesus Christ as my Lord and Savior. I repented of my sins and expressed my desire to be immersed in the waters of baptism.

I can't explain it, but the whole day has a surreal quality I will never forget.

The shore is lined with those who are about to become my brothers and sisters in Christ. Although they're singing hymns of praise to the Lord, I'm lost to the world around me, totally immersed in the joy I'm feeling. I barely hear the words spoken by our minister, Dave. They come as though through a fog. He's asking questions, and the answers form in my subconscious and somehow make their way to my lips.

The waves that were once lapping against my chest now cover me. I hear more words, this time muffled by water.

"I baptize you in the name of the Father and of the Son and of the Holy Spirit."

When my head emerges, air fills my lungs just as it would for a newborn baby, which is exactly what I am. I've been immersed and raised to walk in a newness of life. The air feels different, surrounding me as a cleansed spiritual being ready to take on the world in the name of the Lord.

PART ONE
A FLASH OF LIGHT

ONE

Wednesday

Three days later, I still feel the joy of knowing that I'm closer to my Lord and God than at any other time in my life. I'm basking in that feeling of happiness.

However, a disturbance in my consciousness makes me feel as though I've missed something. What it is, I can't say. But I'm preoccupied about it.

I ask my big sister Debbie whether she saw anything out of the ordinary at the baptism, but she just assures me that the entire ceremony was beautiful. She is so happy for me.

Then I ask my friends from youth group—Matt, Brian, Gary, and Glen. They give me a similar, although less flowery, answer.

I even ask my parents. Dad didn't see anything strange, though, and adds that he's just glad I made the decision. He tells me this is the biggest and best decision a person can make. Mom tears up and gives me another great big hug, blubbering some more about how much she loves me.

Tonight at youth group I'm going to ask our youth minister, Derrick. Pastor Dave will be there too.

But that's for tonight. Right now it's time to go fishing.

I dug up worms last night, and I always dig more than I need because Matt, my fishing buddy and best friend, has a hard time finding worms at his place for some reason. I'm pretty sure I know the reason; he's just too lazy to grab the shovel and do the work.

He's a good friend, though, and I don't mind digging up the worms that are so plentiful down by our garden. In fact, I almost enjoy it, because it means I'll soon be back on the riverbank fishing. I do love fishing.

"Matt's here!" calls Mom from the kitchen.

"Okay, I'll be right down."

Grabbing my fishing hat off the back of the bedroom door, I head downstairs. I find Matt sitting at the kitchen table with a tall glass of cold lemonade in front of him and a plate of Mom's chocolate chip cookies, fresh from the oven—or should I say, half a plate.

"Eat fast or fill your pockets," I say. "It feels like the fish are waiting to come home for supper today and we don't have time for you fillin' your face. So let's go!"

He gets up with a grimace and puts a handful of cookies in his pocket before turning for the door and grabbing his fishing rod. I scoop up what's left of the cookies to stuff into my own pockets. He exits and I'm right behind him, rod in hand.

As we head down the driveway, he turns and walks back to me. "Where we goin' anyway?"

"I thought we'd go down to the old sawmill. The last time I was there, the trout were jumpin' all over the place but weren't biting at spinners or worms. Fly season is mostly over, so I hope worms will be on their menu today." I paused. "Oh, by the way, where are your worms?"

"I dug and dug and dug and only came up with a few. I hoped you had enough for both of us."

I laugh. "No worries, I've got you covered."

Like I hadn't expected that.

It's a good couple of miles to the river and then another half-hour down-stream to the old mill. Once we get there, I let Matt pick the spot where he wants to try first. I'm glad when it turns out to be a different location than the one I have my eye on.

As I get settled into my spot, I bait my hook and make my first cast.

I love fishing for a whole lot of reasons. First, you're communing with nature. Whether on the riverbank or shore of a lake, you're away from what passes for civilization these days. I have to get away from the noise of traffic and hubbub of people milling about doing whatever it is they think they have to do, even though they don't really enjoy it… but it puts food on the table, two cars in the yard, and cable on the television.

Me, I just sit there on a rock with my fishing rod in hand and absorb the peace God provides. The calming ripple of the water as it makes its way slowly toward the Atlantic is joined by the sound of robins singing their sweet melody. I hear the leaves rustle on the gentle breeze and, in the distance, the excited chatter of a squirrel as it scolds an intruder that's transgressed on his peace and quiet. Life is good.

Then reality wakes me up.

I've been daydreaming while at the same time reeling in my line. It's just something you do automatically, like a muscle memory.

Today's fishing rods are designed to relay sensitive changes. Mine jumps ever so slightly in my hands and I snap to full awareness. Adrenaline fires up my nerve endings as I tense for another, hopefully more significant tug through line and rod.

There it is! The rod responds with an exciting bend.

"Got one!"

Matt gives me a thumbs up from twenty feet away. From the firm pressure, I know this is a good-sized fish. Then, confirming my suspicions, I hear the line play out as the drag sizzles. Never has that happened to me before. What have I hooked?

Matt is watching. I can see him out of the corner of my eye. He knows from the bend of the rod and telltale sound of the drag that I've hooked something bigger than we're used to. This is shaping up to be a personal best.

Keeping the tip of the rod up, as I learned early in my fishing education, I slowly gain on this unseen monster of the deep. Closer it comes.

I see a flash of silver as sunlight plays off the reflective scales below the surface. The sight triggers a memory, one I didn't know existed. I'm taken back to that day, back to the lake, back to my baptism… and there it was: a flash of light.

But what caused it, where did it come from, and why am I remembering it now? All these thoughts jam themselves through my consciousness and I lose focus on what's happening in real time. In a momentary lapse of concentration, I stop reeling in what I feel is probably the biggest fish I've ever hooked in my life. I let the tip of the rod dip…

…and there I stand with no fish on the line, no bend to the rod, no resistance at the reel, and no sizzle from the drag.

"What the heck happened?" Matt says excitedly. "You had him! I've been fishing with you all my life and I never in all my days saw you give up on a fish! That is, until today. Again, I'm asking: what happened?"

Taking a deep breath, I sit back on the rock. I wasn't even aware that I stood up.

"I don't know," I say, red-faced.

"What does that mean, you don't know? I saw you! You just gave up! You were doing great… you had him… and then you just stopped reeling him in. You let the rod sag in your hands. Just like that, the fish was gone and you had this blank look on your face." Matt couldn't seem to let this go. "You had him! And you don't know? You feelin' okay?"

I don't know what he wants to hear. "I just lost my focus for a couple of seconds."

I hope he won't ask any more questions… questions I'm not sure I can answer. Maybe I don't even want to.

As luck would have it, he chooses to travel a different road: a road of torment and teasing.

"You just lost what was probably a monster of a fish of a lifetime, because you what? Fell asleep?" He laughs. "You dummy! I can't wait to tell everyone at youth group what the great fisherman did today. He had a brain fart and it cost him a trophy fish. Ha!"

"Well, that fish might still be around. All your hootin' and hollerin' isn't going to help any, so what do you say we get our lines back in the water and see if one of us can hook him again?"

Just like that, Matt goes back to his spot. With hope in his eyes and focused hands, he puts on a new worm. He casts out and waits.

The rest of the afternoon passes quietly. We catch some nice fish, but nothing as big as the one I lost. We stop every now and then and have some of Mom's cookies and chat about what we'll be doing at youth that evening. It's a good day. We keep some fish, releasing others.

We also talk about my decision to get baptized and why I finally did it.

As the shadows lengthen, we decide it's time to head home. Like the walrus and the carpenter, we talk of many things on the journey back. As we part company in front of my house, after dividing up the fish, I go inside.

TWO

"Caught supper for tonight, Mom," I say as I put a line of fish on the sideboard.

"First, you know that I don't want raw fish on my sideboard," she says. "Second, you and your father both know the rules. You catch them. You clean them. I cook them. And we all eat them. So, mister, the knife is in the drawer. Take them out to the shed and take care of the second part of step two."

I laugh as I grab the knife out of the drawer and, fish in hand, walk to the shed.

As I'm cleaning what promises to be a very tasty supper, my thoughts drift back to the events of the afternoon. Why did the flash of silver in the water trigger my memory? What was that flash? Why didn't I remember it happening on Sunday? Why did it seem so important? Lots of questions with no answers!

After finishing up with the fish, I wash my hands, clean up the workbench, and head back to the house.

Mom takes the fish and asks whether boiled potatoes and carrots fresh from the garden will work well as side dishes. I ask her if it would be too much trouble to make mashed potatoes. They're my favorite.

"Since you're supplying the main attraction, and I know how much you enjoy my mashed potatoes, I guess that's not an unreasonable request," she says. "So mashed it is. Supper's in about an hour. Your father and sister should be home by then."

"I'm going up to my room to read the scriptures for tonight's lesson at youth group. Give me a call when supper's ready."

After I've read scripture for a while, I take some quiet time for myself. I keep running through what happened on Sunday and then today, trying to tie the two together. It doesn't work, though. I know something happened at my baptism, but I have no idea what it is. So far nobody's been able to shine any light on the subject.

So what do I do now? I do what I always do when I have a problem I can't solve: I turn to God. I get down on my knees and first give thanks for the life and breath He gives me every day. Then I ask Him for help solving this puzzle that has gotten bigger but no clearer.

Finally, I recite my favorite passage of scripture. Psalm 23.

"The Lord is my shepherd, I lack nothing. He makes me lie down in green pastures, he leads me beside quiet waters, he refreshes my soul. He guides me along the right paths for his name's sake. Even though I walk through the darkest valley, I will fear no evil, for you are with me; your rod and your staff, they comfort me. You prepare a table before me in the presence of my enemies. You anoint my head with oil; my cup overflows. Surely your goodness and love will follow me all the days of my life, and I will dwell in the house of the Lord forever."[1]

I don't know why that seems to help, but it does. It takes the edge off the urgency I'm starting to feel about this whole thing. I remember what Dad used to say: "Put it in God's hands and He'll take care of it." I have never met a wiser man.

"Come on down and wash up," Mom calls. "Supper's ready!"

"Be right there!"

I hadn't realized how hungry I am. All that fresh air and excitement back on the river has whipped my appetite into a frenzy.

I'm not long getting my feet under the table, prepared to do justice to the meal before me. That is, after we say grace and give thanks to He who provides.

My mom is a great cook and I don't know how she does it or where she learned. Grandma is a good cook too, but Mom is *great*. Dad and Debbie comment on the trout and we talk about my trip down to the river. They ask about where we caught the fish, who I went with, and how long we were there.

I intentionally forget to mention the part about the big one that got away. They all would have teased me. Fishermen are notorious for stories about the ones that have gotten away, and for some reason the one that got away gets bigger with each retelling of the story.

I'm also worried they may ask questions I can't answer.

Everyone talks about their day. Debbie went to the grocery store in town and Dad drove to work at the local airport.

Mom looks at the clock. "If you two are going to make it to youth, you better get a move on."

---

[1] Psalm 23:1–6.

Debbie and I excuse ourselves and hurry up to our rooms to get our Bibles. It won't be a long walk to get to church, so we leave right after telling our parents to expect us home around ten o'clock.

On the way, we pass Matt's house. He's been watching the road and comes out to join us as we go by. Usually Leah walks with us too; she lives next door and is Debbie's best friend. But today her mother took her to visit her grandmother. They won't be back until nighttime.

"Was starting to think you weren't coming," says Matt. "It's getting late."

"We were enjoying those trout you guys caught," Debbie says. "We lost track of time."

"Did Captain Ahab tell you about losing Moby Dick?" Matt laughs.

"What are you talking about?" Debbie asks.

"What? He didn't tell you about losing probably the biggest fish he's ever had on his line? He didn't say a word about falling asleep while a trophy fish made its escape? Surprise, surprise, surprise! Well, I'm here to let the whole world know that James Jeffries is not the greatest fisherman in the world... although I still don't think he'll admit it."

Debbie gives him an exasperated look. "That still doesn't tell me what the heck you're talking about."

But they were almost there and Matt decided the whole story—one of fact, not fiction—would take too long to tell.

"I'll tell you after," Matt says.

Debbie sighs. "Boy, you've got my curiosity piqued. This better be good."

I just walk along, not saying a word, mostly because I don't know what to say. This seems to be a recurring theme the last couple of days. I'm not used to it.

We get to the church and gather as usual in the assembly hall. The evening starts with prayer, a song, and the collection.

Derrick, our youth minister, stands. "Tonight we have in our midst a new-born. James, stand up and meet all your new brothers and sisters. How does it feel to be a newborn? I know I speak for the whole group when I tell you how truly happy we are for you. We'll always be here for you, whether it relates to body or soul. A round of applause for your new brother, please."

Everyone claps and we hug and laugh. People make good-natured jokes about me being a baby.

Then we break into small groups. Ours goes to the junior youth room, where we settle down to our lesson on Acts 3 and how much trouble Peter and John got into for doing God's work. It's also about how much trouble we can get into for doing the same thing in the world we live in.

Taking turns, we read portions of scripture and then engage in an open debate on what it means and how it can be applied today. We always have good discussions, and someone always wants to play devil's advocate to liven things up.

I can't say that I'm fully invested in the lesson. I have too much on my mind. How am I going to approach Derrick with the questions I have about what happened on Sunday? Maybe I'll get him and Dave so I can talk to them together. Two heads are better than one, right?

All the while, I watch as Debbie impatiently glances at Matt and makes questioning faces and gestures. I know that I'm due for a little discomfort later, especially when all she gets from Matt is a smile and a hand held up to simulate a stop sign. Talk to the hand. He's living in his glory. He loves being the center of her attention.

As we finish the lesson, Derrick asks me to close in prayer. Everyone bows their heads.

"Heavenly Father, we thank You for this day and for Your Son and Your Word. We pray that by looking into Your Word we will be better able to see the path You've laid out for each of us to follow. We know that every person has a different path that takes them in different directions, but we also know You have given us the Truth, the Life, and the Way to guide us all to the same destination. Please bless us and protect us. In Jesus's name we pray, amen."

With that, everyone starts talking to the one next to them or across the table. It gets a little noisy sometimes.

Debbie gets up and heads for Matt. He sees her coming and immediately stands up.

"I have a story to tell you guys about one of our group," he says in his most authoritative voice. "It happened back on the river today."

Everyone gets quiet. He has everyone's attention.

"Our newest Christian and self-proclaimed fisherman of renown went fishing today with his less than professional sidekick, me. On his first cast, he hooks what we're both sure is a monster of a trout. 'Got one!' he tells me and I turn to see a fishing rod bent further than I thought possible without breaking. I know he's excited. I know *I'm* excited! If his adrenaline's pumping anything like mine, he must be ready for a heart attack. I hear his spool sing as the drag lets out... he cranks the handle to keep pressure on the line. I see him keep the tip of the rod high to prevent losing this monster of the deep… he's making progress and the battle seems to be on his side."

The room is dead quiet. Matt sure is able to hold an audience!

I happen to notice my sister looking at me while Matt regales the others with the fish story.

"Then the strangest thing happens," continues Matt. "He falls asleep. He'll tell you that he just lost focus, but I watched as this blank look came over his face. He stopped reeling in that fish of his—and my dreams too, I have to add. The rod dips until it almost gets wet. I almost cry when the rod straightens out and the line goes slack. It's over! My excitement crushed! What's just happened? 'I don't know,' he says. Well, I'll tell you this much: moments like this don't present themselves very often and you better be ready when they do. I guess Bob Izumi shouldn't feel threatened just yet. The end!"

Laughter breaks out all around me and I join in. What else can I do? People are slapping me on the back and punching me in the arm, all in good-natured fun.

Glen and Brian and Gary are among my most vocal tormentors. They all want to go back to the river tomorrow to watch me lose another big fish.

"Not often someone else tells the story of the one that got away from a fellow fisherman." Gary laughs. "Usually they want to do their own bragging."

"Falling asleep?" Glen says. "Whatever it was you did, it's not usually part of the story."

Brian piles on. "Is there another version where you actually see the monster and it has big red eyes and bushy eyebrows?"

"Okay, you guys. Have your fun," I say, trying to turn this into just another humorous story. "But I really did hook the biggest fish I never did see and that's the truth. You heard it from Matt, who never embellishes the truth. Right!"

By this time, Debbie has made her way to my side. Being my sister and a female, she has more questions. Questions I definitely don't want to discuss in a large group like this.

"Why didn't you say something at supper? How big was this fish? What caused you to lose it? Did you fall asleep? Why'd you lose focus?"

I don't have to answer any of them because she doesn't give me a chance.

Realizing that there's not going to be any time to talk to Derrick tonight, I pull him aside and ask whether he has anything up the next day.

"Not much," he replies. "Why? What's on your mind?"

"Well, I'm not going to ask you to go fishing, if that's what you're thinking. But I do have a few questions I hope you can help me answer. A puzzle I need help with."

"I do love a good puzzle. And you know me, I'm full of useless information." He laughs. "What time do you want to get together and where?"

"How about my place around 9:30? Mom made a whole batch of chocolate chip cookies today and I bet we can put a sizable dent in them tomorrow. If Dave's not busy, you can bring him along too. The more, the merrier. Some of this is heavy duty, I think."

"Boy! Now you have my curiosity piqued. I'll ask him. We'll see you around 9:30, if all goes to plan. Okay?"

Debbie catches up with me at that point. With Matt in tow, we head for home.

"Wasn't too hard on you tonight, was I?" Matt asks.

"If you're picking on me, it means you're leaving someone else alone," I reply, making myself sound like a martyr. "Besides, laughter is the best medicine. And I figure you added a couple of years to everyone's life with that fishy tale you told."

"Hold on there, good buddy. You know as well as I do that most, if not all, of that story is fact. There are questions, some of which I'm still waiting for answers to. I just added a little color commentary for effect."

Before I can get another word out, Debbie interrupts from the peanut gallery.

"Matt! You're going to have to wait for those answers. I've got a whole lot of questions of my own and family comes first. And don't even try to argue!"

We've reached the front of Matt's house.

"Just give me a couple of days to try to figure all this out," I say. "Then I'll fill you in."

"I don't understand. What's so complicated?" sputters Matt. "It was just a fish. Wasn't it?"

Debbie looks at me first, then at Matt. "Let's give him a break. If he wants a few days, we'll give him a few days. But then we want some answers."

Matt goes into his house and Debbie and I continue homeward. It's an awfully quiet trip and I know it's eating her up inside. I'm sure she's thought up a dozen or more additional questions by now.

As we get to our driveway, she stops and faces me.

"You've got two days. Then I want to know what's going on. And don't think that this is going away. Something's up and I don't like being in the dark. You're my brother and I worry about you, you big jerk."

"Try not to worry. There's nothing to worry about, to the best of my knowledge. I'm just a little confused." I smile. "I know you're there for me just like I'd be there for you."

Into the house we go.

"How was youth tonight?" Mom asks.

"Great!" we say in unison. I look at Debbie and she smiles and gives me an assuring wink.

Sitting with Mom and Dad, we watch a little TV before hitting that wall that says bedtime.

When we became teenagers, our parents told us we were responsible for the amount of sleep we got at night, so our bedtimes are self-regulated. Don't get me wrong! We weren't just let loose without a lesson in the responsibility that comes with that kind of freedom. There was no sleeping until noon. No shirking our duties around the house. No skipping out on our jobs. And most importantly, no complaining about how tired we were. We took this verbal contract very seriously.

After hugs all around, and a chorus of good nights, we head off to bed.

It's about 11:30 when I slip beneath the sheets. By the time the clock radio reads 2:30, I still haven't fallen asleep. Thoughts keep swirling around in my head.

What am I going to say to Derrick? What am I going to say to Dave? Will they have any answers? What am I going to tell Debbie and Matt in two short days? Do I have anything to worry about? If not, why am I not asleep yet?

I remember that I'm supposed to put everything in His hands. I recite Psalm 23 in my head and then decide to read a little scripture to calm me some more.

As I pick up my Bible, I flip it open, not looking for a specific chapter or verse; I let things fall where they may, so to speak.

I turn on the reading light on my bedside table and look to see what scripture I've turned to. It's Revelation 20 and the subtitle catches my eye: "The Dead Are Judged."

Interesting, I think, *but probably not something that will bring on sleep real quick.*

I've got to play by my own rules, though. I can't just look for another verse because I don't find this random choice appealing.

When I look at the page, the verse that catches my eye is one at the bottom:

> Anyone whose name was not found written
> in the book of life was thrown into the lake
> of fire.[2]

Don't ask me why I notice this one. I already have enough questions. But this piece serves as the proverbial flock of sheep I've been looking to count. Shutting off my light, I drift off into what turns into a comfortable and peaceful sleep.

---

[2] Revelation 20:15.

THREE

I didn't set the alarm. It's not very often that I do. For years I've relied on my internal clock to get me up when I have a deadline—and this morning isn't a problem. I'm not one of those people who can sleep half the day away, nor would I want to. It also helps that the morning sun, depending on the time of year, shines directly into my bedroom window, which extends from the ceiling almost to the floor.

Rolling out of bed at 6:45, I walk down the hall to take care of mother nature, wash my hands, and head downstairs for breakfast.

"Good morning, Mom!"

"Morning, son!"

"Did I tell you last night that Derrick and Pastor Dave are coming over around 9:30 and that I promised them some of your chocolate chip cookies?"

"You did not. Let me look and see how many cookies are left. Your father always puts some in his lunch when he goes to work, but I think there should be plenty." She checks inside one of her cookie jars. "Yes, there are. It's a good thing I made an extra-large batch yesterday. Why are Derrick and Pastor Dave coming over?"

"We're just going to talk over some questions I have concerning my baptism. That's all."

"Has it got anything to do with that feeling you had that something strange happened?"

Are all moms psychic, or is it just mine? You can't slip anything past her.

"Might have," I say in a noncommittal way.

"If there's any way your father and I can help, just sing out and we'll see what we can do."

"I know I can always count on you guys, and Debbie too. But this time I wanted to call in the big guns just for my own satisfaction."

I heat up some water and grab a glass and bowl from the cupboard. Opening the fridge, I take out the orange juice. From the middle canister on the counter, I scoop out a cup of instant oats, and from the largest canister I take some brown sugar to sprinkle on top while I wait for the water to boil.

A few minutes later, I'm sitting at the table to eat my oatmeal.

"What are you up to today, Mom?"

"Oh, cooking and cleaning, trying to keep you and your sister presentable. Heaven knows that one of you is a full-time job, let alone two. After lunch, I'm going to ladies quilting club at church. What about the rest of your day?"

"Well, I thought I'd stack some of that firewood Jeremy brought over, and after lunch I'll mow the lawn. It's starting to look a little shaggy. Can't have people thinking we don't care how things look. Especially when I'm the one responsible for the grass."

Mom looks out at the driveway. "Car's coming up. That's probably Pastor Dave and Derrick. I don't think you're going to get any firewood stacked this morning..." She stands up. "Don't forget to offer them tea or coffee to go with those cookies. I'll make myself scarce so you have some privacy."

As she closes the door and goes into the laundry room, I hear a knock at the front of the house.

"Come in," I call. "It's open."

"Hi James! How are you?" asks Pastor Dave with that big smile on his face that never seems to vanish, except when he gets into a sermon on sin and temptation.

Derrick is right behind him and voices a hello as big as his six-foot-four stature.

"I'm good," I say. "Mom says if I was any better, there would have to be two of me. And the world just couldn't stand that."

To which we all laugh.

I invite them into the kitchen and tell them to take a seat. At the same time, I offer tea or coffee or something cold with the cookies I promised. After getting their beverages of choice, I place the whole canister of cookies in the middle of the table.

I pour myself a tall, cold glass of milk. In my mind, that's truly the only appropriate drink suitable to wash down homemade cookies.

"Enough stalling," says Derrick. "You said you have something on your mind. Questions and a puzzle, if my mind serves me correctly. What's up?"

"I don't know where to start. It all seems a little crazy and it doesn't make sense."

Pastor Dave spoke in his easy-mannered, comforting voice. "Just take a deep breath and start at the beginning. When did all this start?"

I take that deep breath and swallow hard. "On the afternoon I got baptized, something was off. And when I say off, I have no idea what I mean. It was just a feeling. Not a bad feeling, mind you, but still a feeling. You know, like when a character on *Star Wars* says there's a disturbance in the Force. I've asked Mom and Dad and my sister and some friends and no one noticed anything. No one can help me out. But I still have that feeling. Then Matt and I went fishing yesterday and the strangest thing happened. Derrick, you heard Matt's story about the one I let get away. There's more to it." I take another deep breath. "Okay, here goes. When I was trying to reel in that fish, something happened. I saw the side of the fish flash in the sunlight and all of a sudden I was back to Sunday morning, under the water, while Pastor Dave was baptizing me. I saw a flash of light just like that fish, only brighter. I didn't even remember seeing it until I was fishing with Matt. How come? What's going on?"

I stop talking and look at the both of them, waiting for them to say something brilliant that will explain everything.

At first, they just sit there. Then they look at each other and I assume they're deciding who should jump in first.

Pastor Dave, being the more senior of the two, takes the lead.

"When you said you had a puzzle and questions, you weren't kidding, were you?" he says. "I don't know what to tell you. Is this some sort of sign? And if so, a sign of what? I'm sorry, James, but at this point I can't offer any logical explanation as to what happened or why it happened. What about you, Derrick?"

"I'm afraid I don't have anything to add," Derrick says. "I think the answers are in the puzzle, but we don't have enough pieces to even begin to put it together yet."

"I don't want to make light of this, but it could be a coincidence," adds Pastor Dave. "Your mind could be making connections that aren't really there. They may seem real, but the mind can play some tricks on us. I'm not saying this is what happened, but it could explain it. What do you think, Derrick?"

Derrick inclines his head in thought. "I've known you for the last five years, James, since three years before you were even old enough to come to youth group. You are not a person given to wild stories. You're a level-headed young man. I'm certain that everything happened just as you say it did. Could it be, though, that in the excitement of the moment, and in the emotional state of your baptism, that Pastor Dave is right? Heightened awareness, the joy of the moment, the singing... it could have had an effect on your state of mind."

"I don't know," I say. "It all seemed so real. You think I imagined the whole thing?"

"We didn't say that," Pastor Dave clarifies. "We're just saying it's a possibility, be it right or wrong. Who's to say?"

I nod. "I guess I'll just have to wait and see if any more pieces of the puzzle fall into place. If nothing else happens, I'll just accept that it was a heat-of-the-moment thing." I don't know what else to say. "Anyone want a refill? There are lots of cookies left."

"No thanks," says Pastor Dave. "I think we'll be on our way. I wish we could have been more helpful. Let us know if anything else happens, okay?"

"Thanks for coming and listening. I wish I had more to give you."

"I think we should pray about this first." The pastor bows his heads and we follow suit. "Heavenly Father, we come to You at this time as Your humble servants. Our brother James has some questions and we don't seem to have the answers. We pray that You will help him through this time and supply him with the answers he seeks. May You use Derrick and myself in any way that might help young James. Lord, we submit ourselves to Your will. Guide and direct us and at last save us in the name of Jesus Christ our Lord and Savior."

To which we all add, "Amen."

As they're heading out the door, Pastor Dave turns to me one last time. "Remember, the Lord works in mysterious ways. Even though sometimes we don't understand why, we have to accept it and know that He will never give us more than we can handle. Always remember the verse of scripture that says, 'I can do all this through him who gives me strength.'[3] Pray about this and it will resolve itself."

"Amen to that!" says Derrick.

Off they go, leaving me to feel maybe a little better—but that's a slim maybe. The parting words bring more comfort than the rest of the conversation.

What do I do now? I guess I'll just have to wait and see.

I go to the laundry room door and tell Mom that we're done and my guests are gone.

"How did it go?" Mom asks.

"Pretty good." I want to avoid a bunch of questions that Mom probably won't be able to help with, especially if a minister and a youth minister can't. "What's for lunch?"

"Sandwiches. You sort of occupied the kitchen for most of the morning. Go next door and tell your sister that lunch is at twelve. She went over to help

---

[3] Philippians 4:13.

Leah with a video game she's playing. You know how good your sister is at those things."

Out the door I go. The Scanlons have been our neighbors since before I was born and Debbie and their daughter Leah have been best friends since their days in the playpen together.

I'm about to knock on the front door when I hear Mrs. Scanlon hollering from the kitchen: "Come on in, James. I saw you coming down the walk. The girls are upstairs in Leah's room."

Upstairs, I find Leah and Debbie lying on the bed giggling.

"What are you two up to?" I ask. "I thought you were playing video games."

"We were, but we got tired of it," says Leah. "We've just been talking."

"What was so funny? When I came to the door, you two were yukking it up…"

Debbie smiles. "Oh, you know, just boy talk."

"Nuf said. Mom wanted me to tell you that lunch's at noon. We're having sandwiches."

"Thanks. I'll be home in time."

Leah breaks in. "Oh, by the way, James, we're going to the Sand Bed for a swim tomorrow morning, if you're interested."

"Sure am! Temperature's supposed to be in the high twenties with a humidex in the mid-thirties… a morning in the lake would be a treat."

"Not to mention the company, right?" Leah asks.

"Too true. As soon as I get home, I'll call Matt and the rest of the guys. We'll have a great time." I head out the door, calling over my shoulder, "See you tomorrow!"

Leah looks sadly at Debbie. "Your brother can be a little thick sometimes."

"Aren't you the master of the understatement. A little? Ha! But he is a boy, after all."

At which point they both break out in laughter.

The rest of the day goes as any other day—uneventfully. I get the firewood stacked and the lawn mowed. Then I call all my buddies and tell them about swimming. They're all on board.

First, though, I okay it with Mom. Sometimes you have to keep your parents in the loop or they get upset and start to worry. Wouldn't want that to happen.

FOUR

The next morning, Debbie and I are anxious to get going. It's going to be a great day!

The Sand Bed is on Lewis Lake, which is also where our church holds its baptisms every summer. The church does have a baptistry, but most people opt for the lake when the weather's nice; it feels more like the kind of baptisms found in the Bible, more natural.

The lake is about three and a half miles away, so we decide to ride our bikes. Leah's going to ride with us and Matt will join as soon as we pass his place.

After placing towels and everything else we'll need in our backpacks, Debbie and I head for the door.

"Just a minute you two!" Mom says.

"What, Mom?" I whine. "We're ready to go. Leah and Matt are waiting…"

She hands me a bag. "I just thought I'd pack a little lunch for you and your friends."

I look inside and find that it's packed with cookies and homemade doughnuts covered with icing sugar.

"You're the best," I say as I stuff it into my backpack. I have to give her a big hug, but then we're off.

Leah falls in behind us as we pass, as does Matt when we get to his place. I normally take the lead on a ride like this, and things are normal. Somehow, though, Debbie falls back and Leah rides up beside me.

We soon arrive at the lake, although we aren't the first to get there. Gary and Brian, along with a couple of the girls from youth, Allison and Cheryl, showed up ahead of us.

"Last one in's a rotten egg!" I yell as I drop my bike and backpack and sprint to the water.

That starts a stampede and soon we're all in the water, with no one noticing or caring who the last one in was. We play frisbee football, then partner up and play piggyback dunk. Somehow Leah ends up my partner; I'm not really sure how that happened. Matt partners up with Debbie, and boy does that girl have a competitive streak like you wouldn't believe. Partnered with Matt, who's like a bull in the woods, they win hands down.

Sitting on towels and blankets afterward we tell jokes, laugh, torment one another, share the lunch Mom packed, and just plain have a good time. The morning goes by too fast and it's soon time to leave. But I decide to go for one more swim.

"Want a race?" Matt asks.

"Okay, but you know that I'm a better swimmer than you."

Gary chimes in too. "Brian and I are in!"

"Sure, but there will be no mercy shown," I say in my most serious voice. "Debbie will you do the honors and be the starter and finish line judge."

We're going to race to the swimming platform, about a hundred feet off-shore, then go around it and get back to the beach. The winner gets the last two doughnuts Mom sent with us.

We line up on the sand with Debbie playing the part and lecturing us on the rules.

"No biting, gouging, kicking, or drowning your opponent. Does everyone understand the rules as laid out in the Geneva Convention? All right then. On your mark! Get ready! Get set! May the best brother win. Go!"

The water churns as the four of us hit it together. Not to boast, but I'm the best swimmer of the group by far. Taking the lead almost immediately, I make it to the platform, round it, and head for home with a two-length lead.

Then it happens again: a flash in the water. And it affects me the same way it did on the riverbank. I sort of lose focus. Mid-stroke, I just stop.

What is this? Something seems important, but for the life of me I don't know what it is.

The flash disappears as quickly as it came. I didn't even notice the others passing me, but suddenly they're almost at the beach. I take up the stroke again and head for shore.

I'm greeted with cheers and teasing.

"What happened to 'no mercy shown'?"

"Even the best swimmers have a bad day, but never that bad. Ha!"

"My, these are good doughnuts. Mm-mm-mm!" This comes from Gary, who finished first and is enjoying the prize Debbie awarded him.

I swallow my pride. "Good race, Gary. I guess the best man won."

I go over and shake his hand. Afterward I have to wash off the icing sugar.

"Guess we better get going, sis. Don't want to worry Mom."

"You're right," Debbie agrees. "Let's go."

All eight of us get our stuff together, mount our bikes, and head for home. I know I'm in for a question from the looks Debbie keeps giving me. So far she hasn't said a thing, but I know what's coming. I just don't know how I am going to handle it. I really don't know what is happening or why.

I don't have to wait very long. The surprising thing, though, is that the questions don't come from Debbie. They come from Matt, who was too busy swimming to even see me in the water.

"I don't know what's going on in the universe," he says. "First, the best fisherman I know loses probably the biggest fish either of us will ever have the opportunity to catch, because he just gave up. Then the same guy, who can swim circles around all of us, loses a race—and not only does he lose it, he comes in last! Who are you and what have you done to my best friend?"

Before I can answer, Debbie pipes up. "You were still swimming, Matt, so you didn't see what happened. If I had to put a label on it, I'd say he just gave up. Okay, mister, what's going on? You're not sick or anything, are you?"

Again, before I can say a word, Leah breaks in, almost in tears. "I don't understand any of this. What's going on?"

"Well, I can tell you all that I'm not sick, so you can stop worrying about that. And Leah, I told these two that I would fill them in in a couple of days. Well, that was two days ago, so I guess today's the day. But the time is not now. Let's get together at our house tonight—say, about seven—and I'll tell you more."

"If that's the best you can do, I guess it's okay," Debbie says.

When we get to Matt's house, he leaves us. "So long! See you tonight."

A moment later, Leah departs too, and Debbie and I are putting our bikes in the shed behind our place.

"You're telling the truth when you say you're not sick, right?" my sister asks in a concerned voice.

"No, sis, I'm not sick. I promise. Stop worrying your little head. It'll all be as clear as mud tonight."

I'm trying to add a little levity to put her at ease, but from the look on her face I don't think it has the desired effect.

"What do you want for lunch?" Mom asks when we step into the kitchen.

I smile. "Ooh, you mean there are choices?"

"You can go out to the garden and pull some beets. Or you could bring in a head of lettuce and some tomatoes for sandwiches. Your choice."

"It's too hot for cooking," Debbie says. "And you've already sweated over a hot stove most of the morning making the bread. Sandwiches sound good."

"Besides, who can say no to fresh homemade bread?" I say.

I head out to the garden at the back of the house and bring in a handful of leaf lettuce and two large tomatoes, handing them to Mom.

"I'll give these a quick wash and then it will be time to eat," Mom says.

"Mom, is it okay if Matt and Leah come over this evening?" I ask.

"Sure, they're always welcome."

The sandwiches are great and the homemade bread is filling. We finish with milk and cookies, after which I go back down to the garden to pull enough beets for the next day. I love buttered beets! I also pick some beans and peas, pull carrots, and dig a hill of potatoes for supper.

In the summertime, supper is Dad's favorite meal. He's been working overtime at the airport for a couple of months now due to a staff shortage. He should get some joy out of life, and I've been doing as much as I can around the house to help. So has Debbie. Being part of a family means being part of a team, and true love means seeing a need and diving in to fill that need without being asked. Our parents don't ask for much; doing a little extra is a labor of love.

It's still hours away from supper, so I grab my pail and head for the wild blueberry patch in the field behind the shed. Some people think I'm crazy, but I like picking blueberries. I find it therapeutic—well, that and Mom makes the best blueberry muffins on this or any other planet.

Picking blueberries gives one time to think, and I certainly need that. What am I going to tell Debbie, Matt, and Leah? I can't just wing it, can I?

After four quarts of berries and an hour of therapy, I decide that my best course of action is going to give them the hardest thing to deal with: the truth. The truth will set you free, right? Well, we'll find out tonight.

The rest of the afternoon goes by as most afternoons do, except with some anxiety lurking in the back of my mind about what the evening will bring.

I take the berries in and put them on the kitchen table.

Mom gives me a big grin. "What are you after? You know blueberry muffins are your father's favorite dessert, especially when they're made with fresh wild berries. I probably have just enough time to make a batch so that it's coming out of the oven when he gets home, hot and ready for a smearing of butter. I just hope it doesn't spoil his appetite. He deserves to be spoiled, though, the way he's been working."

I go up to my room and decide to read instead of playing video games like usual. I'm halfway through the latest issue of *Popular Sportsman*, checking out some great articles on east coast fishing, when I hear Mom's voice calling from downstairs.

"James, your father's home!"

"I'll be right down." I hurry down to the kitchen and see Dad sitting at the table. He's already buttering his second hot blueberry muffin.

"I've already thanked your mother for these blueberry muffins, but she tells me you and God supplied the berries," he says. "Thankful to you both. Would you like one?"

I look at Mom and get a nod of approval. "Sure."

Just then, Debbie gets home from her job as a part-time cashier at the local supermarket.

"Those look good!" she says, eyeing the muffins. "Can I have one? I'm starving!"

"Yes, you *may* have one," Mom says. "But don't you three ruin your appetites. We're having hodgepodge for supper and I don't like having leftovers. Supper's in five minutes, so go wash up."

Supper is as delicious as I thought it would be, and Dad and I are on our second helping when we hear a knock at the door. I get up to see who it is and am not surprised to see Matt at the door. He has a habit of showing up early. Granted, he's only fifteen minutes early, where it's usually a half-hour or more.

"Want to come in and have some blueberry muffins with us?" I ask. "Or you could go out back and wait in the gazebo."

He opted to take a blueberry muffin *and* wait out in the gazebo.

"Have it your own way. Leah's not here yet, but she should be soon. We're just about finished supper."

Back in the kitchen, Debbie and I finish our muffins and ask to be excused. Mom and Dad will probably have a cup of tea while sitting on the front veranda swing and telling each other about their day.

Debbie and I go out to the gazebo.

"I hope Leah gets here soon," Matt says, munching on his muffin.

"Not everybody is as early as you," I point out. "It's one minute to seven. She's still got sixty seconds."

"Who's got sixty seconds?" asks Leah as she rounds the corner of the house.

"You, that's who," says Matt. "We've been waiting."

"I'd have been here sooner, but Mrs. Jeffries stopped me and said I had to wait while she got me a muffin." She holds out her muffin. "See?"

Matt is almost drooling. "If you're not going to eat that, I'll take it."

"Put your gluttony on hold, Matt," says Debbie. "We have more important things to take care of. Little brother, you promised us an explanation about what's been going on."

"I don't know where to start," I say. "Each of you knows a little, but none of you know everything. When I'm done, you may be worse off than before."

"What's that supposed to mean?" questions Matt.

"Give him a chance and maybe we'll find out," Leah growls.

"You all remember my baptism, right? Well, do you remember me asking whether you noticed anything odd about that day? It wasn't just you guys I asked. I asked Mom and Dad, and after Wednesday night I asked Pastor Dave and Derrick too. I still had this feeling that something was wrong. But I guess *wrong* is the wrong word... I've just been feeling... off. I'm so confused. Matt and I went fishing Wednesday morning, and you all know how that went, or at least you know Matt's version. Yes, I lost focus on the fish... but the question is why. When I was reeling in the fish, I saw a flash of silver light. I assumed it was the sun reflecting off the scales of the fish, but I'm not really sure. I think I also saw a flash like that at my baptism. I saw it as clear as day." I look to my friend with an apologetic expression. "I'm sorry, Matt. I couldn't tell you the truth because I wasn't sure what happened. Pastor Dave and Derrick came over to talk to me, and the only explanation they could come up with was that maybe I imagined the whole thing. Even that's just a guess. Pastor Dave just reminded me that the Lord works in mysterious ways. Then we went swimming and I stopped in the middle of that race... well, the same thing happened as when I was reeling in that big fish. Another flash of light and then I just lost focus..."

Everyone was looking at me with confused looks on their faces.

"So that's the truth, the whole truth, and nothing but the truth—up to now at least. You can all stop worrying. That is, unless you think I'm going off the deep end. What do you think? Am I losing it?"

It took a moment for them to respond.

"Man, I don't know what to tell you," Matt said after thinking it over. "That's a lot to take in. How much have you told your parents?"

"I bet they don't know as much as we do," Debbie says, sounding almost upset. "They would want to know what's going on. Do you think it's fair not to tell them?"

I shrug. "Tell them what? That I may have imagined the whole thing? It's bad enough that I'm telling you guys, let alone pulling Mom and Dad into the picture."

"I still think they should know," Debbie insists.

"I'll think about it, but don't you say a word. This is a secret. I want to keep it between the four of us for now."

"What's the next step?" Leah asks quietly.

She had been so quiet that I'd almost forgotten that she was there. "What do you mean, next step?" I ask.

"Well, something's going on, and I don't think it's done yet," Leah says. She takes a few moments to repeat my story back to me, ticking off all the key details. "What other facts do we have?"

Debbie smiles at her best friend. "Wow! I'm impressed. Where did all that come from?"

"Solving video game mysteries," Leah says with a laugh.

I'm glad Leah has deflected the conversation away from the issue of talking to Mom and Dad, even though I know Debbie will press me on it again as soon as we're alone.

There's a pause in the conversation as we each put our grey matter to work trying to locate other pieces of the puzzle.

Matt is the first one to come up with an idea. "Each time this thing happens, it's around water. And it always connects back to your baptism."

"But no one remembers anything unusual from his baptism," Debbie reminded him, sounding frustrated. "It's not like we can go back in time!"

"I'm not talking about actually going back in time, silly girl. I'm talking about back to the lake and recreating the whole thing to see if anything happens. What have we got to lose?"

"You know, that's not a bad idea, Matt," Debbie says. "Even for you. By the way, call me a silly girl again and you'll need to seek medical attention."

"Okay, you two," I say, getting between them. "Let's go to the lake tomorrow. Everybody okay with going in the afternoon? Two o'clock at the Sand Bed?"

All our heads nod in excited agreement.

By now it's past ten o'clock and the sky is dark. Where has the time gone? It's time to call it a night.

"I don't know how you're going to sleep tonight," Leah says, looking into my eyes.

"The Lord is my Shepherd," I reply. Debbie gives me a questioning look. "The Twenty-Third Psalm is my go-to scripture when I have trouble getting to sleep. Works like a charm."

"I'll see you home," Matt says to Leah. "See you guys tomorrow. Stop by my place and we'll ride up together."

After accompanying them to the end of the driveway, Debbie and I turn back to the house. I can feel my sister's gaze fixed on my back.

"What?" I ask, turning to face her.

She sighs. "Don't think for a minute that the issue of telling Mom and Dad has gone away. I'll keep your little secret for now, but I make no promises down the road. The minute I think they need to know, they'll be told. Okay?"

"I guess I can't ask for anything more than that."

"You can ask, but you just won't get it."

"Love you, sis."

She smiles. "Love you too, little brother."

We go into the house and say good night to Mom and Dad while filling them in on our plans to head to the lake the following afternoon. After a round of hugs and kisses, Debbie and I go up to our rooms.

Once I've changed, I get on my knees to thank the Lord for life, breath, and a great day, but most importantly for His Son in whose name I pray.

As I slide between the sheets, I put my head on the pillow and close my eyes. My mind immediately takes me back to my baptism, then to the riverside, then to the beach... only for the whole sequence to replay all over again.

It's time for me to turn on my light and go to the Word to see if reading some scripture will help me calm down. I open by Bible to the Twenty-Third Psalm and read it, even though I have it memorized. Then I read Psalm 24 as well.

Putting my Bible down, I finally shut off the light and start the Lord's Prayer. I don't remember finishing it.

FIVE

Saturday

I wake around 6:30, get up, and have a shower. By the time I hurry downstairs, Dad has already left for work and Debbie is just about to go out the door. I look out into the yard and see her ride in the driveway.

"Have a good day!" I shout to Debbie as she gets into the car with her coworkers.

I sit down at the kitchen table, pour some cereal into a bowl, then add some blueberries and milk.

"What are you up to today?" Mom asks.

"Just going to laze around until lunch. Then we're off to the lake. Why? Is there anything you need done? I've got the morning clear."

"Nothing that comes to mind, but I'll be sure to let you know if I think of anything. I think I'm going to put up a couple of batches of pickled beets for the preserve cabinet."

"Guess I'll weed a bit in the garden," I say. "Then maybe I'll pick some more blueberries. It'd be nice to have a couple of bags in the freezer."

I don't tell her, but I want to spend the morning thinking about the afternoon's plans. As I've said, I find berry-picking therapeutic.

"You'll get no argument from me." Mom laughs. "The more in the freezer, the better the chance of muffins, pies, and grunts this winter. So knock yourself out!"

On my way out the back door, I grab my berry pail. My mind is already shifting to the coming afternoon.

When I arrive at the garden, I put down my pail and start pulling weeds in the two rows of carrots. I don't like weeding, finding it tedious, but it has to be done if you expect a good garden.

After about the fifth or sixth time of kneeling with a handful of weeds and not moving a muscle, I give up. I'm a lost cause. Grabbing my berry pail, I walk down to the berry patch, but I keep thinking about the mystery plaguing me. I replay the events of the previous night. It takes two scriptural sedatives to calm my buzzing mind.

It's about 10:30 when I go back up to the house with my pail half full. Mom is in the kitchen. She takes the pail and puts it in the fridge.

"Berries on their way out?" she asks.

"Getting there. Why?"

"You usually pick more than this in the time you were gone."

"I did some weeding first, but the berries are starting to thin out." I sigh. "I'm going upstairs to read for a while. Wake me up for lunch?"

"Sure. We'll have a sandwich and finish off the cookies. We wouldn't want them to go stale, would we? I'll make a couple of fresh batches this afternoon."

I chuckle as I head up the stairs. Flopping on my bed, I grab my Bible and ask God to help me with my problem. I also tell Him that I trust Him to take care of all my concerns.

Like most times, I let my Bible fall open to a random page and scripture. I look down and focus on Psalm 69:26–29:

> For they persecute those you wound and talk
> about the pain of those you hurt. Charge them
> with crime upon crime; do not let them share
> in your salvation. May they be blotted out of
> the book of life and not be listed with the righ-
> teous. But as for me, afflicted and in pain—
> may your salvation, God, protect me.

I find that a bit strange. The last time I did this, a scripture came up about the Book of Life. That was on Wednesday night.

Let's try this again and see what happens, I think to myself.

I place the Bible spine-down on the bed and let it fall open. I'm surprised to see that it again opens to a piece of scripture that mentions the Book of Life:

> Yes, and I ask you, my true companion, help
> these women since they have contended at
> my side in the cause of the gospel, along with
> Clement and the rest of my co-workers, whose
> names are in the book of life.[4]

---

[4] Philippians 4:3.

That's three for three. Now what? Should I try again?

I go through the same procedure, only this time I close my eyes when I let the Bible fall open. Almost nervously, I open my eyes to see the result. The book has opened to Revelation, just like it did on Wednesday night—or rather, Thursday morning. It's a different chapter, though.

> Nothing impure will ever enter it, nor will anyone who does what is shameful or deceitful, but only those whose names are written in the Lamb's book of life.[5]

Four for four! This is starting to get a little spooky.

I'm not a gambler by any stretch of the imagination, but I do understand how odds and streaks work. Right now I would say that somehow the odds aren't making a lot of sense.

How come the Book of Life keeps showing up in random scriptures? I've got to tell the others what's going on. I decide to try it again, only with the others around next time.

"Your sister's home and we're going to have lunch as soon as she washes up," calls Mom from downstairs.

"Okay, I'll wash up and be right down."

Debbie is already at the table when I take a seat. Mom asks me to say grace, so I bow my head and give thanks for all the blessings God has seen fit to bestow upon us. I ask Him to bless the food we're about to eat, the hands that have prepared it, and those who are going to partake of the food. With that, we dig in.

"How was work?" I ask Debbie.

"Pretty busy for a Saturday morning. Most people wait until the afternoon to pick up their groceries, but lately they've been coming in during the mornings. Probably trying to avoid the crowds later in the day." She turns to Mom. "I see you've been busy putting up pickles."

"By the way, you know that thing we've been working on?" I say. "I found something new we can add to it."

Debbie's eyes get big. It's a good thing Mom has gotten up to get her tea or she wouldn't have been able to miss it.

Mom sits down again. "You two still going to the Sand Bed this afternoon? It's cooled off a little and gotten cloudy."

---

[5] Revelation 21:27.

"Yep," I say. "Can we take a couple of sandwiches and cans of pop with us?"

"Yes, you may. Are you going to make the sandwiches or would you like me to?"

"I'll do it, Mom," says Debbie. "You've got enough to do already."

I stand up. "Okay, sis, get to it. I'll go get my backpack and put a couple of towels in it."

Going up to my room, I grab my backpack and put two towels on the bottom and my Bible on top. Next I put on my swimsuit.

By the time I head downstairs, Debbie is just finishing up the lunch and heads up to her own room to suit up. I pack the lunch in my backpack, then zip it up and get our bikes out of the shed.

Debbie doesn't take long and then we're off. Leah is waiting at the end of her driveway and falls in behind us.

"What were you talking about at lunch?" Debbie asks.

"Wait until we get to the lake," I say. "I don't want to have to repeat what happened more than once."

Minutes later, we get to Matt's. He's ready and waiting at the end of his driveway. He falls in beside Leah.

"You guys nervous?" Matt babbles. "Cuz I am. What do you think is going to happen? I hardly slept at all last night. Am I talking too much?"

"Yes, you are!" Debbie says. "Let's just get to the lake and see if we're making complete fools of ourselves or not. Okay? Besides, James has something new to add. But he won't say what it is until we get to the lake. So less talking and more pedaling."

"What do you mean, something new?" Matt asks excitedly.

I don't answer and Matt response by pedaling even harder. He shoots by the rest of us in his hurry.

It's not very long before we get to the lake. Because it's cloudy and a little on the cool side, there's nobody else at the Sand Bed. We have the whole beach to ourselves. We go down to the water's edge.

"This is it," I murmur.

"What about this breaking news you were talking about?" Matt sputters. "What's up with that? You said you would tell us when we got to the lake. Well, here we are!"

I turn back to the others. "Fine. I want to try something, to try duplicating something that's happened too many times in a row to be a coincidence."

I take the Bible out of my backpack, then look around the beach for a nice level spot for us all to sit. As they all watch, I hold the book an inch off the ground, spine-down. Then I gently drop it and allow the pages to fall open.

"Since you're the oldest, why don't you tell us what book and chapter my bible opened to," I say to Debbie.

She leans in. "Daniel 12."

This scripture isn't familiar to me. "Now read whatever jumps out at you," I say. "I'm not a hundred percent sure how this is going to turn out..."

Debbie starts to read: "'But at that time your people—everyone whose name is found written in the book—will be delivered.'"[6]

It's happened again!

I pick up my Bible and repeat the dropping sequence all over again. When it opens, Debbie starts to lean in again, but I stop her.

"Let's let Leah do the honors this time," I suggest.

Leah looks down at the open page and speaks almost timidly: "Revelation 21–22."

"Start reading from any place you choose," I say. "Your choice."

"Okay, let's see what this has to say: 'Nothing impure will ever enter it, nor will anyone who does what is shameful or deceitful, but only those whose names are written in the Lamb's book of life.'"[7]

"Stop there." I pick up the Bible again before any of them can say anything. I then do the same drop.

With the Bible lying open, the two girls seem to realize it's Matt's turn to see where it has opened this time.

He leans in and takes charge. "Philippians 4. You want me to read?"

I just nod.

"'I plead with Euodia and I plead with Syntyche to be of the same mind in the Lord. Yes, and I ask you, my true companion, help these women since they have contended at my side in the cause of the gospel, along with Clement and the rest of my co-workers, whose names are in the book of life.'"[8]

I put up my hand to stop him. "Anyone starting to see a pattern here?"

"The Book of Life," Debbie and Leah say together.

"Yeah, you're right," says Matt. "But are you sure it's not just a freak coincidence?"

I shrug. "Wanna go again, just for fun?"

---

[6] Daniel 12:1.

[7] Revelation 21:27.

[8] Philippians 4:2–4.

Matt nods. "Why not? Just one more time."

I pick up my Bible and do the same as before. When it falls open. I gesture to Matt. "You wanted this, Matt, so you get to do the honors."

He reads: "'Anyone whose name was not found written in the book of life was thrown into the lake of fire.'"[9]

"Now what do you think?" I asked.

He just looks at me and shakes his head.

"Okay, so the Book of Life keeps popping up and seems awful insistent," says Debbie. "But what has that got to do with flashing lights and water? Can anyone connect the dots for me?"

"No idea," I say. "But I just have this strange feeling that it's somehow connected."

"Well, isn't that why we came out here in the first place?" Debbie looks out towards the lake. "You ready for a swim?"

We walk as a group to the shore and step into the water, which is nowhere near as warm as it was the previous day.

I turn to my friends. "This all started the day I was baptized, so I'm going to walk out to about the same spot where that happened. I want one of you to come with me. The other two, stand off to either side so we have a couple of different angles. Okay?"

"I'm going with you!" says Matt.

Debbie and Leah spread out along the beach as Matt and I walk out into the lake. When we get to the spot where I figure the baptism took place, about chest deep, we stop.

"Anything yet?" Matt asks.

"Not a thing, except that I'm starting to shiver. I'm going to lay back in the water like when I was baptized and see if that makes any difference. Stay close, Matt."

I start to lean back in the water. It soon covers my shoulders, then my chin, and then my head is completely below the surface. Just like when I was baptized, I am immersed completely. All along, I feel the coldness of the water and listen for sounds around me. The waves lap against my skin and in the distance a crow calls from the shoreline. I also hear the sound of my friends' voices...

Abruptly that all stops. There is total silence, and with that absence of sound comes a bright light that fills my consciousness and brings with it a peacefulness I have never felt before. With my eyes open, I see light all around me. I recall once

---

[9] Revelation 20:15.

being told that drowning feels just like falling asleep… but the peace and warmth I feel won't allow any fear or anxiety creep into my mind.

I feel hands under my armpits and realize I'm being raised out of the water.

"You okay?" Matt's asking.

"Yeah, no problems at all," I reply. "Did you see that?"

"See what?"

"The light."

"No! Did you see the light again?"

"I sure did, but it was steady this time, not a flash. You didn't see anything?"

"No, not a thing." Matt looks back towards the beach. "How about you girls? Did you see anything?"

"We didn't see any light," Debbie says. "At least I didn't. How about you, Leah?"

"I didn't see any light either, but we all saw you go really limp and start to sink," Leah replies. "We thought maybe you passed out. I was scared you were going to drown."

"No fear of that. I'm part-fish," I assure them.

As I climb out of the water and onto the beach, Matt and I wrap ourselves in towels. I then sit down and they gather around me.

"So where does this leave us?" asks Debbie.

"I'm going back out there again. I know what I saw and felt. There's more to this and I want to find out what it is."

"Well, this time I'm going to be the one beside you," Debbie states firmly.

Matt seems worried. "What if he starts to have trouble again?"

"The truth is, I didn't have any trouble last time," I say. "You thought you saw me in trouble, but I was as happy as a clam. When you 'saved me,' did I come up gasping for air? Was I in any kind of distress?"

"No," Matt acknowledges.

"Then I figure it's okay if Debbie goes out with me this time."

"We're going to keep a close eye on you anyway," says Leah, still concerned. "And if we see anything that even hints at a problem, up you come!"

I get up and head back to the water, which doesn't seem as cold this time. Debbie follows at my side and Matt and Leah move off to either side.

As we get to the spot, I tell Debbie that this time, instead of lying back in the water, I'm going to go facedown.

"Why's that?" she asks

"Don't know. Just a feeling." I put my arms out to the side, then lower my face into the water. As I drop below the surface, I experience the same quietness as last time. Total silence, a warmth, that peacefulness... and then there it is: the bright light that fills my mind.

This time I notice a difference. My eyes are open and I can see the source of the light.

Gathering my feet under me, I stand up and wipe the water from my eyes. Debbie is looking at me with a great big question mark on her face.

"Well, what happened?" she asks.

"Same thing, but with a twist. The light seems to be coming from a spot just beyond where the bottom of the lake drops off. I'm going to dive down and get a closer look."

"You're not going anywhere without one of us, little brother!"

"Fine. You and I will take a closer look. Leah and Matt can keep watch from the beach." I point offshore a little ways. "That's the way I'm headed. You ready, Debbie?"

"I guess so."

We dive under the surface and swim down to the point where the lake bottom drops off. Just ahead, I see the light and feel that same sense of warmth and peace. I wonder, can Debbie feel it too?

The source of the light isn't far, and within seconds I'm right on top of it.

I can't believe what I'm seeing: it's a book, half-submerged in the mud. I look at Debbie, point up, and we both head back to the surface.

As we break back into the fresh air, she looks at me and stammers. "D–did I s–see what I thought I s–saw?"

"If you thought you saw a book sticking out of the mud, then you saw the same thing I did."

We swim back to shore and sit on the sand. As Matt and Leah join us, I see that they're about to explode with questions.

"You're not going to believe this," Debbie says before they can jump in. "We found a book down in the mud. It seems to be where this mysterious light is coming from."

"You've got to be kidding!" Matt says in disbelief.

Leah just stands there with her mouth wide open.

"Debbie didn't see the light or experience what I was feeling, but she did see the book," I say. "There's no doubt that the light was coming from this book... I'm going back out to get the book and bring it back. Matt, you wanna come with me? I don't know if it's gonna take one or two of us to get that thing out of the mud."

"I'm right there with you."

We head back into the water, leaving the girls on the beach to watch with concern in their eyes.

When Matt and I get to the baptism spot, we go under together and Matt follows me to the book. I grab onto it as gently as I can, because I don't know what shape it's in after being underwater for who knows how long. But nothing happens when I tug. Matt scoops the mud away as I continue to apply gentle pressure. Still no movement.

I point up and we surface for air.

"I think we're on the right track, but let's go as easy as we can," I say. "There's no rush."

Matt waves to the girls to let them know everything is fine. Then we dive again. This time, we know exactly what to do and it's not long before I feel the book start to loosen. I give Matt a thumbs up—and then the book comes free.

Tucking it under one arm, I kick for the surface and then head for shore.

The girls come out to meet us. As they watch, I wrap the book in both arms, then lay it carefully down on some grass near the water's edge. I reach in my backpack for a towel to dry it off. But the towel is a waste of time; the book doesn't even appear to be wet. The others are as stupefied as I am.

I'm confused, and I'm not alone. I pick up the book to let any excess water drain off, but there is none. It seems completely dry.

Another strange thing is that it's as clean as a library book—no mud, no dirt, no anything.

Both Debbie and Leah reach out to touch it in wonder. Matt still seems to be in shock.

"What have you found?" Leah asks.

"I don't know," I almost whisper.

It's quite a large book with an ornate cover that almost looks like tarnished brass. The cover and spine are covered with what look like ancient symbols. The cover also contains a drawing of an ancient building. It looks Roman. But what do I know about ancient stuff?

The book is about eighteen inches square and about four or five inches thick. But if it's that big, it should also be very heavy... and yet I've had it in my hands a couple of times and it seems to weigh almost nothing.

Then I notice that it has a latch to keep the cover closed. I try to pry it open, but it doesn't budge.

"Wow, I'm confused," I say. "Any of you got any ideas?"

Matt finally speaks up. "I don't know what you've got, but I'm guessing it's important."

"What are we going to do with it?" Debbie asked. "Should we tell Mom and Dad? Should we call the police?"

"I don't know," I say. "None of that sounds right somehow. My instinct is to keep this to ourselves and see if a little time will help shed some light on it."

"I agree," says Leah. "I think we're all in a state of shock. We shouldn't do anything in a hurry. Have you got a safe place to keep it, James? Someplace where no one will find it?"

I give that some thought. "There's an old dresser at the back of the tool shed. I'll put it in the bottom drawer. It should be safe there. No one has bothered that thing in years."

Debbie nods in agreement. "That should be a safe place."

"So we're all agreed. This is a secret shared only by the four of us, until we all agree on what should happen to this book.

Everyone nods solemnly.

"Then we better head for home, as it's almost suppertime," I say. "We don't want any extra attention for a while. When should we get together again and try to figure what's going on?"

Wrapping the book in a towel, I put it in my backpack.

"Tomorrow's Sunday. We all know where we'll be in the morning," Leah says. "Let's get together right after the service."

Once that's decided, we get on our bikes and pedal for home. It's a quiet trip with not much being said. We're all buried in our own thoughts about how the afternoon has unfolded.

"See you at church," I say to Matt and Leah as they drop off.

Debbie and I soon pull into our driveway. It's a good thing our bikes are kept in the shed, because that gives us the opportunity to place the book in the bottom drawer of the old dresser.

Mom greets us as we come in and tells us to wash up for supper.

The food is delicious as usual, but at the same time uneventful. We all have moments to talk about our day, laughing at the funny things that happened and showing interest in what's going on in each other's lives. Debbie and I stay away from the topic of our trip to the lake. We don't feel right about keeping it secret, but at the same time we feel it's the right thing to do. When Mom inevitably asks, we both say that we had a good time but don't offer up any details. It just so happens that Dad has a very exciting story to interrupt us with, something that happened at the airport, so we spend a lot of time on that.

After supper, we turn on the television and sit together to watch some game shows. Mom mentions that there's a potluck after the service tomorrow and she's made two pies. Debbie looks over at me and we both smile. That will give us lots of time to get together with Matt and Leah and make plans.

The whole evening, I fight the urge to go to the shed and take a closer look at our find: the mysterious book. Around 9:30, we run out of shows fit to watch. Saying our good nights, Debbie and I get our hugs and kisses from our parents and head off to bed.

In my room, I fire up my laptop and check my emails. Not surprisingly, I find emails from Matt and Leah. Both are excited about the book and can't wait to get together. I figure that Debbie probably has the same emails. I give them a quick reply to try to calm them down. Then I sign off.

I slide under the sheet and reach for my Bible… only to realize that it's still in my backpack out in the shed. I get out of bed, slip on my jeans, and quietly go downstairs. All is in darkness. Mom and Dad have gone to bed too.

Like a ninja, I sneak out the back door. I have to open the shed door ever so slowly because it creaks like a haunted house. Inside, I notice a glow from the drawer where I put the book. Should I open it or shouldn't I?

As I slide the drawer open, I feel that I'm not alone. Turning slowly, I almost jump out of my skin to see a dark form in the doorway. It steps towards me… and that's when I realize it's Debbie, putting her finger to her lips.

"What are you doing here?" I whisper.

"Same thing you are."

"I forgot my Bible in my backpack and came out to get it. There was a glow coming from the drawer and I just couldn't help myself. I had to look…"

She comes over beside me. "Then let's look."

I reach into the drawer and gently lift the book out. Putting it on the workbench, I just stare at it. Debbie turns on a flashlight and we both study the cover. I can't get over how beautiful it looks! It's so ornate, with such fine, delicate work in the lettering and figures.

Out of curiosity, I try the latch again. Same thing. It won't budge.

Debbie lays her hand on the cover as though she has a special feeling and needs to touch it.

"Let's put it back," I say after a moment. "We need more time. Plus, we should have Matt and Leah with us before we do anything else."

"I'm so excited," Debbie says. "But you're right. Put it back…"

Setting it gently back into the drawer, I slide the dresser shut. After retrieving my Bible, we go back to our rooms to spend an anxious night thinking about what the next day will bring.

SIX

Sunday

Rising with the sun isn't hard when your bedroom faces east and you leave the curtains open with the bed facing the huge floor-to-ceiling window. Between that and the chorus of robins that greets me every dawn, the day starts better than I could either deserve or expect.

Anyway, I get up and head down to breakfast. Mom is already in the kitchen.

"Beacon and eggs?" she asks. "There's orange juice in the fridge and sliced homemade bread on the sideboard. Make your own toast. Jam is in the fridge."

"Two over easy with four slices crispy, please." I slide two slices of bread into the toaster and grab a glass out of the cupboard for my juice. I love Sunday morning breakfast. We don't have time for it on weekdays, because Dad is off to work so early and we stay out of his way so he can get ready. But on Sunday we have a full breakfast together. Not quite lumberjack, but close.

When Debbie comes down, we exchange a look, each knowing what the other is thinking. Dad comes to the table fresh out of the shower and Mom puts his plate in front of him. After twenty years of marriage, she knows his wants and needs.

"Sunday school is at ten o'clock, so I want everyone ready to leave by 9:30," Dad says as he picks up his juice.

"We know, Dad," Debbie says with joking sarcasm. "We do this every Sunday twelve months of the year."

"I just know that forgetfulness isn't only a problem of the elderly. I've seen evidence of that under this roof."

"Now Justin," says Mom with a smile, "stop teasing the children."

"Children!" I exclaim." There are no children in this house. We're all adults. Right, Debbie?"

Debbie laughs. "Absolutely!"

"Finish your breakfast and get to the shower, you two." Dad laughs along. "I don't want to be late because a couple of adults are dragging their feet."

Soon enough we're all seated in the jeep with Bibles in hand and wearing our Sunday best.

We arrive ten minutes early and head towards our respective Sunday school classes. Sitting with Leah, Debbie and I start to tell her about what happened the previous night. We're speaking in hushed voices when Matt walks in. After being filled in, he seems to be a little put out.

"What's the matter, Matt?" I ask.

"I thought we were in this together?" he almost whines.

"We are. This wasn't planned. It just happened."

He nods. "Yeah, I guess. I just don't want to miss anything. I've never been involved in something like this."

"And you think we have?" I laugh.

That's when Derrick starts to speak from the front of the room. "Open your Bibles to John 1:1, where we'll start the last of the gospels we've been studying..."

Sunday school goes well. As we go to the assembly hall after, I notice an unfamiliar face in the congregation. In a rural congregation like ours, with only about seventy-five attendees on any given Sunday, strangers stand out like a sore thumb.

Pastor Dave comes to the pulpit and, as is his custom, welcomes us and any newcomers. He invites all to stay for the potluck, saying truthfully that there is always more than enough food. With that, the service continues through songs, prayers, communion, message, and the hymn of invitation. The closing prayer includes a blessing on the meal we're about to share.

Pastor Dave then asks everyone to sit because there's some unfinished business. To my surprise, he suddenly asks me to come to the front. I know what's coming, but I guess thinking about it hasn't been a priority considering everything I've been dealing with.

Pastor Dave asks me to turn and face the congregation, which I do.

"James Jeffries, I would like to extend to you the right hand of fellowship and introduce you to your new brothers and sisters in Christ," he says. "We present you with this New International Version of the Bible to help you to continue to seek His Word and grow as a Christian. Would you like to say something?"

"Only thank you and let's eat!" I say with a grin.

"I should have expected something like that from you. Always the joker. It's almost a shame we're going to let you lead the line at the food table, but I guess that's the custom."

After a round of applause, we all adjourn to the fellowship hall. It's like a junior high dance, only with adults, teenagers, and children. We separate and sit in our various groups of interest. Debbie and I sit with the gang from our youth group while Mom and Dad sit with Pastor Dave and his wife Sue and a bunch of the other adults, including the new guy. We laugh and eat and talk about the upcoming school year.

More importantly, we discuss the end of our youth group pledge for the summer. We had pledged to put away our cellphones for the summer and stay off social media—that is, except email—until the start of school. It wasn't a big deal for me. I'm not a big social media guy. But it really hurt for some in our youth group.

I hear some of the girls start talking about the stranger. Everyone is curious about who he is and the girls are all oohing and aahing over how good he looks.

Enough of that. Matt and I slip away silently after a lull in the chatter, and soon Debbie and Leah join us outside. We go over to the double porch swings by the flower garden.

"Tell me all about last night," Matt says. "Don't leave a thing out."

I turned to Debbie and allow her to describe the whole affair, step by step.

"That's it?" Leah asks when she's finished.

Matt sighs. "So really nothing happened. You're still the only one seeing the light and the book still won't open."

"That's about it," I confirm. "Can you both come over after supper tonight? We'll take a close look at that cover and see what we can make of it. Maybe we'll see if we can get the latch to open."

They made plans to meet up at 6:30. Afterward, they wondered how to go back inside while making it look like there was nothing going on.

"Some of the guys are probably wondering why we're spending so much time together this last week," I say. "I wish we could let them in on what's going on, but I really think we better keep it a secret for a while longer. Matt, have you still got your digital camera? We should take some close-up pics tonight."

"Can do!" Matt chuckles. "This is exciting. Don't you think?"

We head back inside where the crowd has thinned out a bit. The dishes have been washed and tables cleaned, wiped down, and put away. Small groups of people stand around chatting and I see Mom and Dad over with Pastor Dave and Sue. They're still talking with the new face.

Curiosity takes me in their direction, and the stranger smiles as I walk up and stand beside my father.

42

"Congratulations, young man!" the man says. "Your mom and dad have been telling me all about your decision last Sunday. I can tell you that it will bring about changes in your life that will astound you. By the way, my name is Michael Donovan."

The newcomer puts out his hand and we shake.

"Nice to meet you, Mr. Donovan."

"Call me Michael, please. Mr. Donovan is way too formal. All brothers and sisters should be on a first name basis, don't you think?"

I smile. "Okay then. Michael it is."

I hate to say it, but here we go again. There is something different about this guy. When we shook hands, I had a strange feeling—yet another disturbance I couldn't put my finger on.

"This lovely young lady must be your sister," Michael says. "The family resemblance is strong. She has her mother's eyes."

"This is our firstborn, Debbie," says Mom. "He's new to the area and has decided to worship with us while he's here."

He extends his hand again and shakes, this time with Debbie.

"Mom, is it all right if Leah and Matt come over after supper?" Debbie asks. "James and I are working on a project with them."

"Certainly! Your father and I are going over to Pastor Dave's for an evening of music and conversation. Frankly, you two would most likely find it boring." Mom smiles at us.

"Thanks, both for the answer and the reason," Debbie replies.

Debbie and I head over to the corner to talk with some of our friends who haven't left yet.

"Where have you guys been all week?" asks Glen.

"We saw you at the lake on Friday," I point out.

"Oh yeah, that's right. I forgot about that."

But we can't stay long. I can see that Mom and Dad are ready to go.

"See you guys at youth on Wednesday," I say. "Come on, Debbie, let's go!"

When we get home, I change out of my good clothes. Coming downstairs, I find Mom in the kitchen. She's putting leftovers from the potluck in the fridge. Needless to say, there were no leftovers of pie. She makes the best pie crust in the world and everyone at church knows it. It's always a fight to get a slice.

"Dad and I will be leaving at about five," Mom says. "I'll leave these leftovers on the bottom shelf so you two can help yourselves for your supper."

"Sounds good to us," I say.

Debbie nods in approval.

"What's this project you're working on with your friends?" Dad asks.

"Oh, just some ideas for next year's vacation Bible school," I lie. "We want to attract more people our age. By putting our heads together, we thought we might come up with some good ideas."

"Who came up with that, Derrick?" asks Dad.

"No. It was our initiative. Derrick doesn't know anything about it." Lying to my dad really bothers me, but I don't know what else to do. "We thought we'd surprise him."

"Excellent! Good to see you putting some effort into your faith and showing concern for others. I'm impressed."

That just made it hurt worse. "Thanks, Dad."

I have to leave the room, not wanting the conversation to lead to any other untruths. I go out the back door and find Debbie sitting in the gazebo.

"I don't know whether I can do this," I say. "I just lied to Dad about what we're doing tonight and it just about tore me apart. I hope we can figure this out quick so we can let him and Mom know what's really going on."

"Me too!" she exclaims. "I don't want to lie to them. It's just wrong!"

We both sit in the gazebo, absorbing the world around us, including the lazy drifting clouds, the birds singing, and the crickets trying to drown them out. It all seems to relieve the pressure we feel and bring things back to order.

I don't know how long we sit there, but Mom's voice brings us back to earth.

"We're going now," she calls from the back door. "You and your friends help yourself to the iced tea in the fridge. There are cookies in the jar."

"Thanks," Debbie calls back. "Bye! See you later."

When we're alone, I turn to Debbie. "What time is it, sis?"

"Five."

"Well, let's eat and get ready for Matt and Leah. We can call them and tell them to come over anytime."

After I place the call, we sit down at the table to enjoy some leftover. My thoughts are still on the book, of course. I'm hoping that when it's laid out in front of us later, its clues will become more obvious. Right now it's a total mystery.

Leah walks in the back door with a serious grin on her face. "I'm excited and worried all at the same time," she says. "Do we have to wait for Matt? You two are finished eating, aren't you? Am I babbling? I usually don't talk this much, do I? Someone say something!"

Debbie gets up from the table and puts her arm around her shoulder. "Calm down. You're sounding like Matt," she says gently. "Yes, we'll wait for him. You saw how upset he got when he thought James and I started without him."

"I guess that's the fair way to do this," Leah says.

"Besides, I just saw him turning onto the driveway," I add. "Let's go out and meet him."

Out the door we go. As soon as Matt sees us, we hurry over to the back shed. I go in first and bend down to open the drawer. Already I notice the soft glow coming from the book. I gently pick up and place it on the workbench, unwrapping the towel.

"Let's take it into the kitchen so we have more room," I suggest.

A minute later, the book is resting on the kitchen table. We all study it closely, touching its edges and running our fingers over the figures on the cover and spine. We're acting as though we're in a trance.

Finally, I look up to Matt. "Did you bring your camera?"

"Sure did." He pulls a small camera out of his jacket pocket and starts taking pictures of every possible angle of the book.

When we're satisfied, we sit back in our chairs. I ask Matt to email the pictures to us so we'll all have access to the book any time we need it. That way, we can study the book and its writing more closely.

"The writing looks like some ancient language," Debbie remarks. "Maybe if we go online, we can find someone who's able to point us in the right direction."

"Good idea, Debbie," says Matt. "Now what about that latch?"

I nod. "I've been thinking about that."

Standing up, I leave the kitchen for a minute and return with a box of my dad's tools, including precision screwdrivers and picks. I lean in to take a closer look at the latch. It's nothing like I've ever seen before. It has no place for a key and I don't notice any buttons.

"How does this thing work?" I ask. "Anyone got an idea?"

"Looks simple, except there doesn't seem to be a release mechanism," says Matt.

I raise one of the picks. "Okay. I'm going to try to force it."

"Be careful," says Leah. "You don't want to damage it."

"Thank you, Captain Obvious," I retort, only to see a hurt look on her face. "Just kidding, Leah."

I insert the pick into the space where the latch and cover meet. My gentle prying doesn't accomplish anything, so I apply more pressure. At first nothing happens, but then I feel some movement and my pulse quickens. The shaft of the pick is beginning to bend!

Removing the pick, I look to see whether I've caused any damage to the latch. Not a mark. No dent, no scratch, nothing.

I switch to a heavier screwdriver and repeat the process but get the same results: bent screwdriver but no dent or scratch on the latch itself.

"Let me have a go," Matt says, taking the screwdriver from me.

I sigh. "Okay, but be as gentle as you can. I've seen you bulldoze your way into things before. Usually something gets broken."

After twenty minutes of trying different tools and angles, we're no closer than when we started.

My next move is to get my backpack and drop it on the floor beside the table.

"If you hear Mom and Dad coming home, let me know so I can get the book out of sight in my backpack," I say, looking first to my sister, then to the others. "By the way, I told them we were working on ideas to attract more teens to next year's vacation Bible school. So if you're asked, that's our story."

We try working on the latch for another couple of minutes, but we're all starting to feel frustrated.

"Boy, we're not getting very far with this," Debbie murmurs.

"I'd suggest making a list of everything we know about this book and how we ended up with it," says Leah. "I brought a notebook and pen. Making the list will help us make connections. Maybe some of the clues will fit together."

"There's that analytical video game mind we've all come to love and respect," I say, drawing a smile from Leah.

First we recall the strange feeling I got at my baptism. Then there was the fishing incident by the riverbank, when I had the first flashback. That was followed by my discovery of all the scriptures concerning the Book of Life, which definitely wasn't a coincidence. Then, on Friday, I lost focus during the swimming race at the beach.

Finally, we discovered the book in the mud under the lake. Except when we brought it to the surface, it was clean and dry.

"That really defies all logic," Leah remarks. "Not to mention, science!"

I nod. "And I don't understand why I'm the only one who sees the light shining from it."

Leah puts down her pen. "Well, I think that about does it. Anyway, I already see a common theme to everything that's happened so far. Do the rest of you see it too?"

"The Book of Life!" we all say in unison.

This is followed by dead silence as we all stare at the book on the table.

After what seems like an eternity, I whisper, "What the heck are we doing with the Book of Life, if that's what this really is? Why me? Why us? My head's spinning."

No one has any kind of answer to these big questions.

"It sure looks like we've got the Book of Life," Leah says, taking charge. "Everything seems to point in that direction. But we can't jump to any conclusions. Let's study the pictures Matt took. We can all focus on one part of the book. James, you're the lead on this, so why don't you take the cover? Debbie, you can take the back cover. And Matt, you take the spine. Let's see if you can find anything online that helps solve this mystery. Meanwhile, I'll research the Book of Life and get as much info as I can find."

Debbie nods in agreement. "If we all do our part, maybe we'll be able to make a breakthrough next time we get together."

The rest of us appreciate Leah's suggestion.

"Uh-oh, I think your parents just got home," Matt says, looking out the window and seeing a pair of headlights turn onto the driveway.

I quickly wrap the book in the towel and gently lower it into my backpack, which in turn I place on the floor next to my chair.

"Matt, put your camera away!" I say before my parents come inside. "We don't need any more questions…"

Matt slips the tiny camera into his jacket pocket just as Mom and Dad come through the front door.

"How are the four musketeers tonight?" Dad asks with a laugh.

"Just great!" Debbie responds. "How was your evening at Pastor Dave's?"

"We had a good time, as always. We weren't the only ones there. Derrick and Amanda came, along with Michael. We had tea and cake and got to know Michael a lot better. He works for a large company as a consultant and has been all over the world. He says he has the best boss and has had the chance to meet thousands of interesting people over the years. He must be older than he looks, though. Or maybe he just never stops!" Mom smiles. "How did you four make out?"

"We got a start on our project," I say, trying my best to stick to the truth. "But there's still a lot of work to do before we're finished."

"If we can be of any help, all you need to do is ask," Dad says.

"We know," I reply. "If we can, we'd really like to accomplish this as a team. You know, just us."

"I can respect that. The offer's still open if you change your minds."

"Anyone want some cookies and milk?" Mom offers.

"We were just getting ready to finish up for the night," Leah says. "Matt and I were on our way out."

Matt looks disappointed. "But milk and cookies!"

I laugh. "You'll live, Matt."

We all get up and head for the door, me with my backpack in hand. As we walk down the driveway, we decide to meet again on Tuesday night. That will give each of us time to work on our separate tasks.

As Matt leaves, Leah hangs back.

"Thanks for taking charge, Leah," I say.

"Treasure hunting is all about finding clues and putting those clues together to see where they lead," she says. "I'm not just a pretty face, you know!"

"I'm beginning see that."

After saying goodbye, I return to the shed to put the book away. Afterward I head back to the house. Mom and Dad are sitting at the table with cups of coffee in their hands. Debbie stands by the stairs.

"Good night, little brother," she says, smiling. "Sleep well."

She knows full well there's not much chance of that.

"What time is it?" I ask.

"10:30," Dad replies.

"Guess I'll be off to bed too. Good night. God bless. Love you."

As I get to the top of the stairs, Debbie is coming out of the bathroom.

"Are you going to be able to sleep tonight?" she whispers. "I don't think I will. There's so many thoughts buzzing around in my head, I can't think straight."

"Just remember that we're supposed to leave all our worries in God's hands. He'll take care of us."

"I still don't think I'll sleep. Good night."

"Good night, sis. Love you."

With my prayers that night, I include a sincere request for God's help. Then I lay my head on my pillow and close my eyes. I have no idea what's in store for me and drop off to sleep instantly. And not just any sleep, but a deep sleep where nothing and no one can disturb me.

At least, that's the way it feels.

My dreams start with that same sense of peace, warmth, and total silence… it's exactly how I felt when I was getting baptized and then again when we found the book at the lake. Then comes the light, bright but also soft, intense but not glaring...

And then I hear a voice calling my name.

SEVEN

"James."

I don't answer, since I've never had a conversation in a dream before.

The voice comes again: "James."

Okay, let's try, I think to myself.

"Yes?"

"I am an angel of the Lord God Most High and He has sent me to tell you that you have been chosen for a task, as Moses and Noah and Jonah were chosen in the past. You will have helpers in your task. Your sister and your friends Matt and Leah will assist you in the accomplishment of this endeavor.

"You do possess the Lamb's Book of Life. The Lord Almighty has placed it in your hands for a specific reason that will become apparent as your task unfolds. As with Moses and Noah and Jonah, there were various stages to the task with which the Lord presented them. Yours will be similar in nature.

"First, you must know that the Lord is with you. As your Pastor Dave said, the Lord will not give you anything you cannot handle. He quoted Philippians 4:13: 'I can do all this through him who gives me strength.' Remember that throughout the Bible those who remained faithful and put themselves totally in the hands of the Lord were rewarded, but those who turned from that absolute commitment met with failure and defeat.

"Do not be afraid! The Lord your God knows that you are young, but so was David when he slew Goliath and then he went on to become king and a great leader. Joseph also was young when he went into slavery among the Egyptians.

"Your sister, Leah, and Matt have been visited by me this night just as you have. They have received the same directive. They know no more or less than you do about this task, but they have been informed that you are to take the lead in this endeavor. You must all know that this information may not be shared with family or friends. It must remain a secret.

"The Lamb's Book of Life is in your possession. The Holy Spirit placed it in the spot to which you were led, with His guidance. Despite being underwater and encased in mud, you observed that it suffered no ill effects or damage. You also noticed that it weighed very little for such a large item. Your attempts to open it were unsuccessful and will remain so until such time as the Lord sees fit for its contents to be revealed. Only the hand of God may open the book. It is not of this world. Therefore, the forces of this world have no effect upon it. The pictures Matt took will be of no use to you because it is not made of a material that will show up on film or any kind of digital imagery. The glow that only you can see will remain with you alone, as this task falls principally on your shoulders.

"For the time being, read the scriptures about the Book of Life. Do not be influenced by the interpretations of man. As scripture says, 'For the foolishness of God is wiser than human wisdom, and the weakness of God is stronger than human strength.'[10] If the wisdom of man could be trusted, there would be but one interpretation and that would be the truth. The truth will be revealed to you in due course, but only with faith, obedience, and trust and through prayer. Rest peacefully and awake with renewed energy and a true purpose of life."

Monday

With daylight coming through the window, my eyes open and I roll out of bed. I go to my knees and thank the Almighty for life and breath. I feel full of life—or as Mom would say, full of vim and vigor.

Even though I vividly remember last night's dream, if that's what it was, I feel no fear, worry, of anxiety. Just peace. Mom once painted a small saying over the veranda steps: "Life Is Good." That's exactly the way I'm feeling.

I shower and head downstairs for breakfast. "Good morning, Mom!"

"And good morning to you, my favorite son. How are you today?"

"If I was any better, there would have to be two of me—and as you've said, I don't think the world could stand that."

That produces a laugh. Mom hands me a bowl of hot oatmeal.

"Dad gone to work?" I ask.

"He left about an hour ago."

As she's saying this, Debbie comes into the kitchen.

"Hi, sis! How are you this fine morning?"

"I am marvendiculous! How about you?"

---

[10] 1 Corinthians 1:25.

"Slept like a baby. Not a care in the world and wrapped in the arms of the Almighty."

Debbie smiles. We both understand exactly what she means.

"Great!" I turn back to Mom. "How about you?"

"I'm good. I don't know that I'm as good as you two seem to be, though."

When Mom leaves the room, I turn to Debbie. "Why don't you call Leah after breakfast and see if she wants to get together with us? I'll call Matt. By the way, did you have a strange dream last night?"

"I most certainly did!"

"We all need to meet again, and soon. I need to know if we all had the same dream."

As Mom re-enters the kitchen, we struggle to act naturally.

While Debbie calls Leah, I get on the phone with Matt. He wants to get into a big conversation, but I cut him off and say that we can talk more when he gets here.

I go upstairs and fire up my laptop to see if Matt has tried to send the pictures he took. Sure enough, I see an email from Matt and there are some images attached. But when I open the first image, all I can see is a flash of white light. Going through the rest only confirms that none of the pictures turned out. The email explains that he only sent the nonexistent images to prove there was nothing to see. He adds that he took a few other pictures to confirm his camera still worked, and it does.

Logging out, I go back downstairs and tell Mom that I'll be out in the shed. I open the door, step inside, and immediately feel a change in the atmosphere. I clear a space on top of the workbench, then open the drawer and pick up the book. I lay it on the bench and unwrap the towel around it.

I just stare at the book in front of me, all the while running through all the events that led up to last night's dream. What does it all mean? What am I going to do?

All these questions running through my head come to a screeching stop when I arrive at a realization: I know what I have to do. I need to go to God in prayer.

Bowing my head, I close my eyes and silently pray to my Creator.

"Heavenly Father, Creator of all that is visible and invisible, I stand before You a sinner who has recently been reborn through the blood of Your Son. As an infant in the family of God, I ask for Your guidance, just as any child needs guidance, to protect me from injury and keep me safe on the path You wish me to follow. Give me the strength to complete the task You have put before me."

I hear a noise and turn to see Debbie enter the shed, followed closely by Leah.

"Hey, you two," I say.

The girls come inside and look at the book.

"Aren't you a little shaken after what happened last night?" asks Debbie.

Leah gives me a concerned look. "I know that I am."

I look out the door and see Matt getting off his bike and heading for us.

"Hey, partner," I say when he joins us in the shed. "How you doin'?"

"Just great, James. Have I missed anything? Have I got news for you guys!"

"You haven't missed a thing and we've been waiting for you. I just got the book out so we could have a closer look…" I trail off, wondering how to proceed. "Before we do that, did you all have the same dream I had? You know, the one where an angel spoke to you, confirming that this is the Book of Life and God has something He wants us to do for Him and that we're a team and that this whole thing is a secret and apparently I'm the one in charge?"

I stop to take a deep breath before I pass out.

"Did the angel also tell you that we wouldn't be able to open the book and that the pictures wouldn't turn out?" Debbie asks excitedly.

"And that you're the only one who can see the glow?" says Leah.

Matt jumps in. "And that we're no younger than some of the people in the Old Testament that God gave tasks to and that if we have faith, pray, and trust, we won't have any problems?"

"He didn't tell me we won't have any problems," I say. "But we can overcome any problems so long as we trust Him and do what He asks, as He asks, when He asks."

So yes, it turns out we all had the same dream.

"Is everybody as nervous as I am right now?" I ask, and all three of them nod their heads. "There's no backing out or changing your minds now. Remember what happened to Jonah when God gave him something to do? He tried to run away from it and that turned out badly."

Debbie furrows her brow. "It sounds like we're going to be spending a lot of time together. How are we going to explain this to our parents and friends without lying to them? I hate lying to Mom and Dad."

"I think our best and truthful explanation is to say we're working on something for the Lord and that it's a secret," I suggest.

"That sounds good," says Leah.

Matt glances at my sister. "I'll just tell them that I like the company."

"Oh, you!" She punches him in the arm. "Okay, that's settled. So now what?"

"Remember what the angel said," I remind her. "We can't open the book. He also said that the task would unfold over time. The only thing we need to do is read scriptures about the Book of Life. He also told us not to let man's interpretations influence us. I guess we should just read all the scripture we can find and pay no attention to footnotes, Bible dictionaries, or reference books to help us out. More will be revealed with obedience, faith, and trust and through prayer. I guess we obey, put our faith and trust in Him, and pray. It sounds like we'll need patience too. God will move us at His speed, not ours."

I pause to let this sink in.

"I want us to all put our hands on the book and pray together for the strength to do this. After a few minutes of silent prayer, I'll close at the end. Okay?"

I get no answer, but three hands join mine on the cover of the book. Everyone's eyes are closed and their heads bowed.

"Heavenly Father, we stand humbly before You acknowledging that You have chosen us for a task. We ask for Your blessing in the performance of that task. May You give us the faith and strength to fulfill Your wishes. As in all things, dear Lord, Thy will be done. We pray this in the name of Jesus Christ, our Lord and Savior. Amen!"

I don't know why, but we each leave our hands on the book for several seconds after I finish.

Opening our eyes, we remove our hands.

"I don't know about you guys, but I feel all warm and fuzzy," Matt says with a grin.

Debbie laughs. "*Warm* and *fuzzy* aren't words you hear very often from the lips of Matt Philips."

"I think we're about to have a lot of new experiences," Leah points out. "And not all of them are going to be warm and fuzzy."

"I know what you mean," I say. "If you think about scripture and the people God gave tasks, I can't remember anyone having a smooth ride. But you never know. Maybe this time will be different. We can only hope and pray and leave it in His hands. Right?"

Matt nods. "Yeah, you're right. We'll just have to wait and see what we're supposed to be doing and take it from there."

"You surprise me, Matt," Debbie says. "Of the four of us, I thought you would have the most trouble with this."

"I've got a few surprises up my sleeve."

After comparing schedules and agreeing to meet again on Wednesday morning, we put the book away and troop into the house. We find Mom in the kitchen, where I detect the aroma of something delicious baking in the oven.

Mom turns as we come in. "If you four aren't too busy with your project, there will be a couple of pans of brownies coming out of the oven in ten minutes."

We grin widely, which is all she needs to know.

I head to the fridge for the milk and Debbie opens the cupboard for the glasses. Neither of us is surprised by the brownies. Mom is… well, just that. She's Mom.

Everybody grabs a chair and takes a seat.

"You know, if I lived here I would probably weigh a ton," Matt remarks.

Mom smiles. "Thank you for the compliment, Matt, but you haven't even tasted my brownies yet."

"I don't know about these other three, but I would be willing to bet this year's allowance on what's about to come out of your oven."

I sigh. "Just leave Debbie and me a few for later in the week, okay?"

While all this is going on, I notice that Leah seems awfully quiet. It's like she's fallen into a trance.

I kick Debbie under the table, which gets me a look. When she's paying attention, I nod toward Leah and hope she understands. Something's not right.

She looks at Leah and then back to me.

"Leah, what are you up to tomorrow?" Debbie asks. "You should come with Mom and me. We're going into town to get school supplies and check out some clothes. A lot of sales on right now. We can probably get some good deals. What do you think?"

"That sounds okay," Leah says. "What time do you want to go?"

"About 1:00." Debbie turns to Mom. "Is that okay with you, Mom?"

Mom nods. "Just fine with me. I'm going to the ladies quilting in the morning. After lunch is fine."

"What about you, Matt? You want to go check out the fall fashions at Birkendales? We wouldn't want to show up on the first day wearing last year's jeans, would we?" Immediately I start laughing.

"Heavenly day, no!" Matt adds with a burst of laughter. "We'd be the laughingstock of the whole football team. How embarrassing would that be?"

"Okay, you two, stop teasing the girls," Mom says. "And James, you can get some dessert plates out of the cupboard for the brownies. And use the placemats. I've seen you and Matt eat and I want a little protection for my tablecloth."

The brownies come out of the oven and Mom cuts them into generous squares. Putting the pan on an oven mitt, she lets us help ourselves. They're warm and soft, moist, and full of flavor. A fourteen out of ten! A chorus of "Mmm, these are good" gives Mom cause to smile. She's always said that the true test of her cooking is whether it's enjoyed by those who eat it.

Leah seems a little more present in the moment as she and Debbie chatter about their planned shopping trip. Matt and I both have seconds and then Mom, after offering the girls seconds, which they decline, takes the pan away.

"I don't want you boys to spoil your lunch," she says. "I'd like to have some left for Justin when he gets home from work. So off you go."

All four of us get up and head outside.

"Are any of you as nervous as I am?" Leah asks. "This seems so surreal. It's like I'm playing a video game and somehow got sucked inside the game."

"I don't know about the rest of you, but I've got to say this whole thing is giving me a case of the willies," Matt says. "A book in the mud at the bottom of the lake and it's not wet or muddy… dreams with angels talking to us. Nothing there to be nervous about, right?"

Debbie shrugs. "But I don't know what we can do about it except see where it takes us."

"I am as confused as the rest of you," I say. "Maybe even more confused. I'm the one who started all this. Flashes in the water, odd feelings about things and places… I just don't know. What I do know is that God is giving us a task and we need to follow it through to the end. Why I'm in charge, I have no idea! I guess we all have a lot of praying to do, and a lot of trust to put in God's hands. But isn't that what we're supposed to do anyway?"

After reiterating our plans to meet on Wednesday, I start back to the house.

Shortly after lunch, Debbie goes into Mom's sewing room where they work on Mom's latest quilt. I mow the lawn and whipper-snip around all the flowerbeds and the foundation.

In my room later, I open my Bible and check the concordance for references to the words *book* or *Book of Life*. I already know of several from my recent experience of randomly opening of the Bible and write them down: Revelation 20:11–15, Revelation 21:27, Revelation 13:8, Revelation 3:5, Philippians 4:3, Psalm 69:27–28, and Daniel 12:1–4. I also find Daniel 7:10, but after looking at it I decide to read the whole chapter.

As I turn to my laptop, Mom calls up. "Your father's home and supper's ready. Get washed up and come on down."

"Down in a minute, Mom."

Cleaning up, I head downstairs. I join Dad at the table while Debbie helps Mom get the hot dishes from the pot to the serving dishes and then to the table.

After they take their seats, Dad asks Debbie to say grace.

We dig in, releasing a clatter of stainless steel on ceramic; the noise only lasts thirty seconds and is followed by silence as we eat. Mom asks Dad how his day went and so begins the typical mealtime chatter. The world seems to be on its normal path—that is, except for me, my sister, and our friends. I think Debbie and I are doing pretty good considering that we're keeping an enormous secret.

I wonder how Matt and Leah are doing. Maybe I should email them after supper and make sure they're all right.

Mom gets up and brings a plate of brownies to the table.

"My!" Dad says. "What have I done to deserve this, Winnie?"

"Just being you is all I need, my loving man."

"You made the dessert, I'll make the tea." He gets up. "You kids want tea or milk?"

"Tea please, Dad," Debbie says.

I shrug. "I'm good with milk."

"No sooner said than done." Dad smiles. "Oh, I meant to ask. How is your project coming along? Remember, your mother and I are always available if you need help."

Debbie nods. "It's a little slow but we're making progress, Dad. We met this morning and we're going to meet again on Wednesday. We all have our own tasks, and hopefully we'll make some headway. Right, James?"

"Fingers crossed!" I say.

Once supper is done and we fail to find anything of interest on television, I go up to my room to do some research on my laptop. Debbie does the same.

But just before we go into our respective rooms, Debbie stops and turns to me.

"Have you had a chance to look up any scriptures?" she asks.

"Yes, this afternoon while you and Mom were quilting. I'll email them to you and Matt and Leah. But you should all look too. I may have missed something."

"Leah seemed a little freaked out this morning."

"I know what you mean," I say. "I think your plan to take her shopping helped calm her down a lot."

I shut the door to my bedroom and turn on the laptop. My first ask is to email the list of scriptures I found to the group.

But then what? The angel told us not to trust man's interpretation, so I can't conduct more research online. It feels like we've hit a roadblock.

That's when I remember something else from the dream: the keys are faith, trust, obedience, and prayer. Which of these seems like the best tool for the problem at hand?

Prayer.

I get down on my knees, bow my head, and go to God for help.

"Heavenly Father, in You I put my faith and in You I put my trust. You have given me a task and I'm unsure what to do next. I pray for Your guidance and trust that You will point me in the right direction. While I'm here, dear Lord, I also would ask for the strength to see this through to the end, and also that You give that same strength to Debbie, Leah, and Matt. Guide us and direct us, dear Lord, so that in us Your will be done. I pray for this in the name of my Lord and Savior Jesus Christ."

Opening my eyes and getting off my knees, I sit back down in front of my laptop. I see that I've already received replies from all three of my co-conspirators. Debbie suggests that maybe all we can do at this point is read those scriptures over and over and maybe even memorize them. Matt's email to me says the same.

Although Leah has arrived at the same conclusion, her reasoning is different. She points out that a lot of video games have deeply embedded clues that only reveal themselves with intense study.

What are the odds that all three would come up with the same course of action? Prayer answered? I shouldn't be surprised. I feel good about this and feel that it's time to obey our instructions and start studying.

Turning to Revelation 21, I start reading at verse one so I can get a feel for what the whole chapter is about. The impact statement comes in the last verse, Revelation 21:27:

> Nothing impure will ever enter it, nor will
> anyone who does what is shameful or deceit-
> ful, but only those whose names are written in
> the Lamb's book of life.

I read this over and over. I think hard and long about what this passage is trying to tell me—tell us.

Committing these words to memory doesn't necessarily mean that I'll under-stand what they mean, though. I learned that in school when asked to memorize a poem and recite it for my classmates the next day. I could remember the words no problem, but the bottom fell out when the teacher asked, "Now what does it means?" It was a hard lesson, but I can be taught.

This is easy, though. All of Revelation 21 is about what comes after judgment day and what it's going to be like to dwell in the house of the Lord forever. What a beautiful place it will be, lit by the glory of God! All that we hold precious here will be commonplace there. Our tears will be wiped away. There will be no more death, no more pain, no more mourning, and no more crying because God Himself will be among His people. Eternity is described in terms we can understand.

Finally, the last verse tells us who will be there—only those whose names are written in the Lamb's Book of Life. A person's name must be found in the book, or there will be no place for them in eternity. Obviously this makes the Book of Life very important in the spiritual and eternal realm. Being able to see whether one's name is inside that book would offer someone great foresight. People would give an arm or a leg to know that!

I can't wait to get together with the others to discuss this piece of scripture. I don't think any of us have really understood the importance of the book that's wrapped in a towel in the shed.

But what in heaven's name does God want with four teenagers? Where is this going?

No, stop that, I think. *The angel said that the truth would be revealed in God's own time.*

I guess I'll just have to be patient and see what happens.

With that, I turn to the next passage, Revelation 20:11–15:

> Then I saw a great white throne and him who was seated on it. The earth and the heavens fled from his presence, and there was no place for them. And I saw the dead, great and small, standing before the throne, and books were opened. Another book was opened, which is the book of life. The dead were judged according to what they had done as recorded in the books. The sea gave up the dead that were in it, and death and Hades gave up the dead that were in them, and each person was judged according to what they had done. Then death

and Hades were thrown into the lake of fire. The lake of fire is the second death. Anyone whose name was not found written in the book of life was thrown into the lake of fire.

To get a clearer picture of what's happening here, I go back and read the rest of the chapter.

Well, it doesn't work!

The strongest impression I get from Revelation 20–21 is that if your name isn't found in the Book of Life, it means you're headed for the lake of fire.

My head is spinning. That's enough for tonight. It's time to get some rest and hopefully clear my head so I can figure out what it is I'm supposed to see in these scriptures. I just need to have faith that the Lord will lead us in the right direction. I have to trust that He knows what He's doing, because at this point I sure don't.

Back on my knees beside my bed, I go to my Father in prayer.

"Heavenly Father, I put all my faith in You. I trust in Your wisdom, Your power, Your knowledge, and Your love. What You ask, I will do. Where You send me, I will go. Guide me body and soul in Your will. I pray that age-old prayer: 'Now I lay me down to sleep. I pray the Lord my soul to keep. If I should die before I wake, I pray the Lord my soul to take.'"

I slide under the quilt and lay my head on the pillow. That same deep sleep of peace and warmth I have felt before overtakes me again. I'm oblivious to the world around me but can feel the reality of my surroundings. That may sound weird, but in this dreamland, if that's what it is, everything seems so clear, sharp, and real—in fact, it feels more real than reality itself.

Despite having described this place as feeling warm, I realize there is no sense of hot or cold here, only an inner peace.

Just as before, a bright light fills my vision and I hear a voice who announces himself as an angel of the Lord.

"You have pleased the Lord your God with what you have done thus far," says the angel. "You are to continue on the path that has been laid out before you. You have read some of the scriptures required of you for this task, but you must read the rest. Remember not to let the interpretations of men sway you in any way. The Lord will guide you and you will interpret as Daniel and with the wisdom of Solomon. I will be with you as a guardian throughout your task, not only for your sake but to safeguard the Book of Life, which is of more value than mankind could ever conceive.

"Tomorrow will give you and your friends the opportunity to finish reading the scriptures ahead of your next meeting. You will finish your reading in the morning and then go fishing in the afternoon. You will go to the same spot where you and Matt went last. At that time, more will be revealed to you. Do not inform the others of this until Wednesday, for this step is required of you alone. Do you understand?"

I recognize the sound of my own voice as it replies. "Yes. I do."

"I will leave you now. You will sleep the sleep of the righteous and awaken refreshed to continue the work of the Lord."

EIGHT

Tuesday

The next thing I know, the sun is shining on my face. I feel great and can't wait to start the new day. Looking at the clock radio, I see that it's 6:45.

I head for the shower, feeling safe that Dad has already left for work and won't need the washroom. Once I'm spic and span, I head downstairs where Mom is preparing breakfast.

"Good morning, Mom! How are you this morning?"

"I'm great, James. How about you?"

"If there's any way to feel better, I don't know what it would be."

She laughs. "Oatmeal, cereal, juice, or coffee? Help yourself."

"Thanks, Mom." I get a bowl of oatmeal and sprinkle it with brown sugar and add a little milk. "Do you need help with anything today?"

"Not that I can think of. I'm going to the church this morning for quilting club, and after lunch I'm going shopping with your sister and Leah. Do you want to come along?"

"No, heaven forbid. I think I'll go fishing. I've got some reading to do this morning, so I'll be up in my room if you need me."

"Oh! Would you take the green cart out to the road before going to your room? I almost forgot that it's trash day today."

"Sure, Mom."

Once I'm finished my breakfast, I take the green cart out and grab a fresh glass of juice before returning to my room. I stop outside Debbie's door and knock softly.

A few seconds later, the door opens a crack.

"Mornin', sis! How are you this fine day?"

"If you really want to know, I feel just great. I've been awake an hour or more. I just about have all those scriptures read. After last night, I didn't have much hope for a good night's sleep, but I guess I was wrong."

"I just had breakfast. I should have lots of time to study the scriptures today, with you and Leah going shopping in the afternoon."

"See you at lunch."

I sit at my desk, bow my head, and ask my heavenly Father to guide and direct me as I get into His Word. Then I open my Bible to the next scripture on my list—Revelation 13:8:

> All inhabitants of the earth will worship the
> beast—all whose names have not been written
> in the Lamb's book of life, the Lamb who was
> slain from the creation of the world.

The meaning is clear: those who are not in Christ are in the world and all it has to offer. From there I move on to Revelation 3:5:

> The one who is victorious will, like them,
> be dressed in white. I will never blot out the
> name of that person from the book of life, but
> will acknowledge that name before my Father
> and his angels.

The one who is victorious over what? The beast? The temptations of the world?

Needing some help with this one, I ask God for understanding and then push on to the next scripture. It's Philippians 4:3.

But when I try to turn to it, my Bible instead opens to a different page. My eyes are drawn to 1 Corinthians 2:10:

> ...these are the things God has revealed to us
> by his Spirit. The Spirit searches all things,
> even the deep things of God. For who knows a
> person's thoughts except their own spirit with-
> in them? In the same way no one knows the
> thoughts of God except the Spirit of God.

Whoa! I guess I just got a bit of the help I asked for. The Lord reveals things to us through the Spirit, and He will reveal what we need when He feels we need it. I feel better, accepting that it's okay if I don't completely understand everything I read. God will let me understand what I need to understand when I need to understand it.

I can see this being a hard sell for Debbie, Matt, and Leah. But I am talking about God and there's nothing He can't do.

Well, back to Philippians 4:3:

> Yes, and I ask you, my true companion, help these women since they have contended at my side in the cause of the gospel, along with Clement and the rest of my co-workers, whose names are in the book of life.

I don't see anything too staggering there and decide to move on to Daniel 12:1:

> At that time Michael, the great prince who protects your people, will arise. There will be a time of distress such as has not happened from the beginning of nations until then. But at that time your people—everyone whose name is found written in the book—will be delivered.

What does it mean to be delivered? I keep reading:

> Multitudes who sleep in the dust of the earth will awake: some to everlasting life, others to shame and everlasting contempt.[11]

That explains a lot. Who would want to live in everlasting shame and contempt? No one! And from what I've read so far, that shame and contempt involves a lake of fire.

Since that's my last passage of scripture, I decide to reread them a couple of times and pray for understanding.

After going through the list three more times, I decide that it's time to take a break. Laying my Bible down, I start to get up...

---

[11] Daniel 12:2.

...when suddenly my Bible falls open. That's strange! I knew my Bible was closed when I put it down.

I lean down and study the page. Now what do we have here? My eyes are drawn to Daniel 7:10:

> A river of fire was flowing, coming out from before him. Thousands upon thousands attended him; ten thousand times ten thousand stood before him. The court was seated, and the books were opened.

Wow! That sounds a lot like the scenes of judgment described in Revelation. Important books are being opened. The text doesn't specifically mention the Book of Life, but I know that it has to be one of the books because it's the most important one; if a person's name isn't found in it, they have no hope.

I add this scripture to the list.

I'm about to stand up when I stop myself. What if there's more? Picking up my Bible, I place it spine-down and let it fall open again. My eyes go to Exodus 32:31–34:

> So Moses went back to the Lord and said, "Oh, what a great sin these people have committed! They have made themselves gods of gold. But now, please forgive their sin—but if not, then blot me out of the book you have written."
>
> The Lord replied to Moses, "Whoever has sinned against me I will blot out of my book. Now go, lead the people to the place I spoke of, and my angel will go before you. However, when the time comes for me to punish, I will punish them for their sin."

I spot two important things here. The first is that God can blot names out of His book. Second, the person who has sinned will be the one who is punished. This gives me lots to think about.

I again rest my Bible on its spine and let it go. This time, the book falls to one side with the cover shut. Just to be doubly sure of the meaning, I do it again. Same result.

I feel safe. My studying is done for the day. I email these new scriptures to the others.

Seconds later, I hear a knock on my door and Debbie sticks her head in.

"Where did those come from?" she asks.

"Remember how my Bible fell open to certain scriptures back at the lake? I did it again, and this is what I found."

"Do you think there are any others?" she asks.

"Not today. I double-checked."

"Okay. Well, it's lunchtime and I think I just heard Mom come home."

Going downstairs, we find Mom putting away her coat and purse.

"How was quilting?" Debbie asks.

"Great! Almost everyone was there. We had sixteen women and had to take turns. You can only get six people around a quilt, three to a side. Sandwiches good for lunch?"

I smile. "Works with us."

"There are leftover cold cuts in the fridge and you can cut some slices off of the loaf in the bread box. I hope you're both okay with milk to wash it down," Mom finishes. "How did you two make out with your reading and studying this morning?"

"Great. I got a lot done," I say. "Ready for fishing this afternoon."

"Is Matt going with you?" Mom asks.

"I thought I'd go alone. I need some time to think. You have your quilting, I have my fishing."

Mom sighs. "And your father has his time in his workshop."

We all laugh, because Dad can disappear into his workshop for hours at a time—that is, when he can find the time.

"I'd better go dig some worms," I say. "If I don't get back inside before you go, have fun shopping. As a hunter-gatherer, I'll see if I can bring home supper. Just in case, though, you could always bring home a pizza!"

I head for the door.

"We haven't had pizza for quite a while," Mom calls behind me. "We'll probably invite Leah to supper too…"

I go into the backyard and head over to my favorite spot for worms. It takes about ten minutes to dig up enough of them. Then I go to the shed for my fishing gear, and of course I have to take the book out of the drawer. Gently putting it down on the workbench, I remove the towel. It hasn't changed a bit—and yes, it's still glowing. I find myself looking at it with even more respect today; it commands a feeling of awe in me, knowing that God's hand is involved.

I place my palm on the book and ask God to strengthen and guide me in whatever He has planned.

With that done, I wrap the book in its towel and place it back in the drawer. Time to go fishing!

I take my bike out of the shed and put my tackle box in my backpack. With rod in hand, I set off. As I pedal along, so many thoughts are buzzing around in my head that I almost miss the path down to the river.

I leave my bike by the path and start walking towards the old sawmill.

Arriving, I take up my favorite spot—the same spot where I lost that monster fish. I get geared up and look out over the river. What a beautiful day! There's hardly a breeze and the river is rolling lazily along. It rises slightly in one spot, covering a boulder that sits just below the surface. Elsewhere, an eddy warns of a sunken log. A robin sings across the water and a crow calls in the distance. I hear the chatter of a squirrel behind me. Life is good.

I take a deep breath of the cool, clean air and make my first cast. Pausing to let my presentation settle in the water, I slowly reel the line back in. I keep an eye on the area where my spinner should be.

I feel a tug on the line but miss setting the hook. Slowing the retrieve, I feel another bite, and this time it's vicious. The rod bends like a horseshoe.

I set the hook, or so I think. Then, as fast as it started, it's gone. There's no pressure on the line. The rod is straight again. The only noticeable difference is my heartrate.

Trying to calm myself, I finish retrieving my line. As it exits the water, I see that the worm is gone. Whatever it was has enjoyed a good snack at my expense!

Needing to rebait the hook, I sort through the worms, looking for the best choice. I'm startled when I hear a voice coming from right behind me.

"That looked like a big fish," he says. "I think he wants to go home with you today."

Almost jumping out of my skin, I turn and see Michael Donovan standing with a fishing rod in his hand.

"You almost gave me a heart attack!" I say. "Where did you come from? I didn't hear you come up. And how did you know about this place?"

"Slow down. I'm an avid fisherman, and Matt told me about the riverbank after church on Sunday. Says it's a good spot to catch some trout. He swore me to secrecy, though! As for not hearing me, I don't make any more noise than I have to when I approach a fishing spot. Besides, I think you were otherwise occupied when I arrived."

"Did you see the bend in that rod?" I exclaim. "I think that was the same fish I lost last time. You got enough worms? I have plenty if you need some."

"Oh, I think I'm good. But would you like to fish or would you like to talk?"

"Let's fish. I want to see if I can hook that monster again."

He smiles at me. "You do that. I'll go so far as to guarantee that you catch that fish today."

"I sure hope you're right!"

"It's not a matter of right and wrong. It's a matter of faith."

"How can faith catch fish?"

"Jesus told the apostles that they would be fishers of men," Mr. Donovan says. "That's exactly what happened… because of their faith." He lets that sink in for a moment. "You were sent here today not to catch a once-in-a-lifetime fish but to receive instruction on what the Lord our God wants of you. The fish will just be a small reward for your obedience."

I know I must look dumb, just standing there with my mouth open and a blank look on my face.

"How did you know?" I ask. "Who told you? Why are you here?"

"Calm yourself, young man. Sit down and I'll answer some of your questions."

Stepping away from the riverbank, I nervously sit on the trunk of a fallen tree. I don't know whether I should demand answers, sit silently and wait to see what he has to say, or get up and run as fast as I can.

"Running won't help," he says. "If you sit quietly, most of your questions will be answered."

Not being able to speak, I nod my head. How does he know what I'm thinking?

"Let's start with a new introduction. My name is Michael, as you know, but that is both who I am and *what* I am. I am an angel of the Lord."

I start to speak, but he cuts me off.

"Do not interrupt. When I am done, I will answer what questions you may have that are within my power to answer. I know what has happened to you and your sister and two friends because I have been the one to make these events happen. The flashing lights, the flashbacks, and the dreams all come from me. The Lord sent me to put the Book of Life into your hands. Why will not be revealed to you today. It will be revealed only when and if the Lord sees fit.

"I give up the book begrudgingly, for it has been mine to safeguard since the beginning. In Daniel 12, I am mentioned. Mine is the duty to protect God's people, but also to protect the Book of Life. It has fallen to me to oversee this next step in the progression of the Book of Life.

"Do not be disillusioned. You are not merely taking possession of a holy text of the Almighty. This task comes with great responsibility. It will require you and your friends to risk life and limb, and even your immortal souls. The Book of Life is an important part of God's plan for mankind and eternity, where there are but two destinations. Because of the importance of the Book of Life in this plan, it is sought by powers that seek to change God's plan.

"God has deemed that when the Book of Life is opened, the end of an age will come—the age of man struggling with the powers of darkness. This is also the age in which those same powers wage war with all that is good in an attempt to steal souls from the reward their heavenly Father has prepared for them. The Father went so far as to send His only begotten Son as the perfect sacrifice for the people's transgressions. These powers of darkness will do everything they can to lay their hands on the Book of Life. This is why secrecy is of the utmost importance.

"As troubling as all this might sound, you must always remember that the Lord is with you. At no time will you be alone. I will be with you also to help light your way and guide you in the will of God and the path He has chosen for you.

"You have been chosen as the leader of your group because your faith is the strongest. I tell you this not to build up your pride and ego, for they have no place in the Lord's work, but so you may know where the greatest responsibility lies. It is not an easy task to lead, but you can do all things with Christ to strengthen you. Remember to pray often and put your faith in God. When tempted, and you will be tempted, always go to that phrase: what would Jesus do?

"You may bring the Book of Life into your house, to your room, where you may safely conceal it in your closet. It will not be detected. Only you and your friends will be able to see it. However, do not make any more attempts to open the book. As I have told you, you will not be able to open it. That is God's will. Now do you have any questions?"

I am so startled by everything he has said that it takes me a moment to get my wits about me.

"You say that we will be in danger from the powers of darkness," I finally respond. "Do you mean Satan?"

"That's one of his many names."

"How can four teenagers fight the power of Satan?"

"As Ephesians 6:13–18 says, 'Therefore put on the full armor of God, so that when the day of evil comes, you may be able to stand your ground, and after you have done everything, to stand. Stand firm then, with the belt of truth buckled around your waist, with the breastplate of righteousness in place, and with your feet fitted with the readiness that comes from the gospel of peace. In addition to all this, take up the shield of faith, with which you can extinguish all the flaming arrows of the evil one. Take the helmet of salvation and the sword of the Spirit, which is the word of God. And pray in the Spirit on all occasions with all kinds of prayers and requests. With this in mind, be alert and always keep on praying for all the Lord's people.'

"Remember these words. Take heart of their meaning as you face everything that is sure to come. Remember this also: I am here. Though you may not see me, be assured that I am here. The short answer to your question is that you are not alone in this. God would not give you a task that He did not know you were capable of finishing."

"How long do we have to be the guardians of the Book of Life?" I ask.

"Until the Lord our God says otherwise. It has not been revealed to me. Therefore I cannot answer that question."

"Is there anything special we should be doing?"

"You were told to study the scriptures, which you have done. You and the others will meet tomorrow to discuss what you have read. Beware of the words of man in your discussion. Further instructions will follow."

He stops speaking and I find myself mesmerized by the power of this tranquil moment by the riverside.

"Our time today is done," he concludes. "You will not see me again for a time, but I will be with you. Catch your great fish and go home."

I watch as he walks into the woods and disappears. I don't know how long I remain there, but it's a long time. Thoughts are whirling around in my head. Even as I prepare to make my next cast, it's done by reflex; my thoughts are elsewhere.

Casting out into the current, I start to reel in my line when the rod jumps in my hands and bends, almost doubling over. With an aggressive upward pull, I set the hook. The pressure on the line is so strong that I can't reel it in. Keeping the tip of the rod up, I maintain good pressure on the handle, slowly reeling in against the drag. Each time I feel an easing of pressure and the drag stops singing, I retrieve more line. As I gain a little, I know I still have a long way to go.

Never have I experienced this kind of fight. It takes all my concentration to keep from losing this fish. He goes deep. He rises suddenly. He is unpredictable.

I don't know how long we battle, but I'm winning. Ever so slowly I gain ground as I reel firmly but gently.

As if to shock me into making a mistake, my opponent performs a surprise jump, higher than any I've ever seen before. I'm in shock, not because of the jump but because of the fish's gigantic size. Maintaining my composure, I keep pressure on the line. It will soon be over.

I bring the fish closer to the bank of the river, knowing that this is where it could get tricky. Smaller fish can be lifted or flicked out of the water onto the bank, but this beast will break my line and escape if I dare try anything that foolish. My only option is to slide it up onto the bank, although it's risky considering I have no dip net.

Maneuvering the tiring fish, I finally make my move. Onto the bank he comes. With my rod in one hand to keep pressure on the line, I drop to my knees to grab the fish with the other. Seeing that the hook has popped free, I drop the rod and use two hands, both of which are needed. This struggle isn't over yet.

I finally breathe a little easier, cradling the huge trout between my knees. Slipping my fingers into a gill, I move the fish to a more secure position farther from the water. This monster is more than two feet long—and that's before adding any fisherman's exaggerations!

The thought passes through my mind to release this prize, but after some reflective thought I look at this as a gift from God.

Mercifully dispatching my catch, I pack up and head for home. I check my watch and am surprised to see that only an hour has passed since I arrived at the old sawmill. I know that can't be right, but I also know better than to question it.

Nothing will ever again be as it should in my life, of that I'm sure.

PART TWO

STUDY THE WORD

NINE

Tuesday afternoon

My pedaling is as effortless as it is mindless, which is a good thing since my mind is elsewhere. It's back at the river, where I just met an angel face to face. It's back in the shed where the Book of Life is wrapped in a towel. It's with my sister and my friends.

What are we going to do? More to the point, what are we going to be asked to do? Michael just said we would risk life and limb, even our souls! A week and a half has passed since I accepted Christ and I knew my life would change, but I didn't have a clue that all this would happen.

A different train of thought takes over. God Himself sent an angel. He has given me, fourteen-year-old me, a task. If God thinks I'm worthy, who am I to doubt it?

Clearing my mind, I go to Him in prayer. In fact, I'm still praying when I arrive home. The driveway is empty, so I know the girls aren't back from shopping yet. I look at my watch and see that it's only 3:30. Why does it feel like two days have passed since the start of the afternoon?

I lean my bike against the shed. Knowing that the book is inside stirs my curiosity and I feel the urge to take another look. I can't help myself.

I slide open the dresser drawer and the glow of the book emanates out through the towel. I gently pick it up, place it on the workbench, and fold back the towel. I stand and stare, feeling weak in the knees. This is just amazing. Four of us are being given a task by God? Wow!

As I pull myself together, I refold the towel and put the book away. I take a deep breath, then take off my backpack and remove the monster fish. Once I've cleaned it, I wrap it and put it in the fridge.

Now what? Should I go get the Book of Life and take it to my room? Should I wait for the others? There didn't seem to be any urgency about this, so I decide to wait.

I hear the sound of tires grating on the gravel in the driveway and look out to see Mom's jeep. As I watch, all three occupants get out and proceed to remove a bunch of bags from the back.

"You guys need some help with that stuff?" I holler from the front door.

"A gentleman wouldn't even have to ask," Debbie says. "He would just get over here and help."

I head over to help with their treasures. "Can always count on you to build my ego, sis. Looks like you had a fun shopping trip."

"We didn't find everything we wanted," Leah replies. "But if we had, I would have put a big dent in my savings."

"Let me take some of these bags for you." I take a bag in each hand. "Mom, are we still having pizza and Leah for supper?"

"Now, James, you know we're not cannibals. We're inviting Leah as a supper guest, yes, but she is not on the menu." Mom smiles. "Your father is picking up the pizzas on his way home. He should get here by six."

"We can save the trout for tomorrow, I guess."

"How many did you catch?" Mom asks.

"Only one."

Debbie starts to laugh. "You caught one fish and think we can make a meal for five out of it? Do you have a few loaves to go with that? You must be losing it, little brother."

"Maybe we should see this fish before we start making too much fun of your brother," Leah points out.

"You really know how to take the fun out of an opportunity to embarrass my sister, Leah," I say. "I will get an apology, but now the element of surprise is gone."

"You aren't telling me you caught a trout big enough to feed all of us?" Debbie blusters. "I don't believe it!"

"The proof isn't in the pudding this time. It's in the fridge. Have a look for yourself."

Into the house we go. Debbie drops her bags on the floor and heads straight for the fridge. She pulls open the door and looks inside. Her mouth gapes wide but nothing comes out.

She looks at me, then back into the fridge. Then she looks back at me.

"Move over and let me see!" Leah shoulders her way past Debbie and peers into the fridge. "Wow! What a fish! Did you catch that in the river? What a monster!"

"I'd like to take a look." Mom peers into the fridge and gasps. "I don't think I've ever seen a trout that big, except maybe on television. Leah, you're more than welcome to share in the bounty the Lord has provided when we feast on it tomorrow. James, your father is going to want to hear the whole story about this."

"Can I invite Matt over too?" I ask. "You know he'll go nuts when he sees that thing."

"Didn't you say he was coming over tomorrow morning? That being said, you may invite him to stay for the day. After supper you can all go to youth group together. That fish is capable of feeding a multitude. What should I make to go with it?"

I shrug. "Just do your usual magic in the kitchen."

"My mom is going to think you're trying to steal her daughter." Leah giggles. "But I'll explain the circumstances to her. I know it'll be all right."

"We have an hour before Justin gets home, so you youngsters find something to do," Mom says. "I'm going to put my purchases away and then run the dishwasher through a cycle."

She takes a bag and heads upstairs.

This gives me a few minutes alone with Debbie and Leah.

"When I tell Dad the story of catching that fish, I'm going to have to leave a lot out."

"What do you mean?" Debbie demands.

Leah gives me a questioning look.

"Parts of the story have to be kept secret, if you know what I mean," I said.

"That's just it! We don't know what you mean." The pitch of Debbie's voice rises.

"Are you saying what I think you're saying?" questions Leah.

"Oh, I most certainly am, but we don't have time to get into specifics," I say. "Mom will be back down soon. Just know that what happened today will blow your minds. Tomorrow morning I'll give you a complete rundown, when Matt's here."

"I don't know if I can wait 'til tomorrow," Debbie pleads. "I won't sleep a wink tonight. Can't you even just give us a hint?"

I shake my head. "No. One thing leads to another and then another and suddenly you have the whole story and Matt is left out. Remember, we're in this together."

"Going shopping helped calm my nerves, but now I'm just as wound up as before," Leah says quietly. "There's a difference, though. I'm more excited than scared this time."

"Am I ever glad to hear you say that," I say with a smile. "You had me worried the other day. I didn't know if you were going to be able to handle this. So I was hoping for a reboot. Glad to have you back."

"Glad to be back. I appreciate that you were worried about me. If it makes any difference, I worry about you too. All of you."

"You still here?" Mom says as she comes back into the kitchen. "Well, there's no reason you girls can't set the table. By the way, put out extra napkins. James and his father can be messy eaters."

Everyone laughs.

"All right," I say. "Have your fun. I'm going out to the shed to put away my bike and fishing gear."

This draws questioning looks from both Debbie and Leah. I just shake my head as I go out the back door.

I put away my tackle and bike and find myself staring at the dresser. I badly want to open the drawer and take out the glowing book. I want to see it and touch it.

Instead I shake my head and head back for the house. When I step into the kitchen, I notice that Leah is absent.

"She took her packages home and is going to remind her mother that she's having supper with us tonight," Debbie says. "Why? Did you miss her, little brother?"

Mom raises an eyebrow. "Something going on that I don't know about?"

"Only in the overactive female mind," I reply.

Debbie winks. "Oh, we'll see."

I give her my best what-the-heck look just as Leah steps through the front door.

"It's all set with my mom," our friend says. "She wants to know how much she owes you for babysitting, Mrs. Jeffries. I told her you want a hundred dollars but only in cash and that I would deliver it. She didn't bite, but she did laugh. Is there anything I can do to help?"

"No, dear. Everything's ready. All we need now is Justin and the pizza." Mom stops and listens. "Speak of the devil and who should appear? I think I just heard him roll into the driveway. Everyone, sit at the table with a fork and knife in your hands and look hungry."

Dad comes through the door carrying two large pizza boxes and immediately notices us at the table. He starts to laugh.

"I don't know whose idea this was, you poor starving waifs, but any one of you could be culpable. Company excluded, that is, Leah. Although I see you seem to be a willing participant!" Dad puts down the pizza. "I'll wash my hands. Debbie, you can say grace. Before anyone faints from hunger please."

Debbie asks a blessing on food, family, and company and then Dad opens the boxes.

"Dig in, you're on your own," he says as we all reach for slices. "How was everyone's day?"

Mom jumps in and talks about the shopping trip. "A second mortgage should just about pay for what we picked up," she says, smiling widely. "I'll let James tell you about fishing."

"You've heard the phrase 'a picture is worth a thousand words'?" I say. "Well, instead of telling you how fishing went, why don't you just look on the bottom shelf of the fridge?"

"How many did you catch?"

"Just look in the fridge, Dad."

Getting up from his chair, he goes to the fridge. All the time he keeps his eyes on us, knowing that something is up. After looking inside, he turns back to me with a big smile on his face.

"You caught that!" he exclaims, although it sounds almost like a question.

"Sure did!"

He closes the door and comes back to the table. "Tell me all about it, son."

For the next few minutes, I tell my fish story, careful not to divulge any details that might lead to questions I can't answer.

"Good for you, son," Dad says when I'm finished. "You can now tell everyone that you've outfished your father. We have to get some pictures, though. You know how people like to tease about fish stories being embellished. We need documented proof so there can be no doubt. Have you told Matt yet? I can't believe he's not over here talking a mile a minute."

"Not yet," I say. "He's coming over tomorrow and I wanted to surprise him. I'll ask him to stay for supper so he can enjoy the trout with the rest of us."

"I'd like to be here when that boy lays his eyes on that trout, but I guess I'll have to wait." Dad looks over at Leah. "How's our little church mouse? Quiet as ever, I see. You look a little preoccupied today. Is everything okay?"

"Oh fine, Mr. Jeffries. You know me. I just like to sit and take it all in. We had a good day at the mall. We have so much to be thankful for."

"Amen to that!" Dad says.

Before long, the table has been cleared off and everyone's gone into the living room with tea. I take my mug and settle on the floor in front of the fireplace. Debbie is showing Dad what she bought that day while Mom and Leah talk about their own mall excitement.

Dad listens closely, or maybe he's like me and only pretends to listen. Whichever it is, he's good at it.

In a break in the conversation, he finally turns to me. "Go get your rod and reel and we'll take some pictures. And while you're out in the shed, bring a tape measure. I almost wish you hadn't cleaned that beast so we could weigh it too. I think it has to be the biggest fish ever to come out of the river."

"Be right back, Dad."

I get my rod, reel, and a tape measure… but before I can come back inside, I get held up by the usual urge to open the drawer and take a quick look at the book, even though I know Dad's waiting.

Before I can do anything about it, I manage to push aside that urge.

Dad and I spend a half-hour taking measurement and pictures. When we're done, I take the camera to my room to download the pics to my gallery. But none of these are going out until Matt sees the trophy fish for himself.

As I come back down, I'm just in time to see Leah leaving.

"See you in the morning, James," she says.

"Can't wait."

Am I crazy or does that bring a soft sort of smile to her face? Looking around, I notice that everyone's eyes are trained on me. They're all wearing smiles.

"What?"

"Oh nothing," Debbie says with a smirk on her lips and a twinkle in her eyes. "Nothing at all."

"There's a ballgame on," Dad reminds me. "You want to go to the den and watch it? The women want to watch a baking show."

"Lead the way, father of mine."

The ballgame ends at about 10:30 and Mom and Debbie have already been in to say good night. Dad and I wash up and head for bed.

"You had a good day, son," he says. "Don't forget to thank Him for it. Good night. God bless. Love you."

"I won't forget, Dad. Good night. God bless. Love you too."

Back in my room, I turn on my light and close the door. I change into my pajamas, shorts, and a T-shirt. Then I go to my knees with head down and hands folded and begin to pray. Humble before my Creator, I thank Him for all that He has blessed me with. Slipping under the covers, I lay my head on the pillow.

But before I can fall asleep, the next thing I become aware of is that sensation of peace I keep experiencing. It wraps itself around me and I feel comfortable and safe. Through that feeling comes a voice I have heard several times before. It's Michael the angel. I feel no anxiety or fear.

"James, you are doing the Lord's work and He is with you," the angel says. "Tomorrow you will gather with your friends and start a journey into the true meaning of the Book of Life. You are all young, but as this task goes on you will reach a spiritual maturity well beyond your years. You will be guided by the Holy Spirit on your path to that maturity. At times, you and your friends will experience doubt. You will experience conflict. You will experience fear. But you will also feel peace and joy and take pride and understanding in what you're doing. Whether the times are good or bad, always remember that the Lord is with you. Always remember to go to Him for help and strength. If you stay connected with the Lord, you will have the same success as Noah, Moses, David, Daniel, and others like them. The key is to love the Lord, have faith in Him, and trust Him. You can and will do all things through Him who strengthens you.

"Remember that the words of man, including other people's interpretation of God's Word, may not be as the Lord has intended. Read 2 Timothy 4:3–5: 'For the time will come when people will not put up with sound doctrine. Instead, to suit their own desires, they will gather around them a great number of teachers to say what their itching ears want to hear. They will turn their ears away from the truth and turn aside to myths. But you, keep your head in all situations, endure hardship, do the work of an evangelist, discharge all the duties of your ministry.' What does it matter if you please man but in the process displease your heavenly Father?

"The Lord has tasked me to be your guardian angel, so to speak. I will be with you, not always visible but there nonetheless. The scriptures you will discuss tomorrow will take the whole day. In fact, it will require more time than that. Do not hurry through or skip past any of those scriptures. Each is a piece to the puzzle that, when assembled, will take you to the next stage of your task. Understanding will be given to you as you learn the true importance of the Book of Life."

There is a period of silence and I listen for more.

"I will leave you now," the angel finishes. "May God be with you."

TEN

Wednesday

I wake up and look at my clock. It's 6:30. Time to get up.

I take a shower, get dressed, and go downstairs for breakfast. As usual, I find Mom in the kitchen.

"Morning, Mom." I smile. "Whatcha got for breakfast today?"

"Bacon, eggs, and toast. The only choice I'll give you is how many slices of bacon you want and how I should cook your egg."

"Two. And over easy, if that's okay."

"Certainly is. The toast and bacon are warm in the oven. There's juice in the fridge and tea on the stove."

I walk towards the fridge, pouring myself a glass of orange juice.

"Your sister asked me to tell you to get her up no later than 7:30," Mom says. "And your father left a note with some chores he hopes you can do before Matt and Leah come over. It's on the table."

Mom slides two perfectly cooked over easy eggs onto a plate and hands it to me.

"Thanks, Mom."

I carry the plate over to the table and sit down. Taking Dad's handwritten note, I read as I eat. Dad wants me to clean up the garden.

"This looks doable," I murmur before swallowing a mixture of eggs and bacon and washing it down with orange juice.

"If you want to tend to the garden, I'll make sure your sister doesn't oversleep," Mom says. "Deal?"

"Done deal."

"By the way, I have a Women's Missionary Society meeting later this morning and won't get home for lunch. Why don't you youngsters warm up some leftover pizza or use the rest of the cold cuts?"

"What would we do without you?" With breakfast done, I get up and walk over to her. I give her a big hug. "You sure are one of God's blessings to this home."

She swats at me with a towel. "Oh you."

I put on a pair of boots, grab a pair of gloves, and head toward the shed. My plan is to get the wheelbarrow and a hoe.

Even before I get there, I find myself waylaid by that same urge again.

Take a look at the book. You know you want to.

This time I'm not in a hurry. As soon as I enter the shed, I go to the dresser and slide open the drawer. I pick up the book, its glow visible through the towel, and gently put it down on the workbench. I unwrap the towel as though it's made of tissue paper. My awe seems to grow every time I gaze at the book. This is the work of the hand of God. It still boggles my mind that I, James Jeffries, am beholding a piece of biblical history. It makes me feel insignificant and special all at the same time.

I touch the book with a fingertip and experience that same peacefulness I felt the previous night. I slide my finger up the cover and let the whole palm of my hand rest on it.

There it is again! The flash of light that started this whole thing.

I don't know why God has chosen me and my friends, but I trust Him. I rewrap the towel around the book and gently place it back.

I pick up a hoe and I take it and the wheelbarrow to the garden. Pulling the vegetables that are past due and weed the rest takes about an hour, after which I stand back and look over my handiwork with satisfaction. I dump the old plants on the compost heap and put my tools away in the shed, having to overcome my urge to take the book out all over again.

As I walk back to the house and enter through the back door, I see Debbie sipping a cup of tea at the table. Mom is nowhere in sight.

"Any left in the pot?" I ask.

"Should be another cup at least."

"Where's Mom?"

"Getting ready for WMS. The meeting is scheduled for 10:30."

"Have you heard from Leah?"

"No. You heard from Matt?"

"No." I hesitate for a moment. "Did Mom tell you that she won't be home for lunch?"

"Yeah. She mentioned pizza and cold cuts."

I take a moment to look out the kitchen window towards the shed, thinking about the book again. "I think we should set up at the kitchen table."

"You think it's wise to bring the book in here?"

"Yes, and I'll tell you why when Matt and Leah arrive."

"Tell your sister what?" asks Mom as she steps back into the kitchen.

"Just an idea I have for the project we're working on," I tell her. "I think she's going to like it. We plan on working here in the kitchen, if that's okay."

"Sure. It will put Matt closer to the cookie jar. That boy sure does like my cookies."

"Not to burst your bubble, Mom, but Matt just likes to eat," I say. "I have to admit, though, that he seems to have a special attraction to eating *here*."

Debbie frowns at me. "What's that supposed to mean?"

"Nothing."

Mom nods along. "Well, you're all set for lunch, and snacks too. I'm off to the church. Remember, we're having trout for supper."

And with that, she's gone.

She must have met Leah in the driveway because no sooner has Mom left than Leah walks in.

"Your mom waved to me as she left," Leah tells us. "Where is she off to?"

"WMS this morning," Debbie answers.

Leah sighs. "Oh, I should have known. My mom was heading that way when I left."

I stand up and walk towards the back door. "Matt should be here soon. While we're waiting, I'll go get the book."

"You're bringing the book in the house?" Leah asks.

I nod.

Just then, Matt walks inside. "Last one to arrive again, I see. You guys always tease me about being an early bird... what have I missed?"

"James was just going out to bring the book in for our session," Leah says.

"Bring the book in the house?" Matt's eyes widen. "Really!"

"Why is everyone so surprised?" I ask. "Did you think we would be doing this out in the shed? Besides, the angel told me it's okay to keep the book in my room from now on. He says it'll be safe there."

They all answer in unison: "What? When did this happen?"

"I'll fill you in." But first I retrieve the book from the shed, carrying it into the kitchen with great reverence. "Debbie, why don't you unwrap the book on the table?"

"I can't believe how nervous this makes me." Debbie's hands shake as she folds back the towel. "Can you still see a glow from it?"

"Yeah, I can. But first, I think we should say a prayer." Their silence is the sign of agreement. We all bow our heads. "Heavenly Father, You've given us a task and we're here today to work on it. Please guide us and direct us, give us strength, and open our eyes and our minds to see what you want. We thank You for any and all help You send our way. We ask this in the name of Jesus Christ, our Lord and Savior. Amen."

We all open our eyes.

Matt jumps right in. "When did the angel talk to you again?"

"That same angel appeared to me in a dream Monday night. He said God was happy with us so far. Then he reiterated our instructions to study those scriptures. He reminded me again that we are not to rely on the interpretations of man. Then he told me to go fishing where Matt and I were the other day."

I look to Matt, but my best friend doesn't say a thing. I've got everyone's attention now.

"I couldn't tell you, Matt, because he said I had to go alone." I nod towards Leah and Debbie. "While you two were out shopping, I went to the same spot by the old sawmill. I was putting on a worm when a voice called to me out of nowhere. I almost jumped into the river. Looking to my left, I saw Michael Donovan standing there with a fishing rod in his hands. It turns out he's Michael, an angel mentioned in the Bible!"

They all react with wide eyes, but I keep going.

"First I was speechless. He explained that God has tasked him with looking after the Book of Life. Taking possession of it, he said, is great responsibility and will require us to risk life and limb, and even our immortal souls. The Book of Life is an important part of God's plan for mankind and eternity. Its opening will begin the end of an age…"

Over the course of the next few minutes, I pass on every detail of my conversation with the angel, trying my hardest not to leave anything out.

"When I asked him how long we would have the Book of Life, Michael said that he didn't know. I asked if we should be doing anything special, and he just told us to keep studying the scriptures. Further instructions would follow." I take a big, deep breath. "That's about it. Any questions?"

I look around the table at a trio of stunned faces.

Matt is the first to speak. "Any questions? I don't know where to start!"

"Let's just settle down," Leah says calmly. "I think this whole thing just got very real, but we don't have a whole lot of answers."

"There's one thing I'm surprised Matt hasn't asked about," Debbie remarks.

"And what's that?" Matt asks.

My sister looks him right in the eye. "You've forgotten all about that fish, haven't you?"

"You're right! I did. I guess this angel stuff is way more important than any fish." Matt turns to stare me down. "Well, what about it, James? Did you catch it?"

"Look on the bottom shelf of the fridge, Matt. You'll see."

Matt gets up and goes over to the fridge. When he opens the door and bends down to see the bottom shelf, I can almost hear his jaw hit the floor.

"What a monster!" he exclaims. "Don't tell me you caught this on your trout rod."

"Twenty-nine inches long, nine inches deep, and five inches thick—and that's what we're having for supper." I clear my throat. "But enough about fish. Let's get back to why we're here: scripture. I thought we'd start with the older passages and work our way up to the new. That puts Exodus 32 first on the list. You want to read it, Matt?"

"Okay, but just know that I'm gonna want to go back and hear the whole fish story from beginning to end later." Matt opens his Bible and finds the scripture in question.

> So Moses went back to the Lord and said, "Oh, what a great sin these people have committed! They have made themselves gods of gold. But now, please forgive their sin—but if not, then blot me out of the book you have written."
>
> The Lord replied to Moses, "Whoever has sinned against me I will blot out of my book. Now go, lead the people to the place I spoke of, and my angel will go before you. However, when the time comes for me to punish, I will punish them for their sin."[12]

I turn to Leah. "What do you think?"

"This is the first passage in the Bible that talks about God having a book," she says. "It isn't called the Book of Life specifically, but many people assume that's what it is. If you compare this scripture to Revelation 20:12, for example, it makes you wonder. We can't be really sure."

---

[12] Exodus 32:31–34.

"And you, Matt?" I ask.

"It reminds me of the old days when my grandparents and great-grandparents kept all the family names in the family Bible," he says. "But if someone did something really bad, their name could be removed. Back then, that was a big thing… and this is a whole lot bigger, obviously, since we're talking about God's punishment. But I agree with Leah. It's hard to tell whether this is referring to the Book of Life or another of the books mentioned in Revelation. What do you think, Debbie?"

"Here's the thing," says Debbie. "James found this scripture the same way all the others turned up, by letting his Bible fall open. If all the others were about the Book of Life, I'm pretty sure this scripture is too."

Leah nods solemnly. "I never thought of that, but you're right."

"What I got out of it is that God can and will remove names from the Book of Life and punish those who sin against Him," my sister continues. "He wouldn't let Moses take the blame for the people. He gave us free choice and we all have to answer for our own decisions. You know, it's the choices and consequences that Derrick is always talking about."

"I've got to agree, sis," I say. "How could this verse be talking about anything else but the Book of Life? It's a big thing for God to remove a name from the book. The names aren't written in stone. He wouldn't remove a name without good reason."

Everyone nods and my gaze shifts back to the open Bible.

"Let's move on to Daniel 7," I say. "Leah, you want to do the honors this time?"

"Sure," she says as looks through her own Bible, opening the pages to a bookmark.

A river of fire was flowing, coming out from before him. Thousands upon thousands attended him; ten thousand times ten thousand stood before him. The court was seated, and the books were opened.

Then I continued to watch because of the boastful words the horn was speaking. I kept looking until the beast was slain and its body destroyed and thrown into the blazing fire. (The other beasts had been stripped of their

> authority, but were allowed to live for a period of time.)
>
> In my vision at night I looked, and there before me was one like a son of man, coming with the clouds of heaven. He approached the Ancient of Days and was led into his presence. He was given authority, glory and sovereign power; all nations and peoples of every language worshiped him. His dominion is an everlasting dominion that will not pass away, and his kingdom is one that will never be destroyed.[13]

Stopping, she looks at me for direction, but it's Debbie who offers her take on the passage first.

"It certainly sounds like judgment day to me," Debbie remarks. "It's just like in Revelation when the books were opened. The last of those books was the Book of Life, and that's when eternity begins for those whose names are found there. It mentions a dominion that won't pass away or ever be destroyed, and a beast that's slain and thrown into the blazing fire. That has to be Satan. The other beasts mentioned must be those who do Satan's work."

"I can't really add anything," Matt says. "The rest of the chapter interprets this dream Daniel had. It falls in line with what we read in Revelation."

"I think this is the first time the Bible uses the phrase 'son of man,'" Leah adds. "Jesus called Himself that more than once in the New Testament."

I nod reflectively. "That's true. This scripture is more about the end of days than it is about the Book of Life, but the books are there and their opening marks the beginning of the end... and also the beginning of eternity. The Book of Life plays a prominent part."

We're ready to move on and I turn to Debbie and ask her to read from Daniel 12:1.

> At that time Michael, the great prince who protects your people, will arise. There will be a time of distress such as has not happened from the beginning of nations until then. But

---

[13] Daniel 7:10–14.

at that time your people—everyone whose
name is found written in the book—will be
delivered.

"It certainly sounds like a prophecy," Matt begins. "I think it means that
even when times are at their worst, anyone whose name is found in the Book of
Life is going to be saved. After all, isn't that why Jesus came, so we could have
eternal life? He came to seek out and save the lost. We know from Revelation that
if a person's name is found in the Lamb's Book of Life, they will live for eternity
in heaven with the Father."

Suddenly, Matt's face lights up, as though a lightbulb has gone off in his
mind.

"That part about Michael," he adds. "Do you think it refers to the angel
who's talking to us? Is this the same guy as the archangel who battled Satan?"

Leah jumps in. "I don't think it matters who the angel is. Our task has to do
with the Book of Life, not the identity of a specific angel God sends to help us.
We can't get sidetracked by non-issues." She taps her fingers together thought-
fully. "That said, I think you're right about the prophecy. If your name is in the
book, you're okay. What will be the most distressing time in history? It'll come
on the day of judgment when everyone who's denied or rejected the Father, Son,
and Holy Spirit realizes the fate they've chosen for themselves."

"I think you're right on both counts," I say. "Whether our Michael is an
archangel or not, I'm just glad to know he's around. Anyway, this scripture may
be short, but consider what it says: the end will be stressful, but not for those
whose names are found in the Book of Life. It's pretty simple when you stop and
think about it."

When no one seems to have anything to add, I read from Philippians 4:3.

Yes, and I ask you, my true companion, help
these women since they have contended at
my side in the cause of the gospel, along with
Clement and the rest of my co-workers, whose
names are in the book of life.

There's a moment of silence as this one sinks in.

"What I get from this is that we should help one another as brothers and
sisters in Christ," I say. "Paul mentions women and men. He mentions loyalty

and the cause of the gospel. He mentions the names written in the Book of Life. Has the purpose of the gospel changed since then? Should our loyalty be any different? Whose names are in the book? Those who work for the Lord. What do you guys think?"

After a minute of careful consideration, everyone is satisfied with this and ready to move on again.

"We're getting into the nitty-gritty now," I say. "Matt, it's your turn to read. Let's check out Revelation 3:5."

> The one who is victorious will, like them,
> be dressed in white. I will never blot out the
> name of that person from the book of life, but
> will acknowledge that name before my Father
> and his angels.

"A couple of things," Leah says. "First, think about the phrase 'the one who is victorious.' To me, that seems to refer to anyone who has been able to withstand the trials and tribulations of this world and come out the victor. Anyone who faces all the temptations Satan throws their way and is able to resist—or, after slipping, makes it back to the path God lays out for us. The one who is victorious is the one who walks with Jesus. No one has ever been able to face Satan alone, though, and come out on top. Secondly, this victorious one will be dressed in white and their name will be found in the Book of Life. Not just that, but they'll be acknowledged by the Son to the Father and the heavenly hosts. Wow!"

I can't help but smile. "That's pretty deep!"

"Can you imagine?" my sister says, sounding almost giddy. "Think about it... Jesus saying to the Father and the angels, 'This is Debbie and she did well.' Can you imagine anything better?"

"You'll notice that it says 'I will never blot out the name of that person,'" I add. "Let's keep this in mind as we move forward."

We all turn to Leah, whose turn it is to read, this time from Revelation 13:8. Leah has already turned to the correct page.

> All inhabitants of the earth will worship the
> beast—all whose names have not been written
> in the Lamb's book of life, the Lamb who was
> slain from the creation of the world.

I lean forward. "I want to start this off because it goes directly to what I just said about blotting out names written in the Book of Life. What is this scripture talking about when it refers to the Book of Life? It says that this book belongs to the Lamb that was slain from the creation of the world. That's Jesus! That makes this the Lamb's Book of Life.

"Notice that this verse doesn't claim that every name was written in the book from the time of creation. It says that the book belonged to the Lamb from the time of creation. Those who believe in predestination think that if a person's name was in the book from the beginning, they can't do anything to remove it. Those same people think that if a person's name wasn't in the book from the beginning, nothing they can do will get their name added. But here Jesus says that He will never blot out the name of those who are victorious.

"What about those who aren't victorious? In Exodus, Moses seemed to think that names could be blotted out. God didn't dispute that, but He does set the record straight. He says that we ourselves can be responsible for that happening.

"As far as adding names to the Book of Life, let's look at Acts 2:42–47."

> They devoted themselves to the apostles' teaching and to fellowship, to the breaking of bread and to prayer. Everyone was filled with awe at the many wonders and signs performed by the apostles. All the believers were together and had everything in common. They sold property and possessions to give to anyone who had need. Every day they continued to meet together in the temple courts. They broke bread in their homes and ate together with glad and sincere hearts, praising God and enjoying the favor of all the people. And the Lord added to their number daily those who were being saved.

"There are two really important words from that passage: *added* and *saved*," I continue. "Elsewhere the scriptures talk about numbers being added, like in Acts 2 on the day of Pentecost. It only mentions names being added, though, not added and saved. It sounds to me like the Book of Life is constantly being edited.

Since God is the author and editor, I think we have to consider it reasonable that names can be added or removed, but only by Him."

Matt's face has turned white. "You're scaring me, James. Where did all that come from? I've known you all my life and you've never been that deep or made that much sense—ever."

"I think there's a reason God wanted you to be our leader for this task," Leah says. "And I think He just showed us how He can give us what we need to help us along the way. Not to take anything away from James—because I think you're a smart, intelligent guy—but that was out of your depth. You've got to admit that!"

I lower my head in full agreement with her.

"God will lead us," Leah adds reverently. "God will guide us! We should recognize His hand when it's there to lift us up."

"That explains a lot." Matt nods to himself. "If you stop and think about it, we're all out of our comfort zones. But…"

All of our eyes turn to him expectantly.

"Well, I don't need a watch to know it's time to eat," he finishes. "My stomach is rumbling!"

Debbie lets out a laugh. "What a surprise that you should be the one to bring that up. Okay, let's break for lunch. What's your pleasure—cold cuts or leftover pizza?"

"You know me," Matt says with a big smile. "My favorite thing to eat is food. So it makes no difference to me!"

"Sometimes you make me wonder." Debbie shakes her head. "I'll put both on the sideboard and we can all help ourselves. If you want your pizza hot, you know where the microwave is."

"Before we get to that," I say, "Leah, why don't you close our time this morning and give thanks for the food?"

We all put our hands on the book while she prays.

Leah begins. "Heavenly Father, we thank You for this day, for life and breath, for family and friends, for Your Word, and for the task You are leading us into. Please help us to be worthy of Your trust and grant us the strength, knowledge, and courage to fulfill Your desires. We ask Your blessing on the food we are about to eat. We ask this in the name of Jesus Christ, Your Son and our Savior. Amen."

Debbie lays out a selection of bread and cold cuts on the table. The pizza is set beside the microwave and a carton of milk awaits us in the middle of the table.

"Anyone want tea or coffee?" Debbie asks. "The coffeemaker and pods are ready. Help yourselves."

We all chow down, at least Matt and I do. The girls are a lot daintier than we are. While we eat, we discuss what we've covered so far and how it all relates to the Book of Life and our understanding of the importance of the book in God's plan.

"We've only got three scriptures left, but I would say they are the most important," I say. "They're all in Revelation and I don't think we're going to have enough time to do them justice before Mom gets home."

We make a plan to get together on both Friday and Saturday evenings. Two evenings should just about do it, I think.

We finish lunch and help Debbie clear the table. Then we sit, once again ready to get back to the Lord's work.

"Debbie, why don't you start off the afternoon with a prayer?" I suggest.

She bows her head and prays. "Dear God, we thank You for choosing us, Your children, for this task. We ask that You guide and direct us so we bring honor and glory to You in what we say and do. Amen."

After a short pause, she starts to read from Revelation 17:8:

> The beast, which you saw, once was, now is not, and yet will come up out of the Abyss and go to its destruction. The inhabitants of the earth whose names have not been written in the book of life from the creation of the world will be astonished when they see the beast, because it once was, now is not, and yet will come.

"I think our main concern here is the Book of Life," Matt says. "The verse talks about those whose names have not been written in the book since the creation of the earth. They lived under the old covenant and weren't God's chosen people, or they chose to reject Him and disobey the first covenant He made with the Jewish nation before Christ died and rose again. It also refers to those who haven't accepted Christ under the new covenant. The word *astonished* is probably a huge understatement. Satan has ridden mankind hard and for a long time. It will be a terrifying wakeup call when man sees who they have been following. The Abyss obviously is a reference to hell, and that's where the beast comes from.

He is going to his destruction along with those whose names aren't written in the Book of Life."

Leah, whose head has been down, lifts her chin. "I think Matt is on the right track, but I think we have to take into consideration what happens before and after this verse. Not that it has anything to do with the Book of Life itself, but there are implications for those whose names are written in the book and those whose names are not. The woman mentioned in Revelation 17:7 is the mother of all sin and the beast carries her about so she can spread her evil among man. Then there are references in the following verses to hills and kings and horns, referring to past, present, and future history. We should pay special attention to Revelation 17:13–14."

> They have one purpose and will give their power and authority to the beast. They will wage war against the Lamb, but the Lamb will triumph over them because he is Lord of lords and King of kings—and with him will be his called, chosen and faithful followers.

"This is talking about those whose names are in the Lamb's Book of Life," Leah continues. "The Book of Life is the record of those who are called, chosen, and faithful. That alone makes it the most important book on earth, or in heaven or hell."

At this point, Leah takes a deep breath and stops.

"I don't know what to say," Debbie muses. "You and Matt both said James was talking way out of his depth, but did you listen to what both of you just said! I don't think I've ever heard a preacher talk with as much power and conviction as all three of you have today. I may be the oldest in this group, but right now I feel a little overwhelmed."

I quietly watch our little group take this step toward spiritual maturity, letting scripture and the hand of God guide us to this spot from which we can launch ourselves deeper into the task God has placed before us.

I clear my throat and look around the table. "I think we can stop for today. I don't know about you guys, but this has been exhausting for me. It's 2:30 and Mom will probably be home soon. Let's put our hands on the book for a time of silent prayer."

We all place our hands on the book and bow our heads. Not knowing what's in the others' prayers, I thank God for what we've just been through. I ask Him to help strengthen us because we all seem a little overwhelmed.

After a couple of minutes, I pray aloud. "Heavenly Father, I want to thank You again for choosing us for this task. I know Your hand is here today because we've said things well beyond our comprehension—and not only said them, but understood them. I pray in the name of Jesus Christ, our Lord and Savior. Please continue to guide and direct us. Amen."

Debbie gets up to put on some water for tea. She also reaches into the fridge for some milk to go with the cookies.

"I like the way you think," Matt says to Debbie with a big grin on his face.

"You just like food and anyone who will put it in front of you," she teases.

Meanwhile, Leah follows me upstairs to see where I'm going to store the book. It seems important for more than one of us to know its hiding place.

Once in my room, I open the closet door and place the book on a shelf.

"Aren't you going to put it somewhere out of sight?" Leah asks, sounding a little anxious that I'm not giving it the care and respect it deserves.

"Michael told me that we don't have to worry about it being discovered while it's in the house," I say. "I'm going to trust his word. After all, if you can't trust an angel, who can you trust?"

"I suppose you're right. Makes me a little nervous, though." Leah looks up and makes eye contact with me. Her voice sounds more confident now. "But I trust you and you trust Michael. I guess I'm worrying for nothing."

But from the look in her eye, I can see there's something else she wants to say. I brace myself for what I suspect is about to come.

ELEVEN

"James, I don't know if Debbie has said anything to you, but I'm so glad we're working together." Leah lowers her eyes again. "Even before all this happened, I was hoping we could spend some time… you know, you and me. Now God has us working as part of a team, and it makes me happy. And nervous. I guess what I'm trying to say… is that I really like you."

There's an uncomfortable pause.

I swallow hard and find my voice. "I really like you too. I sort of thought you liked me just from the things you've said and the way you look at me sometimes, but I was afraid I was inventing things in my mind. I didn't want to talk to Debbie because she's my sister and your friend and a girl and… well, you know what I mean."

"I guess so," she says. "Debbie knows how I feel about you and she teases me all the time about it. I don't think she wants either one of us to get hurt."

I'm getting ready to say more when we're interrupted by the sound of Debbie yelling from downstairs.

"What's going on up there?" she calls. "You two need a chaperone? How long does it take to put a book on a shelf?"

"Hold your horses!" I yell back, then turn to Leah and speak more softly. "We'll talk about this more when we have a chance to be alone. Let's go down and join the others."

With that, we head down the steps and return to the kitchen. We're just in time to hear Mom's tires crunch along the gravel in the driveway.

"Good thing Mom didn't come in to find you two upstairs together in your bedroom," Debbie says quietly. "I know she trusts us, but she still has some pretty strict ideas about what's acceptable and what's not."

"I'm so glad that didn't happen," Leah agrees. "I like your mother a lot and I wouldn't want her to think I was that kind of girl. Anyway, James and I were just talking."

"I know that, and you know that, but I'm not the one who's blushing as red as the two of you are right now." Debbie laughs. "You're trying to justify the situation."

Matt averts his gaze. "I think I'm gonna stay out of this whole conversation…"

"Stay out of what conversation?" asks Mom as she comes through the door.

"Oh, Debbie was just teasing me again," I say. "As usual."

"How did you four make out with your project? Any headway?"

"We made progress," says Matt. "But we have a long way to go yet, Mrs. Jeffries. Can I help with anything that needs to come in from the jeep?"

"Why thank you, Matt. Aren't you the gentleman." Mom smiles and gives me one of those why-didn't-you-say-that looks. "Well, I'm going to start getting supper ready. That fish is going to take at least an hour to bake and I have some ideas for spices. Then there's the veggies and an apple crisp for dessert. You girls want to give me a hand while the boys go outside to stay out from underfoot?"

Debbie nods enthusiastically. "We sure will, Mom!"

"I can take a hint," I say. "What about you, Matt?"

"I can be pretty oblivious sometimes, but even I got that loud and clear. Let's grab some cookies and head for the hills."

Matt and I head out the back door. I grab the axe from the shed as well as a stick of firewood.

"We might as well split some kindling while we wait," I suggest. "Unless you can think of something else."

"I got nothin' except maybe a question. What were you and Leah talking about while you were upstairs?"

"I could tell you it's none of your business, but that probably wouldn't work. I'll tell you—if you swear it stays between just you and me."

"Cross my heart and hope to die."

"Okay then. She told me she likes me and I told her I like her too."

"As in boyfriend-girlfriend like?"

"I guess so. We didn't get very far into it before Debbie called us down."

"Wow. I wish I had guts like that. You know I like your sister. What do you think she'd say if I told her how I feel?"

• • •

In the kitchen, a similar conversation is going on between the three females. Leah feels a little guilty over Debbie's teasing and decides to open up about it.

"Mrs. Jeffries, something happened this afternoon and I'd like to talk to you about it."

"Yes, Leah, what is it?"

"Well, James and I were putting some stuff away up in his room and I told him that I like him." Her eyes dart around the kitchen nervously. "Nothing happened. I just told him that I like him."

"That's fine, dear. What did he say?"

Leah answers in a shy, almost embarrassed tone of voice. "He said he liked me too."

After she says this, a big smile suddenly appears on her face.

"I can't say I'm surprised," Mom says. "I've been watching you two grow up together and you seem like kindred spirits. I'm happy for the both of you."

Leah looks over to Debbie, who is listening quietly.

"I'd appreciate it if you and Debbie would keep this a secret between the three of us," Leah says. "I don't know if James wants anyone else to know."

"You don't know what you're asking," Debbie says with a twinkle in her eye. "Do you know what kind of fun I could have with this? I didn't know that friendship could be so costly."

"You can count on us both," Mom says in a serious voice. "Right, Debbie?"

Debbie pouts. "Oh, I suppose so."

• • •

Back at the shed, I split a block of firewood and sit down on the chopping block.

Haven't we got enough on our minds? I wonder in the long silence. *Now we've gone and added another complication.*

At first I have no idea what to tell Matt, but eventually I figure out what to say: "There's only one way to find out and that's just to tell her. I get no read off Debbie, but like most guys I can be pretty thick when it comes to understanding girls. So don't set your clock by me."

"I don't know if I'm ready to take that kind of chance. What if she doesn't like me?"

"Oh, I think she likes you all right. But does she *like you* like you, if you know what I mean?"

"I do and that's what makes me so nervous."

"Seems to me you've got two choices. Number one, do nothing. Number two, do something. The ball's in your court. My take on it is pretty simple: no guts, no glory."

"Easy for you to say. It's not your guts that could get spilled on the ground and trampled."

"True. I'm not being much help, am I?"

"You certainly are not. Not that I blame you. Girls! Who can figure them out? I think I'm just going to play it safe and keep my mouth shut. Maybe I'll get a sign." Matt lets out a long sigh. "Let's split some kindling. Maybe the exercise will help clear my mind!"

I hand him the axe and stand back. As he splits kindling, I gather it up and put it in the kindling box. Pretty soon the box is full to overflowing, but Matt keeps swinging the axe. He's like a machine. I should stop him, but I know that this will help me work through the emotional stress he's under. Every guy should have a woodpile to go to for just such times. The world would be a much better place.

My mind turns to thoughts of Leah and what we said to each other. Where is this going to take us? I know one thing: we can't get distracted from the task God has given us.

I wish we knew what the task is, I think. *How close are we to finding out?*

I tell myself we'll be closer to an answer once we go over the two remaining scriptures on our list.

The kindling is way past overflowing now so I tap Matt on the shoulder. "Let's go in and clean up. If the women don't need any help, maybe we can play video games until Dad gets home."

"Sounds like a good idea. I'm in."

We clean up in the sink in the mudroom by the back door.

"Mom, do you guys need any help?" I ask, peeking into the kitchen. "If not, Matt and I are going up to my room."

"I think we can manage, but thanks for asking," Mom says teasingly, as though she's talking to little children. "You boys run along and play."

We go up, not having to be told twice.

Once in my room, Matt asks where the book is. I show him the shelf in the closet and then explain what Michael said about it being safe here.

"Want to get the book down and study it a little?" Matt asks.

"It does seem to have some sort of draw," I say. "When I'm near it, I feel like I want to be closer, to touch it and study the cover and think about what's inside. I wonder if my name is in there. Or yours and Debbie's and Leah's. What about Mom and Dad and the rest of our parents? Are their names in there?"

I reach up and take the book down with great care and respect. Gently I place it on the bed and ease back the towel it's wrapped in. The glow somehow seems even brighter than ever.

"It's kinda hard to believe you can see it glow," Matt says. "But no harder than believing all the rest of the things that have happened lately. I want to pick it up and hold it for a minute. Do you think that'd be okay?"

"Sure, go ahead."

Matt leans down and gingerly takes the book in his hands. He holds it at arm's length, turning it left and right, then up and down.

"I can't believe how light it is. A book this size should weigh ten or twelve pounds at least. I don't think it weighs half a pound. Freaky!" He pulls the book close to his chest and hugs it tightly. "I don't know why I'm doing this, but it just feels right. Gives me a warm fuzzy feeling, like everything is all right in the world and I'm loved. Does that make sense?"

"I've had that feeling a lot lately. Usually happens when Michael shows up in my dreams."

To our shock, the door suddenly opens and Mom appears there. "Your father just texted from town," she says. "He'll be home in about twenty minutes. You boys want to get washed up for supper?"

She's standing right there in the doorway and Matt's right in front of her holding the book to his chest. I brace myself, ready to offer some explanation...

But then I realize she doesn't see it, even with Matt turning bright red and looking for a place to hide.

"Sure, Mom," I croak. "We'll be right down."

When we're alone again, I turn to Matt with a dumbfounded expression.

"Can you believe that?" Matt gasps. "Why wouldn't she say anything?"

"Micheal said the book will be safe here, that it won't be discovered," I say. "So I figure Mom didn't say anything because she didn't *see* anything. But that was definitely an adrenaline rush!"

"I didn't know what to do. I just froze. I'm still shaking."

"It just goes to show you that when Micheal says something, he backs it up. Now put the book back on the shelf and let's go downstairs."

In the kitchen, we find Mom, Debbie, and Leah already sitting at the kitchen table.

"Well, don't you three look overwhelmed with work," I tease.

Debbie just smiles. "We're having trout fresh from the river, garnished with a medley of vegetables from the garden, followed by a warm apple crisp topped with thick cream. All this from the kitchen of master chef Winnie Jeffries and sous chefs Leah and Debbie. What are you gentlemen having? I believe there are some hot dogs in the refrigerator."

"You crack me up, sis. Does smell awful good in here."

"You have to make up your mind, James," Mom says in a patronizing tone. "Does it smell awful or does it smell good? It can't be both."

I sigh and look down at the floor. "Okay, I'm just gonna shut my mouth 'til there's some food to replace my foot."

Matt laughs at me. "I just love watching you taking it from the women."

"You want in on this, Matt?" Leah asks.

"No! Was just saying, that's all. Leave me way out of this…"

"If you four are finished, make sure you're all washed up and ready to eat," Mom says. "I hear Justin coming down the driveway and the food's ready whenever he sits to the table."

Only a few minutes later, Dad walks in and calls loudly, "Honey, I'm home!"

We've become used to this announcement over the years, and as he enters the kitchen he stares at the five of us sitting around the table.

"It seems like our family grows on a daily basis." He steps closer. "Hello, Matt, it's good of you to join us—although I may be a little worried about the grocery bill if this turns into a habit." He looks to our other guest. "Hello, Leah. You are always welcome at our table."

Matt smiles. "Thanks, Mr. Jeffries, and I'll try not to eat too much."

"Oh, don't do that!" Dad waves him off. "Mrs. Jeffries likes to see young men with healthy appetites. You'll get me in trouble if she thinks you're holding back on account of me. No, no, no… have all you want."

"Justin, will you please wash your hands and sit down?" Mom says impatiently. "We don't want that lovely fish to dry out, do we?"

"We certainly do not!" Dad exclaims. He turns to Matt. "What did you think of that leviathan James caught? Quite impressive, isn't it?"

"I couldn't believe my eyes. I wish I had been there with him."

With the help of Debbie and Leah, Mom takes the dishes out of the oven and lays them out on the table. The women then take their seats as we all fix our eyes on the feast.

"Since you provided the main course, James, I would ask you to say grace," says Dad.

I bow my head. "Heavenly Father, we thank You for the many blessings You have provided. We thank You for family and friends. At this time, dear Lord, we thank You for the food before us and ask a blessing on it and the hands that prepared it. May it nourish our bodies as our Your word nourishes our souls. We ask this in the name of Your Son, our Savior Jesus Christ. Amen."

"Well done, James." Mom passes the platter of trout to Leah. "We'll let company serve themselves first."

"Try to remember there are others to follow, okay, Matt?" teases Debbie.

Matt accepts the platter from Leah. "You're so funny."

We all finish filling our plates—well, I say filling our plates, but the plates of the males of the species seem to be fuller than the ladies. It's quiet for a while as we dig in.

Then Matt breaks the silence.

"Mmmmm! This is delicious… and I don't mean just the fish. Everything is great. Mrs. Jeffries, do you need another son? And please don't tell my mom I said that."

"Why thank you, Matt," Mom says. "It's always nice to be appreciated. God provides. I just take what He gives and do my best to make it acceptable."

At this point, we all jump in to heap praise on Mom. She modestly accepts it but insists she's just using her God-given talents.

"By the way, I saw Michael at the airport today," Dad remarks. "He told me to say hi. Apparently he was heading out on a business trip… although isn't it strange that he never seems to have any luggage with him? Anyway, he's going to be back at church this Sunday and looks forward to seeing us all in the house of the Lord. He seems like a very nice man."

We all nod and agree that he seems kind and easygoing.

"Are you three going to youth tonight?" Dad asks.

"Right after supper," Debbie replies.

"Speaking of dessert," I interrupt out of nowhere, "didn't someone mention apple crisp? Matt looks like he's about ready for it."

Leah elbows me. "Don't lay this on Matt. We know it's you who wants dessert."

"Am I that transparent?" I say with a chuckle.

"Since you brought it up, you can fetch it from the stove and put it on the coaster while I move the trout," Mom says.

While I'm putting the apple crisp on the table, she's getting the cream from the fridge. It's a good thing we have a large table, but even so Mom has to move dishes out of the way.

"The feast continues!" Matt exclaims.

Debbie laughs. "And we know who the court jester is."

"Less talking, more eating please," Dad says.

Once we've finished up with dessert and tea and coffee, having extended even more compliments to the chef, we all help clear the table.

TWELVE

The four of us enter the church with our Bibles tucked under our arms. We quickly notice our other friends, including Gary and Glen and Brian.

"Hey, look who's here!" Gary cries out. "It's the four musketeers. Haven't seen you guys since last week. What's new?"

We greet each other warmly.

"By the way, Glen and Brian and I saw the email you sent us with the pictures of that monster fish," Gary says. "Where did you get that picture? It can't have been real."

At this, Debbie and Leah peel off to join some of their friends.

"It certainly was real," Matt jumps in. "I was over to James's tonight and we had some of that trout for supper."

"Really?" Glen asks. "That wasn't photoshopped?"

I shake my head. "Totally legit."

"I wish I had been there when you caught it." Brian lets out a whistle. "Where did you catch it?"

"You know better than to ask that," Matt says. "No fisherman gives up his best spots. Maybe some decent spots, but never the best spots."

"Can't blame a guy for trying." Brian laughs. "Anyway, it's almost time to start. We'd better get in there."

Once inside the fellowship hall, our three guy friends take seats at the back. That's what people usually do in church, I've observed; they hope not to be noticed.

Derrick comes in and goes to the front where he stands quietly until we settle down.

"Good evening, all you bright and cherry faces!" he begins. "I'm glad you're here this evening. For those of you sitting way at the back, you know what I want… so just move to the front, okay?"

So much for not being noticed!

After the program and everyone is starting to break up and go their separate ways, Derrick comes over to me.

"James, have you thought any more about that thing we talked about at your house last week?" he asks.

I appreciate his being discreet. I don't need a bunch of my youth friends asking about what's going on.

"I've thought about it quite a bit actually." I try my best to evade the question without having to actually lie. "I don't have anything new to share, but thanks for asking. In the meantime, I'm working with Debbie, Matt, and Leah on a project. I don't want to say much, though. We promised each other to keep it secret for now."

"Now you've piqued my curiosity!" Derrick smiles and changes the subject, respecting our vow of secrecy. "Are you getting anxious for school to start? I know you're involved in the football program, and so are most of your friends."

"Yeah, we should have a great team this year. A lot of us younger players didn't see much playing time last year. With six seniors having graduated, though, we should have a better chance now to show our stuff."

"I hear you're a darned good running back."

"I do okay," I reply, not liking to attract much attention to myself.

Having overheard that last comment, Matt chimes in. "I'm here to tell you that James was the best running back in the whole league last year. He won't admit it cause he's too humble to blow his own horn!"

Some of our other friends are gathering around now, heaping on the praise.

"Okay, okay, it's time to go out and play a little basketball," I plead. "Leave me alone."

As we walk, Debbie gives me a punch to the shoulder. "Keep this up and Dad will have to cut a bigger doorway so we can get your head through the door…"

We all have a great time on the basketball court outside the church, and before long it's time to head for home. Debbie, Leah, Matt, and I start walking down our street. We confirm our plans for Friday.

"It seems like a long time from now," Leah says sadly. "Every time I close my eyes, I see the book. Or I dream about it or hear the voice of that angel talking about it. You would think I'd be exhausted from lack of sleep, but I haven't felt this rested in years."

"I know what you mean. The fitful sleep hasn't kept me from waking up fresh as a daisy," says Debbie before changing the subject. "What do you think about what Dad told us? You know, about seeing Michael at the airport."

"It's going to be strange seeing him at church, knowing what we know," I admit. "What should we call him? How do we treat him? The Bible talks about entertaining angels, but I don't think any of us ever thought we would knowingly be in the presence of a real honest-to-goodness angel. It's going to feel bizarre on Sunday."

"I don't think we have to worry about it," says Leah. "God has gotten us this far. We can trust Him to guide us through."

I turn and stare at her. Didn't she used to be the nervous one? Now she's the one giving us calm, sound advice.

"Sometimes you impress the daylights out of me," Debbie says to her friend. "Here we are panicking over meeting an angel face to face, and you just tell us to trust God. It's so obvious! How can we be so dumb?"

"Yeah," Matt says. "It's so obvious and we overlooked it completely."

I nod. "That's one of the key things Michael has said from the beginning: trust God. If you stop and think about it, all success stories in the Bible involve people putting their trust in God, and all failures come from failing to trust Him. The pattern goes as far back as Adam and Eve."

We walk for a while in silence, thinking this over.

"It does seem like a long time to wait until Friday night, though," I murmur. "Maybe we could meet tomorrow afternoon instead."

It turned out that everyone was either free or could change their plans to make it work. Privately, I plan to ask Dad if we can use his den.

Within a few minutes Matt and Leah have both peeled off. Debbie and I walk the final fifty yards in silence.

"Leah felt so guilty about being up in your bedroom that she told Mom about it," Debbie reveals as we walk up the driveway. "She also told her what she said about liking you. Mom's okay with it and even thinks you and Leah make a nice couple."

My mouth drops open in surprise and she breaks out into a huge grin.

"You should see your face," she says, laughing. "What a lovely shade of red! Come on, little brother, you know she's great. Admit it!"

"She sure is something. I just don't know if now is the right time to start a relationship, considering what's going on in our lives. You know what I mean."

"I think she understands that the task ahead has to take priority. She's pretty focused on it, don't you think?"

"I just don't want to hurt her, and I know she doesn't want to hurt me."

"You know God has a plan for us," Debbie says. "But I don't think our love lives are a major concern to Him right now. We can't let them be a distraction."

We go into the house and are immediately greeted by Mom and Dad. We talk to them about our plans to work with our friends over the next few days, and I ask about possibly using Dad's den, since it'll be more comfortable than cramming around the kitchen table.

"You certainly may," Dad agrees. "I'm anxious to find out what this top-secret project is all about."

Debbie smiles. "Well, we've got nothing to leak to the press just yet, but I can assure you it'll be a blockbuster."

"I'm going to take a shower and hit the pillow," I say. "Good night. God bless. Love you."

I'm halfway up the stairs when I turn back. "Oh, Mom, better make sure the cookie jar is all stocked up. Matt asked about it..."

She laughs and nods her head. "Made fresh this evening. I'm surprised you didn't smell them when you came in."

"I don't have Matt's nose for food!" I turn and head back down the steps. "I think I can postpone that shower for at least a glass of milk and a couple of cookies. Anyone care to join me?"

Debbie follows me to the kitchen. "Ouch, you've twisted my arm."

After our snack, I shower and go to my room. I change for bed but can't help myself; I take the book down off the shelf and hug it close to my chest, just like Matt did that afternoon. He's right. That warm, peaceful feelings flows over me.

There's something else, though. It doesn't jump right out, but as I think about it I sense a subtle feeling of power. I don't know how else to describe it. It's way beyond my experience.

All my thoughts come to an abrupt halt as I hear the voice of Michael inside my head.

"Why are you worrying about matters over which you have no control? You have a task to perform for Your heavenly Father. Fulfill that and you will have done the will of God."

I shake my head, go to my knees, and thank the Lord for another day. The book goes back on the shelf.

I then slide between the sheets and put my head on the pillow. I'm pooped and fall asleep right away, wondering whether I'll have another dream.

The next thing I know, Michael's voice is speaking again.

"James?" the angel says. "James, are you with us?"

"I'm here, Michael." I hesitate for a moment. "But who's *us*? Is there someone else?"

"Debbie, Matt, and Leah are all part of this conversation."

That surprises me, but the more I think about it, the more normal it seems. This isn't the first time we've shared the same dream, after all.

"I wish to tell all four of you that the Lord your God is pleased with what you have done so far, but this is just the beginning," says Michael. "The most important scriptures remain to be studied. Much will be revealed in them about the importance of the Book of Life, not only to all mankind but also to the powers of darkness. Read carefully. Open your minds and hearts to the Word. Concentrate fully on what each of you bring to the discussion.

"I am aware of what transpires in your lives and I would ask you not to let the affairs of your own hearts interfere with the work of the Lord. Leah, you and James have revealed to each other your feelings. God understands love, for He is the Creator. Love would not exist without Him. Your love for each other has His blessing, but it must be secondary to your love for Him. The first great command is: 'Love the Lord your God with all your heart and with all your soul and with all our mind.'[14] You must adhere to this without fail.

"Matt and Debbie, although you have not declared it, I am aware that you as well have feelings for each other you have not shared. These feelings will grow stronger every day until they are brought into the light. What grows in the darkness will itself become dark; therefore it must be exposed to light.

"I say these things as a warning. You must not let your love for each other interfere with your love for the Lord and the task He has given you. Do not let your feelings lead to embarrassment, for the strongest powers in heaven and earth are found in true love. True love can only come through God.

"Matt, you have embraced the book and felt a change. James, you have done this as well. More will be revealed after you complete your study of the scriptures. Debbie and Leah, you must also embrace the book to become aware of its power.

"I will leave you now, but I will see you on Sunday. May the peace of the Lord be with you always."

---

[14] Matthew 22:37.

Thirteen

I don't remember another thing until I awake the next morning to the sound of quiet tapping at my bedroom door. The door gently opens and Debbie stands in the opening.

"Are you awake?" she asks.

"I am now. What's up, sis?"

"You were in on that dream last night, weren't you?"

"Yes. And so were Matt and Leah." I whistle to myself. "Hard to wrap your head around it, isn't it? He laid out some pretty heavy-duty stuff."

Debbie pauses. "But why did he say those things about me and Matt? And telling us not to be embarrassed… how could either one of us not feel embarrassed over our feelings being exposed like that? How do I face Matt this afternoon? What do I say?"

"Hey, slow down. First, do you feel like that towards Matt?"

"Yes, of course. But I wasn't ready for Matt to know yet."

"Well, he does now. And to put your mind at rest, I can tell you that he feels the same way. Does that help?"

"A little, I guess," she mutters. "How do you know? Have you guys been talking?"

"Of course, just like you girls have been talking. Stop and think about exactly what Michael said. It's better for this to be out in the open than for it to fester. It's not healthy for your uncertainty and doubt to grow into jealousy or something worse. This way we're free to do the Lord's will without being held hostage by our own emotional baggage."

"This definitely isn't the way I saw my first relationship starting off. Not in a million years."

"Neither of us did. Matter of fact, I didn't see myself in a relationship at all 'til Leah sprang that on me the other day. But it felt right, even good." I yawn. "Now go back to your room and try to get some more sleep."

Debbie raises her eyebrow at me. "What are you talking about? It's almost 7:30. Dad's gone to work and Mom's got breakfast on the table. It's time to get up, lazyhead."

I can hear her laughing as she heads downstairs.

I'll blame it on being preoccupied, but I failed to notice the daylight in my room. Up I get, dress, and head downstairs. Mom has a pot of oatmeal on the stove and bread in the toaster. I also notice the delicious smell coming from the oven.

"Oatmeal to stick to your ribs and toast with homemade strawberry jam to sweeten your disposition," Mom musically offers.

Debbie laughs. "You should fill up on the toast and jam."

"What do you mean?" I ask. "I'm my usual happy, brighten-the-room self, aren't I, Mom?"

"No fair! She's biased!" Debbie says.

"You two are very entertaining this morning." Mom sighs. "You have company coming this afternoon, so I made up a list of things to do. After breakfast you can divide it up however you want. I think that's fair. Oh, and by the way, that smell from the oven is banana bread. As soon as that comes out, there will be cookies enough to refill the jars. After all, Matt's coming."

"You keep this up and he may never leave," I tell her.

Debbie smirks. "You always said you'd like a little brother."

"I have never said that, ever," I say indignantly. "Who could ask for a better sibling than you?"

At which all three of us break into laughter.

After breakfast, Debbie and I look at Mom's list and split up the chores. She tackles the kitchen-related ones while I vacuum the whole downstairs and then tidy up Dad's den, which takes all of five minutes. Dad is by nature very organized.

When this is all done, I ask Mom if there's anything else that she can think of.

"Nothing in particular. Why? What do you have in mind?"

"I think I'll go for a run. School's starting soon and I want to be in shape for football tryouts."

"Is it okay if I join you?" Debbie asks. "I should be getting into shape for field hockey. I sort of let things slip this summer."

"Sure, but remember: I take no prisoners."

Mom just reminds us to be back for lunch because she's leaving for quilting at 1:00 and wants to spend a little time with us before we leave.

"I get to see you so little," she says wistfully. "I get spoiled in the summer and hate to let go of you again in the fall."

We promise to be back by noon.

On the veranda we do our stretches, then jog down the driveway and turn right. Debbie wants to talk so we set an easy pace. We stay together for the next half-hour, pushing each other to maximize the workout. After a certain point we part company, since our training won't be compatible.

"I'm home, Mom," I say when I return to the house afterward. "Debbie's not far behind. I'll shower before she gets here."

"Lunch will be ready at noon."

As I head into the bathroom, I hear the door shut and Debbie announce her arrival. By the time I get to the kitchen, Mom has set the table. I plunk myself onto a chair.

"Need any help, Mom?"

"As a matter of fact, you could drain the pot with the peas in it. If you don't mind."

"Not a problem. What we havin'?"

"Cream peas on toast. Your father doesn't like it, but you and your sister do. Figured this was a good time."

Debbie enters the room with a towel around her head and takes a seat. "Did I hear someone say cream peas on toast? Mmmm, I approve. It's been a long time since we've had that."

"Are the peas drained, James?" Mom asks. I nod. "Good. Debbie, if you'll say grace…?"

Debbie bows her head and gives thanks. After her amen, we dig in.

We idly chat about the upcoming school year and our expectations, both from our perspectives and in terms of what Mom would like to see us accomplish. She reminds us that our birthdays are coming up next month and asks whether we have any special requests. Debbie would like to have a few friends over and just play some music. She doesn't seem to mind if I join in.

"Here comes the hard part," I say, turning to Mom. "Do you think we could have one of your chocolate cakes? You know, with your boiled icing? You know how much I love those."

She looks at me with a glint in her eye. "Again?"

"What do you mean, *again*?" I ask, a little confused.

"Why don't you look under that tin-covered cake plate on the sideboard?"

Getting up, I lift the cover and to my surprise see a chocolate cake with boiled icing. "Wow! Great minds think alike."

"I just thought that you and your friends might enjoy a nice cake."

"You mean I have to share it? That's pushing love-your-neighbor to the brink…"

"I also know you were raised to do the proper thing, no matter how much it hurts," Mom says.

Debbie lets out a hoot. "The Mom guilt trip using Christian ethics. You're toast now and you know it."

"I guess I have to admit that sharing will make me savor every bite a little more, since there won't be much left over. When it comes to Mom's cake, quantity doesn't change the quality. And there's no such thing as too much of a good thing." I release a protracted sigh. "This doesn't let you off the hook for my birthday, though, Mom. I'd still like another chocolate cake."

Mom smiles at me. "I think that can be arranged."

As Mom gets ready to leave for quilting, Debbie steps in to clean up the lunch dishes. We give her a hug, and then she's out the door and headed down the driveway.

It's time to get ready for our afternoon meeting. I carry the Book of Life from my closet to Dad's den, then get the cookie jar from the kitchen, along with the banana bread and a picture of lemonade. I set everything on the coffee table.

"We'll save the cake for a last-minute surprise, okay?" I say as Debbie and I return to the kitchen to wait for the others.

"Okay, but I won't let you forget it. It would be a tragedy not to share with Matt and Leah."

My reply is sheepish. "The thought never crossed my mind."

I look out the window and see Matt coming. The clock shows that it's 1:30.

"Here comes the early bird," I remark.

"What am I going to say?" Debbie says, starting to feel nervous again. "This is already awkward and he isn't even here yet. You've got to help me out, little brother. He's your friend."

Before I can reply, Matt comes through the door. I can feel the tension. When people say it's so thick you could cut it with a knife, they're not kidding. Neither he nor Debbie say a word. They just stand there sort of looking at each other and the floor at the same time.

"Okay, you two, it's time to face some facts," I begin. "You like each other. I know that. You know that. Leah knows it and Michael knows it too. Leah and I had a better start since we actually talked to one another. You two sort of got it dropped on you in a surprise reveal. One benefit of it is that neither of you has to work up the guts to say something to risk rejection. Another is that Micheal says it's okay so long as it doesn't interfere with God's plans. That's the downside too, if you want to call it that. We all have to put the relationship thing on hold until this task is finished."

They continue to stand around, avoiding each other's gaze.

"Now get it over with," I say. "Give each other a big hug."

Matt turns on me in irritation. "You jerk!"

"He is a jerk, but he's right," Debbie says.

"Aren't I always? Now where's that hug?"

They each step closer to one another. That's when I witness the most awkward hug I've ever seen.

Leah walks through the door. "What's going on here?"

Debbie laughs. "James just killed the elephant in the room."

"I think I know which elephant you're talking about," Leah says. "I was wondering how this would work out. I'm glad for all four of us. But the work of the Lord has to come first."

"James basically just said the same thing," Matt agrees. "This must be one of the sacrifices and sufferings Micheal mentioned that we'll have to face. So let's suck it up and move on. We've got work to do."

I nod. "Let's move into the den. Debbie and I have things ready, including cookies and lemonade. There's banana bread fresh from the oven, and a surprise finish after that."

"Are we going to eat all afternoon or work at these scriptures?" Leah asks.

"Haven't you ever heard of multitasking?" Matt laughs. "I can eat while I'm reading, thinking, and even listening. I don't talk while I'm eating. Momma says that's rude."

We're all chuckling as we head into the den and take seats. The Book of Life sits in the middle of the coffee table, emitting a warm glow. I ask everyone to lean in and place their hands on the book while I open with prayer.

As they take their hands off the book afterward, I pick it up.

"As you know from what Michael said last night, Matt and I have already embraced the book and felt something. We all need to do it." I turn to Debbie. "Now close your eyes and squeeze it tightly."

I give her the book as she closes her eyes. She wraps her arms around the book and embraces it. I didn't notice it when Matt was hugging the book, but an expression of peace comes over Debbie's face. She looks almost like a sleeping baby.

When she's done, she opens her eyes and immediately hands the book to Leah.

Leah repeats exactly what Debbie did and wears that same look of peace on her face.

"What do you think?" I ask when it's finished.

"That's so nice," says Leah. "I don't know what it is, but there's a power there. It's like being curled up in a warm quilt."

Debbie nods in agreement. "I know exactly what you mean. I don't know how you can feel so at peace and at the same time feel such a deep feeling of power."

"I think we all have a little better understanding of what we have here," I say. "This is a possession of the Father that He has put in our hands. That's why we feel peace when we hold it, because it contains the names of those who will spend eternity at peace with their heavenly Father. At the same time, it's connected to God Himself, the greatest power of all, a power so great that the whole universe is the result of His hand. He is the Creator. That's the simple explanation. We will never understand, and are probably never meant to understand, anything beyond that."

"I think I'm developing a new respect for you, my friend," says Matt. "You've come up with some incredible revelations. I can hardly believe this is coming out of your mouth."

"I know what you mean, Matt, and you're included in that also," Debbie adds. "But one thing we have to remember is that God is in this with us. He's with us every step of the way. Let's give credit and thanks where it's due."

"Amen to that!" Leah exclaims.

Without further ado, we get down to business. I ask Leah to do the honors and read the next scripture from her own Bible. She turns to the correct page and begins to read from Revelation 20:11–15.

> Then I saw a great white throne and him who
> was seated on it. The earth and the heavens
> fled from his presence, and there was no place
> for them. And I saw the dead, great and small,
> standing before the throne, and books were
> opened. Another book was opened, which is

> the book of life. The dead were judged according to what they had done as recorded in the books. The sea gave up the dead that were in it, and death and Hades gave up the dead that were in them, and each person was judged according to what they had done. Then death and Hades were thrown into the lake of fire. The lake of fire is the second death. Anyone whose name was not found written in the book of life was thrown into the lake of fire.

She puts her Bible down, still open to that scripture.

With that, Matt begins to speak. "The throne mentioned here can only refer to the judgment throne, and the person seated upon it is the judge. What follows supports this. The earth and the sky flee. Why? Because on judgment day there will be no more need of an earth or a sky, as we'll be gathered before the throne of judgment. The next verse says as much. When the writer talks about 'the dead, great and small,' that has to mean that no one will be absent or escape judgment. We will all stand before the throne and answer for how we've lived our lives. It then says that books are opened. Which books? These books are those that are devoted to works. Many think that because they've lived well and been kind, loving, and generous, that'll be good enough on judgment day. Some people think that being a good person is the main requirement of our coming judgment. But this passage tells us that people were 'judged according to what they had done.' From that, we can conclude that works will be part of the judgment.

"Other things will be part of the judgment—like how we've lived, what we've done, and whether we've loved our neighbor as ourselves—because there are other books. This passage says so. However, it doesn't say specifically what these other books contain. Over the years, man has come up with supposition and conjecture about the contents of these books, but God didn't give us any direct insight. If we're honest, we have to admit that we don't know.

"Accepting that truth will lead us to another truth. The last book opened will be the Book of Life, at which time the dead will be judged and their lives and works taken into consideration. Death and Hades will be thrown into the lake of fire, because that has always been their destiny. There will be no forgiveness or salvation for them.

"Those remaining, meaning those who have been judged according to what they've done, will then face a reckoning. Revelation 20:15 lays out the final piece of judgment: 'Anyone whose name was not found written in the book of life was thrown into the lake of fire.' The end, no appeal, done for eternity, no coming back! It doesn't matter what's in the other books. The final judgment will come down to whether a person's name is found in the Book of Life."

At that, Matt stops and looks at each of us intently. We're all sitting in our seats with our jaws in our laps. This just came out of our friend. We're flabbergasted.

Debbie is the first to speak. "You said something earlier about feeling amazed at James for the words coming out of his mouth. Well, I want to tell you, Matt Philips, you just went to the head of the class. Wow!"

"Anyone who doubts that God can work through us should have been sitting where I'm sitting for the last ten minutes," Leah says with admiration. "All doubt would be gone."

Matt seems as surprised at himself as any of us. "I wish I could take credit, but you all know as well as I do that those words only came *through* me, not *from* me. By the way, Leah, could you pass the cookies?"

"And he's back." Debbie laughs. "You guys keep going while I slice some banana bread and serve it up with some butter."

Matt smiles. "My kind of woman!"

Debbie gives him a scowl but sets to work on the banana bread, slicing it up as neatly as possible.

"I have a question," says Leah. "In Revelation 20:11, who is it that sits on the throne of judgment? Is it the Father or is it Jesus?"

The answer comes to me through inspiration.

"We read in John 5:26–27, 'For as the Father has life in himself, so he has granted the Son also to have life in himself. And he has given him authority to judge because he is the Son of Man.' Then again, in Acts 10:42, we read, 'He commanded us to preach to the people and to testify that he is the one whom God appointed as judge of the living and the dead.' Finally, we can look to 2 Timothy 4:1: 'In the presence of God and of Christ Jesus, who will judge the living and the dead, and in the view of his appearing and his kingdom, I give you this charge.' These three scriptures make me believe that Jesus will be the judge on the throne. But in the grand scheme of things, does it make any difference? We know that we'll be judged and that it's God who will judge. Whether it's the Father, Son, or Holy Spirit, who are all God, it won't make a bit of difference.

Too often we get all tangled up in matters we aren't meant to understand, like the nature of the Trinity. We seem determined to understand, but in reality we never will."

"You're absolutely right, James," Leah agrees. "Where did those scriptures come from? Did you look them up last night?"

"They just came to me. There's no doubt in my mind that the Lord is working through us and in us."

"I was wondering that too, about who the judge is," says Debbie. "James, your answer takes that question off the table, but let me replace it with another: are there two Books of Life? We have the new and the old covenants. One is based on the Law, referring to the Ten Commandments and the many other laws God gave the Israelites. The other is based on the birth, death, and resurrection of our Lord and Savior Jesus Christ. Are the names of God's chosen from the old covenant written in the same Book of Life as the names of those who have accepted Christ and had their sins washed away by His blood?"

"Several scriptures, including the passage we've just read, mention other books that come into play on judgment day," I point out. "Nowhere is it even hinted at that there may be more than one Book of Life. We have to remain focused on *the* Book of Life and not get sidetracked. Let's remember what we just read in Revelation 20:15: 'Anyone whose name was not found written in the book of life was thrown into the lake of fire.' This doesn't say anything about multiple Books of Life. I would also point out that this scripture deals with the judgment of death and Hades and the dead. The living will be dealt with in our next scripture…"

I trail off, realizing that I have so much more to say. But for now I think it makes sense to take a short break. It seems like the perfect time for that surprise I told them about earlier.

"I'll be right back," I tell them. "I won't be long. Keep thinking this over."

I hurry over to the kitchen and get the cake plate. When I come back into the den, everyone is staring at me.

"What's this all about?" Matt asks.

"Matt, you don't know how much this hurts!" I place the cake plate down on the coffee table and lift the cover.

Matt gasps. "Is that one of your mother's chocolate cakes? With boiled icing? And you're sharing it with us? I'm shocked! I know how sacred this is." He turns to Debbie. "You knew about this?"

"Honestly, I didn't know whether he would go get the cake without a little prodding," Debbie says. "Well done, little brother. Sometimes you surprise me."

Everyone leans forward to get a closer look at the delicious cake. Matt's mouth is practically watering.

"The fact is, James has surprised me a lot lately," Debbie continues.

"I think we can all agree on that," Leah says. "But I'm in the dark about this cake. What's so special about it?"

Debbie grins. "Oh! You'll see. James, you want to do the honors?"

"That's cruel," I say, feigning pain. "Sharing is torture enough. Now you want me to serve it too?"

"Okay. I'll make the first cut and then everyone can help themselves." Debbie picks up a knife and slices the cake neatly down the middle.

"I'm not shy." Matt takes the knife and slices off a generous piece for himself. He places it on the same plate that just a few minutes ago, it seems, held the banana bread.

Before any of us can fill our own plates, Matt is already two bites deep, moaning as though he's died and gone to heaven.

"Oh! This is a slice of heaven!" Leah exclaims as she savors her first bite. "I understand all the fuss now. Matt, slow down and enjoy it."

Matt talks with his mouth full. "Sorry, but this is just too good."

"Glad you like it," I say. "I'll pass that on to the chef."

As we all settle back in our seats, enjoying the cake, I return to the business at hand. We still have a lot of studying to get through.

"So this is what I'm thinking: the lake of fire is the second death. Those who know that this is their eternal destination probably won't want the Book of Life to ever be opened. Or they'll want to get their hands on the book to manipulate when or how the judgment comes to pass. That would make this the most sought-after book in all of history, physically and spiritually."

Even as I say this, my gaze settles on the book, glowing with even greater intensity than ever. Is this really happening?

"This book sitting in front of us is a treasure that people, never mind the powers of darkness, would move heaven and earth to possess," I say so quietly that it comes out almost as a whisper. "Even those who don't believe in God or an afterlife would be intrigued by it. All four of us have held the book and experienced the peace and power it brings. That feeling comes from God, the author of the book. It makes sense that the book is endowed with His power. It just makes sense.

"I can understand why people would be obsessed with possessing this book, because honestly that's the same thing I feel every time I think about it," I admit. "I'm deeply drawn to it. When I held it last night before bed, I couldn't help thinking about whether my name is written inside. Or your names. Or our parents... these thoughts filled my head! Then I heard Michael's voice telling me to stop worrying about things I have no control over and to focus on the task the Lord has given me.

"If it helps, we all know ourselves and how we live. That should give us peace. Do we really need to look inside the Book of Life to satisfy our doubts? We need to have faith, trust in the Lord, and believe in our parents."

The ticking of the clock above my dad's desk draws my attention and I look up to see the time. Mom will be home soon.

"Matt, would you close with prayer?" I ask.

Matt bows his head and humbly asks for God to continue blessing us. He also prays for strength, understanding, and wisdom as we study His Word.

As he finishes, I once again hear tires on the gravel in the driveway and know that Mom has gotten home. I pick up the book and walk towards the stairs, clutching it tight against my chest.

I walk right past Mom as she enters through the front door. I wave and smile, not the least bit concerned about her seeing the book.

She just waves back.

FOURTEEN

After putting the book on the shelf in my closet, I return downstairs and find everyone gathering in the kitchen. Matt is helping the girls put away the food and dishes from our afternoon snack. Mom is sitting at the table watching.

"I've called the Scanlons and the Philipses," Mom says. "They're coming over for supper tonight at about 6:30. Justin is stopping on his way home to pick up Chinese food. Does that sound okay?"

"Who am I to argue?" Leah says with a big smile.

In fact, that plan sounds great to all of us.

"We have about two hours," Mom continues. "James and Matt, you'll need to put two extra leaves in the table. Girls, I'll need help setting the places. Then you four are on your own for a while. Oh, is there any cake left? We can serve that for dessert."

"Humph," I grumble. "Come on, Matt. The leaves are in the pantry."

Matt follows me into the pantry where we get a couple of table leaves and install them in no time. We then leave the women to set the table, heading outside to shoot some baskets by the shed.

• • •

As the table is being set, Mom turns to Leah and Debbie.

"Leah, I didn't know whether you've told your mother about James, so I didn't say anything to her at quilting. You know how stories can spread, even among good Christian women."

Leah smiles. "I appreciate your being so considerate, Mrs. Jeffries, but Mom and Dad already know that James and I have feelings for each other."

"Oh. That makes this a little awkward," Debbie says, feeling a little sheepish. "Mom, have I told you that Matt and I are at the same place in our lives as James and Leah?"

"Why no, daughter, you have not. Tell me more."

"It's not serious, but since we've been hanging out so much together lately… I guess we both sort of like each other… and it sort of came out last night. I meant to tell you, but I guess things got busy and I just forgot."

"I can forgive you. Besides, I like Matt, so we don't have a problem there." Mom puts her hands on her hips. "Aren't you four something! My best advice is to just go slow and remember to let the Word guide you every day."

"Thanks, Mom. You're great! I thought you might make me suffer for not telling you right away."

Mom shakes her head. "No. You're early in the love life game, so I'll go easy this time. As you mature, there will be times when you can be sure I'll torment you, but probably not as bad as you and James will torment each other."

Debbie laughs. "Of that I have no doubt."

"I wonder if Matt has said anything to his parents?" Leah queries.

"You're kidding, right," Debbie blurts out. "Boys don't talk to their parents about things like that. Do they, Mom?"

"All boys are different," she says. "Some are open with their feelings, but I would say they're in the one to two percent group. Sports, cars, work… now those are things they'll talk about a lot. But their feelings? They're usually kept way back on a dusty shelf. Some will bring them out once in a while. You have to go slow and not force the issue. That just gets them defensive. Then they withdraw into their shell like a turtle."

Leah and Debbie giggle at that image, wondering what their futures have in store.

When they're finished setting the table, Mom gets out the kettle to boil water. "Let's have a nice relaxing cup of tea in the living room."

They accept.

• • •

Outside, Matt and I are playing one-on-one and practicing foul shots while we talk some more about the book.

"It sure would be nice to know what comes next," I say. "You know, after we get finished studying the scriptures."

I take a shot and watch the ball sail perfectly through the center of the basket.

"Our last passage of scripture is pretty big compared to what we've covered so far," Matt says as he gets the ball. "Not only that, but it's got some pretty deep messages."

"I know what you mean."

"Have you stopped to think about what's happening to us?" Matt lines up a shot. "We're not stupid, but our analysis lately has gone far beyond our IQ level, don't ya think?"

"I look at it this way, Matt. God is giving us everything we need in order to complete the task ahead. In the Bible, did God send out people to do His work without giving them the necessary tools to do the job? Did Jesus send out the disciples to preach the message of good news without making sure they received the Holy Spirit first? No. God looks after His own, and right now I guess that's us."

It's my turn to run for the ball, which ricochets off the backboard and lands in the grass near the garden.

"Makes me worry a little about what's next," I say. "Michael said there would be danger involved, and so far this has been a cakewalk…"

Before Matt can answer, Debbie pokes her head out the back door.

"You boys want tea?" she hollers.

"We'll be right in, sis." I put the ball away and Matt and I head inside.

The tea is already poured as Matt and I grab seats on the sofa. Matt picks up his cup and is reaching for some cookies when Debbie slaps his hand.

"You were offered tea. I don't remember anything being said about cookies."

I smile at her. "Back up, little sister. I had to share that cake, and now you're going to share these cookies. After all, Matt is a growing boy."

We all laugh as we sip the tea.

The next thing we know, there's a knock at the door. Mom gets up and greets the Philipses and the Scanlons. Ushering them into the living room, she offers more tea, which they gladly accept.

"You could get hurt if you reach for the cookies," Matt warns his parents.

This produces some questioning looks from the newcomers and an outburst of laughter from the rest of us.

"Justin should be home any minute now," Mom says, and a moment later we hear that familiar crunch of tires outside. "Speaking of the love of my life, here he is now."

Dad comes in through the front door carrying two large bags of Chinese food. He places them on the kitchen counter and turns to greet everyone.

"I'm just going to clean up a little," he says, already heading for the stairs.

By the time we've gotten ourselves ready and laid out the food, Dad is back and taking his place at the head of the table.

"James, would you ask a blessing please?" he says.

We bow our heads as I give thanks and ask a blessing on the food, the company, and my family.

The meal is spent in general conversation—the kids, his work, her work, what's going on at church, etc. The topic of my great catch comes up as well. Mr. Scanlon and Mr. Philips are both avid fishermen and want to see the pictures and hear the full story over dessert.

"We girls will leave you men to your fish tales and manly exploits while we retire to the living room, if that's okay with you," Mom says as she pours still more tea for those who want it, and coffee for those who don't. "Help yourselves to cake, banana bread, and cookies. Don't be shy. Right, James?"

"I suppose," I say in my best poor-pitiful-me tone, lowering my head.

"What's that about?" asks Mr. Philips once the women have left.

Matt jumps right in. "That chocolate cake is James's favorite. It pains him every time he has to share it."

"In that case, I'll have to try a piece," Mr. Philips says. "To see if he's justified."

Left with lots of sweets to eat and a large pot of tea on the stove, we resort to man talk. My fish comes up immediately and I have to run up to my room for my laptop.

Coming back, I put the laptop on the table and show them the pictures.

Mr. Philips and Mr. Scanlon are amazed at the size of the trout. All kinds of questions follow, and lots of teasing too. Even Dad takes some jabs for having a son who can outfish him.

"I notice none of these pictures are from the riverbank where this behemoth was caught," Mr. Philips points out. "Mind sharing that little piece of info with us, James, or is it a secret?"

Matt just shakes his head. "Dad, you know better than to ask a fisherman where his favorite spot is. I know, and James knows, and that's probably one too many."

"True, it's a time-honored tradition to hold fish spots sacred, but I guess it wouldn't hurt to let you know. The place I caught that fish is back on the..."

I name the river and then stop. Everyone around the table stares at me expectantly, waiting for me to divulge the details. Instead I just smile and sit back in my chair.

Matt starts laughing and then the rest join in.

"Well played, son," Dad says with a grin. "There are only twenty-seven miles and both sides of the river to pick from. But that does narrow it down some."

We talk about many things—weather, church, hockey season, football, and how Matt and I think our school team will do this year. Around nine o'clock, Mrs. Philips comes back to the kitchen.

"Bill, I think it's time to go home," she says. "Justin has an early morning and so do you."

Right behind her is Mrs. Scanlon, who echoes the same sentiments.

As they're heading out the front door, I remind Leah and Matt that we have another work session tomorrow. Dad allows us to use his den again, this time in the evening.

"I'm eager to see this big project you're all working on," says Mrs. Philips as they walk down the front step.

Debbie and I just smile and nod before returning to the kitchen to help Mom clear the table and load the dishwasher.

As I'm getting ready for bed that night, I draw the Book of Life down off its shelf and lay it on my bed. Kneeling, I put my hands together around the book and rest my head on the cover. I remain in that position, absorbing the peace that seems to emanate from it…

I must fall asleep, because my mind starts to swirl. I don't mean that I'm dizzy; it's like lying down in a field on a summer day and staring up at the sky as the clouds drift by without a care in the world. In this serene state, my subconscious is filled with matters I don't understand. And yet I feel comfortable with that. I'm surrounded by an expanse of joy, happiness, worship, and praise.

Maybe I'm not explaining this well, but how do you explain something when you don't know what it is you're trying to explain? It should be confusing, but it isn't. It should be overwhelming, but it isn't. All I can say is that I feel no discomfort, no worry, and nothing negative.

When I finally raise my head and open my eyes, I find myself still kneeling at my bedside, my arms around the book. I return the book to the closet and then slide into bed. I close my eyes without a worry in the world.

FIFTEEN

Friday

I'm shocked to open my eyes to the rising sun and not the voice of Michael calling my name. Despite the lack of angelic communication, I feel refreshed and rested, ready for another day the Lord has blessed me with. I thank Him as I rolled out of bed, grab my clothes, and head for the shower. When I'm "all clean and nice," as Mom used to say when I was little, I walk down to the kitchen and find it just as I would expect. Mom is working her magic and Dad has already left for work.

"Good morning, Mom. Whatcha doin'?"

"Oh, just putting things away from last night and getting ready to do some baking. Bread and cookies today. Could you get me about six good-sized potatoes from the garden sometime this morning? I have a large roast thawing for supper and new potatoes will go well with it."

"No problem. Anything special for breakfast this morning?"

"Not today. I have a lot on the go, so it's just cereal or toast. Help yourself."

After breakfast, I go out to the garden. There's nothing as fulfilling as harvesting what you've grown with your own hands, and rolling new potatoes out of the ground has to be one of my favorite harvests. They are so clean and white, even though they've just come out of the ground.

Is that how God looks at us? Those who have been washed by the blood of His Son are spotless, clean, and white, even though they come from a world of sin. I've never thought about it that way before.

"James! The phone's for you," Mom calls from the back door. "It's Matt."

"I'll be right there."

Picking up the bucket of potatoes, I head for the house. As I pass through the kitchen, I put the potatoes on the sideboard.

I pick up the phone, which is resting on the hall stand. "What's up, friend of mine?"

124

"I don't have anything to do today. Any chance we could meet for lunch instead of waiting for supper?"

"I'll check with the others and let you know."

"Okay. Talk to you soon."

I end the call and go back into the kitchen. Debbie is seated at the table with a piece of toast in one hand and a cup of tea in the other.

"About time you were up, sleepyhead," I tease.

"Who can sleep with all the racket you make?"

I tell her about Matt, who also prefers to meet sooner rather than later. She agrees to call Leah and I agree to talk to Mom about the change in plans.

As expected, everyone is on board. After another round of calls, we confirm the new time.

"You better get some more potatoes," Mom remarks. "Sounds like we may be having company again for supper. Six more should do it."

I go back outside to get the potatoes. When I come in, Debbie has already left for a run—but if I hurry, I can still catch up.

"Any interesting dreams last night?" she asks when I fall into step alongside her, having run at top speed for almost a mile to match her pace.

"Nothing like that," I say, huffing and puffing. "But I did have a closer... uh, relationship experience with the book."

"What does that mean?"

I explain to her what happened and describe how it felt.

"I think we've barely scratched the surface with this whole Book of Life thing," she says. "I've seen a lot of movies where kids get involved with something out of their league and end up in major trouble when their curiosity overcomes their common sense. That's not what's happening here, but it still makes me a bit nervous. There is no script. I'm being held together by prayer, faith, and the fact that I'm not alone in this."

"It sure takes the boredom out of the end of the summer, doesn't it?"

We run in silence for a little while, concentrating on our breathing as the sights and sounds of the neighborhood pass us by.

"To be honest, I'm trying not to think so hard," she says. "It hurts my head not knowing what will happen next."

"And don't forget that we're going to see Michael again on Sunday."

"Yeah."

Once again, our conditioning regiments are different and end up taking us in opposite directions.

When I get back home, I go up to my room to change. My eyes are drawn to the book, like always. It's shining even brighter today. Not only brighter, but I can feel its warmth even from outside the closet.

I take a step forward to pick it up…

"All in good time, James. In good time."

I immediately recognize the sound of Michael's voice in my head and back off. For now I'll just have to wait and see what comes next. I guess God wants me to exercise a little patience.

After showering, I go downstairs and discover the kitchen table covered in warm biscuits fresh from the oven, homemade applesauce, and a jar of Mom's strawberry jam. Debbie and Mom have started without me.

Looks like I'm going to put back on all those calories I just burned off!

"I'm going to give you young people some privacy this afternoon," Mom says. "I'm driving into town to do some grocery shopping. The roast and veggies are in the slow cooker, so there's nothing for you two to take care of except concentrate on whatever it is you're doing."

"You're the best, Mom!" Debbie and I say in unison.

We clear the table and load the dishwasher as Mom gets ready to leave. Just as she's about to depart, Matt is on his way in.

"Where's your mom going?" Matt asks, looking behind him as Mom drives the car onto the street. "I thought maybe she was going to cook some more today."

"Matt Philips, you are an empty pit." Debbie laughs at him. "Why you don't weigh two hundred pounds just amazes the daylights out of me."

"Why, Debbie, you should know by now that I'm a growing boy with a high metabolism."

She smirks. "We know you're something. I still think you're a bottomless pit…"

"I agree," Leah says as she walks in and takes off her shoes.

Matt scowls, but the rest of us can't help but break into good-natured laughter.

"All right, all right, we'll stop picking on Matt," I say. "We have far more serious fish to fry."

Matt and Debbie go upstairs to retrieve the book from my closet.

"Leah, why don't you and I go to the den and get the chairs arranged and the coffee table cleared off?"

"Right behind you, James."

We open the door and step into Dad's den. Immediately our mouths open in surprise at what we see.

"Don't say a thing," I tell her. "Wait and see how long it takes Matt to notice."

Shortly, Matt and Debbie come into the den. Debbie puts the book down on the table and Matt plunks himself into a chair. From the look on Debbie's face, I know that she has seen the same thing as me and Leah.

The three of us all stand in place, glancing at each other, and waiting. It doesn't take long for Matt to feel the extra attention on him.

"What? What did I do now?"

"Just gauging your powers of observation, Matt," Debbie says.

As he looks around, he finally sees it: a giant platter of cookies and dough-nuts placed on Dad's desk along with a picture full of lemonade with ice cubes floating to the surface.

"You're mother's a saint, James!" Matt says with reverence.

Debbie laughs. "Mom knew you were coming and thought you might like a little refreshment, I guess. She spoils you worse than her own kids!"

"I'm okay with that. I'll just grab a doughnut before we get started…"

We all get out our Bibles and turn to Revelation.

"Anyone want to lead off?" I ask.

Leah volunteers to read. She picks up her Bible and starts reading from Revelation 21:22–27.

> I did not see a temple in the city, because the Lord God Almighty and the Lamb are its temple. The city does not need the sun or the moon to shine on it, for the glory of God gives it light, and the Lamb is its lamp. The nations will walk by its light, and the kings of the earth will bring their splendor into it. On no day will its gates ever be shut, for there will be no night there. The glory and honor of the nations will be brought into it. Nothing impure will ever enter it, nor will anyone who does what is shameful or deceitful, but only those whose names are written in the Lamb's book of life.

"I don't think we've included enough of that scripture," Debbie says when Leah finishes her reading. "I think we have to start at the first verse of the chapter. Leah's already read the most important part, but the earlier verses set the complete landscape of the picture being laid before us. For example, what is the city being talking about? What temple? Do you see what I mean?"

I nod in agreement. "Okay. Let's go back and read from the beginning of the chapter."

Matt flips back a page and starts reading aloud.

> Then I saw "a new heaven and a new earth," for the first heaven and the first earth had passed away, and there was no longer any sea. I saw the Holy City, the new Jerusalem, coming down out of heaven from God, prepared as a bride beautifully dressed for her husband. And I heard a loud voice from the throne saying, "Look! God's dwelling place is now among the people, and he will dwell with them. They will be his people, and God himself will be with them and be their God. 'He will wipe every tear from their eyes. There will be no more death' or mourning or crying or pain, for the old order of things has passed away."
>
> He who was seated on the throne said, "I am making everything new!" Then he said, "Write this down, for these words are trustworthy and true."
>
> He said to me: "It is done. I am the Alpha and the Omega, the Beginning and the End. To the thirsty I will give water without cost from the spring of the water of life. Those who are victorious will inherit all this, and I will be their God and they will be my children. 8 But the cowardly, the unbelieving, the vile, the murderers, the sexually immoral, those who practice magic arts, the idolaters and all liars—they will be consigned to the

fiery lake of burning sulfur. This is the second death."

One of the seven angels who had the seven bowls full of the seven last plagues came and said to me, "Come, I will show you the bride, the wife of the Lamb." And he carried me away in the Spirit to a mountain great and high, and showed me the Holy City, Jerusalem, coming down out of heaven from God. It shone with the glory of God, and its brilliance was like that of a very precious jewel, like a jasper, clear as crystal. It had a great, high wall with twelve gates, and with twelve angels at the gates. On the gates were written the names of the twelve tribes of Israel. There were three gates on the east, three on the north, three on the south and three on the west. The wall of the city had twelve foundations, and on them were the names of the twelve apostles of the Lamb.

The angel who talked with me had a measuring rod of gold to measure the city, its gates and its walls. The city was laid out like a square, as long as it was wide. He measured the city with the rod and found it to be 12,000 stadia in length, and as wide and high as it is long. The angel measured the wall using human measurement, and it was cubits thick. The wall was made of jasper, and the city of pure gold, as pure as glass. The foundations of the city walls were decorated with every kind of precious stone. The first foundation was jasper, the second sapphire, the third agate, the fourth emerald, the fifth onyx, the sixth ruby, the seventh chrysolite, the eighth beryl, the ninth topaz, the tenth turquoise, the eleventh jacinth, and the twelfth amethyst. The twelve

gates were twelve pearls, each gate made of a
single pearl. The great street of the city was of
gold, as pure as transparent glass.[15]

"The first verse of this chapter has a huge impact," Debbie notes. "There's going to be a new heaven and a new earth because the old ones will be gone. The passage has to be describing a period of time after judgment day. Everything that follows supports this. There will be no more pain, no more tears, and no more suffering, all of which will have passed away with the old order. This is the reward for those who are victorious, which we have already discussed.

"The middle section of this passage describes the new Jerusalem as a beautiful city in terms we can understand. There will be precious gems and minerals. It will be a super clean, almost sterile setting, without even a speck of dirt. The twelve gates of this city are a testament to God's chosen people, the Israelites who for thousands of years worshipped Him as their one true God and remained His people despite bumps in the road. The city's twelve foundations are a testament to the apostles who became the foundation for Christianity, with Jesus as their cornerstone.

"Then we get to the end, which says the city will have no temple. Why? Because God will dwell within men. People will be the temple. There will be no sun and no moon. Again, no problem! The radiance of the Father and the Son far surpasses any other kind of light.

"Next we read that this city's gates will never be shut, and there will be no night. The prince of darkness will be thrown into the lake of fire with sin completely defeated. There will be no reason to close a gate because there will be nothing and no one to keep out. Those who are impure, shameful, or deceitful will have gone to the reward they chose. Only those whose names are written in the Book of Life will remain."

We all look at the book lying on the coffee table, struck again by how amazing it is that we have it in our possession.

"This book we have in front of us contains the names of everyone who will be saved, from the time of creation to the present day." Debbie lets out a huge sigh. "Okay, I'm done. That was exhausting."

Leah leans over and puts an arm around her friend's shoulder, giving her a hug.

"Debbie, you just put the icing on the cake," I say. "But I think we should take a short break and let our minds digest all this before going any deeper."

---

[15] Revelation 21:1–21.

Matt perks up. "Did somebody mention cake and icing?"

"There's no cake or icing." I smile. "Just doughnuts and cookies and lemonade. You'll have to make do."

Matt hangs his head and we all laugh.

"While we're taking a break, I want to tell you all about something that happened to me last night," I say.

"What is it?" Leah asks.

"While I said my prayers, I rested my head on the book with my arms around it and my hands folded. I must have drifted off..." I trail into silence for a moment, remembering how I felt. "You know that feeling you get when you hold the book, or the way you feel when Michael is talking to you? This experience was even greater and more intense. It was beautiful! I don't have the words to describe what it felt like. I wish I did. I don't know... it was like being connected with all the souls who have their names written in the Book of Life, feeling their happiness and peace."

The others are watching me with wide eyes.

"I want the rest of you to have this experience for yourselves. Debbie, take the book to your room tonight and see if you can duplicate it." I look to Leah and Matt. "Maybe you can take the book other nights. We'll have to ask Michael if this is allowed."

"That sounds incredible," Debbie says in a quiet voice.

"Another thing. This morning, the book looked much brighter than usual... and warmer too. Then I heard Michael speak to me: 'All in good time, James. In good time.' Debbie, did you or Matt notice any difference when you brought the book down today?"

Debbie gives this some thought, then nods. "It *was* warmer, come to think of it. I wonder what that means."

"In good time, sis, in good time. That's what I was told and that's what I'm telling you... all of you. I'm hoping that we can get some alone time with Michael on Sunday. I've got some questions, and I'm sure the rest of you do too."

Leah has been silent for a long time, but she suddenly comes to life.

"We seem to be gaining ground," she says. "Debbie opened that last chapter wide open so we can better understand what eternity will be like. But our task is to research the Book of Life. Where does it fit into all this? It's only mentioned in the last verse of Revelation 21, but I think it has a big impact. Those whose names are found in the Book of Life will be bathed in the glory of the Lord. They will live in this beautiful place with God while those whose names aren't in the book will end in the lake of fire. That's a pretty important separation!"

"In the period of time Revelation 21 is describing, judgment day will have come and gone," Matt reminds us. "The Book of Life has already been opened by then. Judgment has been passed and the book has served its purpose."

I reach out and touch the cover of the book. "Have any of us really looked closely at the cover? Now that I look at it with fresh eyes, the front seems to depict a large structure that looks like a temple with twelve gates. And there's writing on the gates. I'm willing to bet that if we find someone who can translate ancient Hebrew, we'll find out that each one bears a name of the twelve tribes of Israel."

I turn the book over and look at the etchings on the back. I trace the lines.

"These are the foundations of the temple that we see on the front," I continue. "Each one has some writing on it, and I have no doubt that these are the names of the twelve apostles. Why put the gates on the front and the foundation on the back? Well, the twelve tribes of Israel, God's chosen people, came first. He made His first covenant with them. The apostles came later, signifying the foundation Christ laid in the second covenant, of which He was the cornerstone. He came for all mankind, not just the Israelites."

"Wow! You're so right," Matt exclaims.

"How did you come up with that?" asks Leah.

"It just came to me while you guys were talking," I say. "I'm not claiming any credit. In fact, I'm not taking credit for anything I've said or done lately. I'm sure the Spirit of God has been moving in each one of us."

We all hear the sound of a car in the driveway.

Debbie looks at the clock on the wall. "Oh my! Look at the time. How are we going to get the book back up to your room, James?"

"Have faith, sis. Let's just go out to the kitchen and say hello."

I pick up the book and head for the kitchen, followed by my three totally confused co-conspirators.

"Hi Mom!" I say. "Have a good afternoon?"

"I certainly did. How about the four of you?"

"We accomplished a lot," Debbie answers.

Leah smiles widely. "Yes, we did."

"I just need to run up to my room," I tell Mom. "I'll be right back."

When I come back, Mom is inviting Leah and Matt to stay for supper. She's making roast beef and veggies. They agree, but only after they check in with their parents.

"You four go clean up the den while I finish getting everything ready for supper," Mom says. "It should be ready by 6:30."

From the den, we pick up the dirty glasses and empty plates.

"James, I realize that Mom and Dad can't see the book, but don't you think that was a little brazen?" Debbie asks. "Standing there with the book right in front of Mom? That's gutsy."

"It's not brazen or gutsy," I say. "It's faith. Micheal said that the Book would be safe here and I believe him. After all, he is our guardian angel now."

"Speaking of guardian angels, maybe we should ask Michael about that on Sunday."

"I think we should keep our questions focused on the task at hand." I hesitate. "But you're right. I would love to ask that question."

Once we've got the den in order, we head back to the kitchen. Mom has set the table and turned on the tea kettle.

While we wait for Dad to get home, the four of us return to the den.

"What time are we meeting tomorrow?" asks Leah. "If we meet in the afternoon again, it means your mom will probably have us all stay for supper. I don't think that's fair to her."

"We've been here a lot lately," Matt agrees. "Not that I don't like being here... but James, your mom is a saint. We shouldn't take advantage of that."

Instead we make a plan to meet after supper.

Soon Mom calls into the room to tell us that Dad is home and we'll be eating in fifteen minutes. We wash our hands and then sit down in the kitchen.

After dinner, we help clear the table.

Dad invites everyone to stay for a board game—and before we know it, it's 9:00.

"Guess it's time to fold up the tents and head home," Matt says as we put away the game pieces. "Have any plans for the morning, James? Thought maybe we'd go fishing again. Season's getting short."

"Actually, I had been thinking you and I could go fishing," Dad says to me. "But you can come too, Matt. We'll make it a threesome."

"Fine with me, Mr. Jeffries, just so long as you promise not to outfish me. Your son seems to enjoy doing that every time we go."

"You're on, boys, but no promises." He smiles at us. "I've got a spot all picked out. Somewhere neither of you have ever been."

Matt and Leah head for home and Debbie and I go up to our rooms. I get the book down from the closet and meet Debbie in the hall.

"I told you what I did and what happened last night," I say. "What do you think you'll do? Any ideas?"

"I'll probably do the same thing and see what happens."

"Well, good luck, sis. Just remember that God is with us in this." I give her a kiss on the cheek. "Good night. God bless. Love you."

She says the same to me, then goes into her room and closes her door. As I go to bed, I drop down onto my knees and say my prayers, including an extra exhortation for Debbie.

• • •

Debbie changes into her nightclothes and places the book on her bed. She kneels, puts her arm around it, and lowers her head onto the cover. As she starts to pray, she begins to sense an odd sensation; it's like she's floating, without a care in the world. She remembers what James tried to describe and immediately understands why he had so much trouble. This is just beautiful, overwhelmingly beautiful, but without being overwhelming. Love, peace, and warmth settles over her.

Amidst this, Michael's voice calls out to her: "Debbie?"

She hesitates, sort of caught by surprise.

"Debbie?"

"Yes," she answers timidly.

"Debbie, you have entered the Book of Life, in which are found the names of those who will be spared the second death. Everything you see, everything you feel, everything that surrounds you now is the peace of the Almighty. This is the peace experienced by those whose names are written in this book as they await the day of its opening, the day on which judgment will be passed on the living and the dead. The Book of Life cannot be opened. Only the hand of the Almighty is able to open it. And yet you and James and Matt and Leah have been blessed with the ability to see within. You do not understand what you see, for it is not something the mortal mind can comprehend. Take joy in the knowledge that you would not be granted this access if your names were not written in the book. But be warned: this does not mean you are assured that your names will remain in the Book of Life. You may share what you see with your taskmates and them alone. More will be revealed as you prove yourselves worthy of the task and of the trust He places in you. May the peace of God be with you."

Then nothing.

She remains on her knees, her head nestled on the book, her arms wrapped around it. Eventually the clock on her nightstand reads 3:30. She crawls beneath the sheets, cradling the book in her arms, and falls into a deep, uninterrupted sleep.

• • •

Across the hall, I have gone to sleep—but in that sleep, I hear that familiar voice call my name: "James?"

"Yes, Michael."

"James, you have had an experience with the Book of Life. Your sister Debbie is having a similar experience now. Leah and Matt must have the same experience, but they must have it in this house. Debbie will tell you more. Each time you enter this realm, you will learn more as the Lord sees fit.

"You have noticed a change in the book. It seems warmer to the touch and brighter to your eyes. The reason for both of these phenomena is the same: as names are added, the book becomes warmer and brighter. As names are removed, the book cools and loses some of its intensity. You remain the only one who has the ability to see this glow.

"Tomorrow you will have Leah and Matt engage the book as you and Debbie have. A time of turmoil is coming and you must all ready yourselves for it. Your preparation in the Word of God is not yet complete. Focus on that and the rest will fall into place.

"I will see you on Sunday in church. We will not talk of guardian angels. It's not pertinent to the task at hand and you must not invite any distractions. Our time this night is over. May the blessing of the Lord be with you and give you the strength to fulfill this task."

SIXTEEN

Saturday

I don't know if my visit from Michael came early or late in the night, but when I open my eyes it's 5:45. I head downstairs and find Mom at the stove. Tea is brewing and toast, jam, and juice are waiting on the table.

"Worms are in the can," Dad says from his seat. "Grab a bite and let's go."

"I'll get the rods out of the shed, Dad."

"Check the front step, James. They're already there."

"I don't know who it's harder to get ahead of, you or Mom. How are you both so organized? Not that I mind. Are we ready then?"

"Guess so."

We go to the truck, picking up our gear off the veranda. On our drive to Matt's, Dad asks what I've been doing to get ready for football season. I tell him that Matt and I plan on starting a conditioning program next week.

"You're leaving it a bit late, aren't you?" Dad says. "You know there'll be a lot of newcomers looking for positions on the team. Competition could be fierce."

"I know, Dad. Matt and I have kept busy and done a lot of swimming at the lake. I think we're in pretty good shape. We just have to put on the finishing touches."

"I hope you know what you're doing."

Dad pulls over and Matt puts his gear in the bed of the truck. He gets in the rear and gives us a "Good morning."

"Where are we going?" Matt asks.

"It's a secret place," Dad answers. "I need you to swear yourselves to secrecy about its location too."

I smile as I turn to look at Matt in the back seat. "Oh, you don't have to worry about us, Dad. We know how to keep a secret. I give Matt a wink. "Don't we, Matt?"

"We most certainly do." Matt responds with a big grin on his face.

"Now that we've got that settled, we're almost there," Dad informs us.

He turns onto an old logging road that Matt and I have ridden past a thousand times. He drives just far enough into the bush that his truck won't be seen by passersby.

When he stops, we get out and gather up the rods and backpacks.

"Okay, Dad, how far do we have to walk?" I ask.,

"About five minutes, James."

He's right and soon we're baiting hooks and settling in to what we hope will be a successful day. The sky's a little overcast and there's a slight westerly breeze. The birds are singing. The river flows peacefully. And best of all, the trout are biting. Life is good.

We have a fantabulous day fishing, talking, and eating the lunch Mom packed for us. The only sad thing is that we eventually have to pack it up. After picking up the trout we're keeping, we walk back to the truck and head for home, dropping Matt off at his place on the way.

Debbie is on the front veranda when we arrive. She stops me while Dad goes straight inside.

"How did the great hunter-gatherers do?" she asks as she strolls over to the truck.

"We hunted and we gathered and now it's time for you womenfolk to prepare the feast." I hold up a string of nice trout.

"Mom said we'd be having trout for supper," Debbie says. "She has potato salad and a green salad ready to go. By the way, James, who caught the most fish?"

"Why are you asking me?"

"Because I know the answer will be hard for you to admit. And Dad is too modest to torment you. So who caught the most?"

"Smarty pants! I guess you already know."

"Yes, but I want to hear it from your lips."

"Okay, okay… Dad caught the most. As much as it hurts me to say so, he won by quite a bit."

Debbie glances at our catch. "Are these all cleaned and ready?"

"Just give them to Mom. They're ready to go. I'm going to have a shower and change."

"Use the downstairs shower. Dad went upstairs." Debbie leads the way back inside the house. "By the way, he and Mom are going to a movie in town tonight. We'll have the house to ourselves. And I have some pretty interesting things to share."

"Yeah, me too. Tonight can't come too soon."

After showing, I return to the kitchen, the nerve center of our home. The whole family is already here.

"Sit down, you three," Mom says from the stove, right where I left her this morning. "Get your salads on your plates. They'll be joined by fresh trout rolled in cornmeal, with a few secret spices added, and panfried in butter."

"You've got me drooling, Mom!" I remark.

Debbie smiles. "You should be writing menu descriptions for restaurants."

Mom serves up the trout and says grace before digging in. Debbie tells us about her day and Dad and I describe our excursion to the river. As for Mom, she had a nice and quiet in the house. She got a lot of work done in the morning and then spent some time with tea and her Bible on the veranda in the afternoon.

As we finish up, Mom gets up to serve tea while Debbie and I clean off some of the dishes.

Mom looks out the window over the sink. "Here comes your early bird."

"What? It's only six o'clock." Debbie sighs. "Matt does hate to be late."

A moment later, I meet Matt at the front door. "Hi, early bird."

"Am I early?"

"Not only that, but you're just in time to join us for dessert," Mom calls. "Have a seat, Matt. James, get your friend a small plate and a cup while I take the apple pie out of the oven."

"What apple pie?" I ask.

"The one that's been keeping warm while we had supper. I was hoping the smell of the fish would mask my little surprise. Debbie, would you get the pie server out of the drawer? I assume everyone wants pie."

"Matt, would you like tea or coffee?" Debbie asks.

"Milk is just fine for me." Matt grins. "I guess it pays off to be early sometimes."

As I pass Matt's plate to Mom, I laugh. "You're like a great white. They can smell blood in the water from miles away. You can smell food from about the same distance."

He blushes a bit.

Finishing our pie, we hear a soft knock at the door. From my chair in the kitchen, I can see Leah standing outside.

"Come in and join the party!" I call. "Want some warm apple pie fresh out of the oven?"

"Oh my goodness!" Mom exclaims. "I completely forgot about the vanilla ice cream in the freezer."

"Nothing lost, Winnie," says Dad, pushing his empty plate away. "The pie was delicious even without the ice cream."

We all agree.

"How 'bout it, Leah," I say again. "Pie?"

"No thank you. I had a big supper. I couldn't eat another bite."

"Maybe later?" I suggest.

Matt looks up in excitement. "Later?"

"Oh, stop it, Matt!" Debbie giggles.

Dad stands up. "Well, if your mother and I are going to get to the theatre on time, we should get moving."

"Don't worry about the dishes," Mom says. "I'll take care of them later, or maybe in the morning. Okay, kids, you have a productive evening. We'll be back about 10:30."

Pretty soon they're on their way down the driveway in Mom's jeep.

"Let's go to the den," I say. "Debbie, you want to go up to your room and get the book?"

"So Debbie actually had the book overnight." Leah asked. Then she asks a few rapid-fire questions. "How did that go? Did anything happen? Can we each have a turn?"

"Slow down, Leah." I lead them into the den. "I'm just as much in the dark as you two, although I did have another visit from Michael last night."

Matt paces around the den, refusing to sit down. "I'm just buzzing. Can hardly sit still."

"Sit down anyway," Debbie comments as she comes in with the book and places it on the coffee table. "Where do we begin, James?"

"Let's start with you. What happened last night? Did you feel anything?"

"You have no idea!" she gushes. "James, you told us about your experience and I have to say that you were right when you talked about how completely overwhelmed you felt with peace and love. It goes way beyond my ability to describe. No words come close... and then a voice spoke my name."

At this, we all come to the edge of our seats.

"It must have been Michael," Debbie says. "He tells me that I'm in the Book of Life... actually *inside* it! The feeling we get is the same feeling of joy and peace of those whose names are written there. I was also told that if our names weren't written in the book, we wouldn't be able to go there. Can you imagine? That means my name is written in the Book of Life! All of our names must be.

Of course, there's no guarantee our names will stay there. That depends on the choices we make throughout our lives. That's about it."

"That's about it? Where do I start?" Matt exclaims. "This is a lot to take in. First, to know your name is in the Book of Life, and then to know you're going to have access to what's in that book… I'm just turned upside-down and inside-out right now!"

I turn to Leah. "You're awful quiet. What's going through your head?"

"I don't know what to think, James. Matt's right about it being a lot to absorb, but I think we have to accept this as part of God's plan for us. So what comes next? Do Matt and I take the book home and repeat the things you and Debbie did? I'm just a little confused."

"Well, don't be," I say. "I had a visit from Michael last night and he told me some things."

"You didn't tell me you had a visit from Michael!" Debbie exclaims.

"Face it, sis, this is the first time today we've been in company where we could talk about it."

"True."

"Michael told me that Leah and Matt have to experience the book too, just like me and Debbie. He also said that it has to happen in this house, although he didn't say why. We'll figure out how we're going to do that. He also said we'll learn more each time we visit the book. He also explained why the book seems brighter and warmer…"

I go on to recount all the details of the message.

"So I guess we'll need to arrange a sleepover," Leah remarks.

"I think I have something simpler in mind," I say. "Leah, why don't you take the book right now and go up to Debbie's room? Put the book on the bed. Then close your arms around it, lower your forehead to the cover, and start to pray. No questions. Just do it!"

Without a word, Leah picks up the book and heads for Debbie's room.

• • •

Leah enters and shuts the door behind her, then places the book on the bed. She gets to her knees and follows the rest of the instructions, wrapping her arms around it and putting her forehead to the cover. She clasps her hands, closes her eyes, and starts to pray.

Within an unknowable period of time, she feels a wave of peace, love, and tranquility, the same indescribable sensations the others felt. The peaceful pandemonium and total comfort amidst chaos makes no sense, but her mind tells her that this is as it should be.

"Leah."

Nervous with anticipation, she answers timidly. "Yes."

"Leah, God has given you a task which He is revealing to you in stages," Michael explains. "One of these stages is to reveal to you what is held within the Book of Life. The book will not be opened to you, but you will be allowed inside. You will have no understanding of that which you experience. Becoming more familiar with the book will change you. You will know more, but never all. You will understand little. The mind of man has not the capacity to comprehend the will of God.

"I will now take you once more into the Book of Life. Feel it. Let the comfort of it caress your soul. Let it fill your heart with joy. Bathe in the peace of those whose names are found within it. Then I will leave and you will awaken to share this experience with the others."

True to these words, Leah awakens and goes back downstairs to the den, carrying the book.

• • •

"What are you doing back so soon?" Matt asks. "You just went upstairs a minute ago. Didn't anything happen? Maybe you didn't give it enough time."

Debbie shushes him. "Be quiet, Matt. Look at her face. Have you ever seen her look so at peace before in your life?"

"Oh! Debbie, it was so beautiful… and at the same time so wildly confusing with peace," Leah says. "And I had a feeling of… I don't know, being in the arms of someone who will hold and protect me from all harm. I just loved it!"

"Did anyone make contact?" I ask.

Leah smiles beatifically. "Yes. Michael's voice explained that we would be taken into the book and each time know more, but never all. He said our minds don't have the capacity to understand the will of God."

As this sinks in, we all realize that it's Matt's turn. He takes the book from Leah and walks out of the den.

"All right," he calls over his shoulder. "Here I go."

• • •

Matt takes the book from Leah and heads upstairs. When he gets to James's room, he does the same as all the others before him. As he starts to pray, he feels the same sensation.

And then comes the voice of Michael.

"Matt?"

"Yes."

"You knew what to expect today, but you didn't understand the impact of what you would actually feel. Bathe in that sensation. Absorb it into your soul and feel it in every cell of your body. To know but not know, to feel but not understand. Give it time, give it prayer, and give it into His hands. All will be right in the world, physically and spiritually. There are names in this book, but you will not know them; there are faces, but you will not see them. Knowing whose names are not written in the Book of Life is a cause for sorrow, and there will be no sorrow for those whose names are found in it. As with Leah, I will return you to the book so you may again experience the love of God, which defies any physical or psychological feeling you can have in this life. Allow yourself to absorb this feeling. You will feel like you're floating in a warm lake with the blue sky overhead, large fluffy clouds drifting by and birds singing serenely in the background. If you listen closely, their songs are hymns of praise to the Father and the Son and the Holy Spirit."

Matt awakens to a clear head and feeling of great peace.

Gathering himself, he goes back downstairs with the book and rejoins the others in the den. He places the book on the table and sits down.

• • •

"Well?" Debbie asks. "What happened?"

"The same as for the rest of you," Matt says. "I don't think I have ever felt this good in my whole life. How long was I gone?"

"About five minutes," I tell him.

"Felt a lot longer than that… and at the same time, not nearly long enough. Michael's voice came to me too, telling me to absorb the feeling into my soul and body. I was to know and not know, feel but not understand. I was told that if we put everything in the hands of the Lord, all will be right with the physical and spiritual world…" He smiles widely. "Boy! I'd like to do that again."

"It's only eight o'clock," I say. "Why don't we take a break. Does anyone want pie or cookies or tea or lemonade?"

Leah gets up. "I'll help."

"No thanks, I'm good," Matt says to me.

We all just freeze and stare at him.

"What!" I exclaim.

"You just turned down food, Matt Philips. Are you all right?" Debbie sounds worried.

"To be honest, no. I haven't ever felt this good or satisfied, not just with food but with everything," Matt tells us. "It just feels good to be alive, close to you guys, and, most important, close to God."

Debbie sighs in relief. "Amen to that."

Leah and I bring in a tray containing a picture of lemonade and plate of cookies. We all get relaxed, knowing that in a few minutes we'll be back to studying the scriptures, as Michael as instructed us to do.

"If memory services, we left off our studies at Revelation 21," I say. "What comes next?"

Leah starts us off. "From all the scriptures we've been reading, we can see how important the Book of Life is to mankind. If your name is in it on judgment day, you spend eternity with our heavenly Father. If it's not, you spend that same eternity in a lake of fire. Judgment day is going to be a sort of black-and-white affair. But until then, we all have the opportunity for our names to be added to the book. Or removed. It's only too late after we draw our last breath. Then we can't change the outcome. Will God make any exceptions or grant any pardons? It's not up to us to even speculate. We can't read God's mind, and that's not what we're here for. As for when the book will be opened, we know it can't be opened by man or beast. We can only look after our own lives and make decisions for ourselves. That being said, I don't think we need to be worried about anybody taking possession of the book."

"Wait a minute," Matt jumps in. "Couldn't a man take the book and give it to Satan? What then?"

"Matt's right," Debbie says. "Satan has used humanity as pawns ever since we got kicked out of the Garden of Eden. If Satan wants the book, he'll use everything at his disposal to get it."

"There is no if," I agree. "Michael told me that Satan wants the book. But I still don't think he can open it. We've been told more than once that only God can open the book. Satan must want it for other reasons, and I have some theories as to why. I'll keep them to myself for now, since I don't know for sure. But this book sitting before us is ancient and contains priceless information. Forces way beyond our imaginations would like to possess it. We may just be four teenagers, but we are the ones God has instructed to look after the Book of Life. That should make us feel kind of proud, but kind of humble at the same time."

Debbie nods to herself. "You said it! It's a huge responsibility. Why did God decide to use us?"

"Why did He choose David to fight Goliath?" I ask solemnly. "Why did He choose Noah to build the ark? Why did He choose fishermen to be His disciples and spread the good news after His resurrection? Ours is not to reason why. Ours is to trust in His infinite wisdom and accept what He gives us to do, without question."

"I know that," Debbie says. "I still can't help but wonder."

"Well, Debbie, I look at myself as the weakest link," Matt says. "But I know the Lord has a place for me in this task. I'm ready for whatever comes our way."

Leah makes eye contact with Matt. "Remember you said that. I have a funny feeling we'll be having challenges we've never seen before. We'll just have to trust, have faith, and pray."

"That's right, Leah," I say. "Matt has the right idea. God is using the four of us. We're all in this together. There are no weak links. Like the three musketeers, we're 'All for one, and one for all.' Except in our case it's 'One for God, and all for God.'"

In the ensuing silence, I clear my throat.

"To be honest, I think we're finished our scripture study," I continue. "At church tomorrow, we can ask Michael for more direction."

Everyone nods.

"Unless any of you have something to add, let's all lean in, put our hands on the book, and have a time of prayer. I'll lead off. If any of you wants to jump in, feel free."

We all lean in, put our hands on the Book, close our eyes, and begin to pray. When I get through, each of the others adds their own thoughts in prayer.

"We ask all this in the name of Jesus Christ our Lord and Savior," I say in closing. "Amen."

Matt gets up. "It's almost ten o'clock. I should be heading home."

"Me too," says Leah.

All four of us begin to tidy up the den and get ready to go our separate ways.

"I'm going to sleep with the book on my bed tonight to see whether any more details will be opened up to us," I say.

"You're so lucky," Matt says. "I can't wait to do that again. It felt so good."

Leah can't help but grin. "I don't know what heaven's going to be like, but if that was a little taste… well, I can't wait."

"But wait you will, Leah," Debbie says with a laugh. "And so will the rest of us. Apparently God's not done with us yet."

SEVENTEEN

After the den is tidied up, I grab a jacket off a hook by the front door and offer to walk Leah home.

"It's just next door," Debbie chides.

I sigh. "Well, if Leah would prefer to go alone, then I'll stay."

Leah seems to turn a pretty shade of pink. "I don't mind. I'd like the company."

"You gonna walk me home, Debbie?" Matt asks through a big grin.

"Get out of here, all three of you," Debbie says in a bluster. "I'm heading upstairs for a shower. I'll put the book in your room on the bed, James."

"Thanks, sis."

Down the driveway we go. I say good night to Matt when the moment comes for me to walk Leah to her door.

I take Leah's hand in mine and she sort of leans against my shoulder as we take those last few steps. When she reaches the first step, she turns and kisses me on the forehead.

"I'm glad we're doing this together," she says. "I don't know how I would ever have found the strength otherwise."

"I know what you mean. It just goes to show you that God knows what He's doing." I give her a kiss on the cheek. "Good night, Leah. See you at church."

With that, I turn and head back for my house. As I walk, her soft little voice catches up with me: "Good night, James."

Just as I'm about to go in through the front door, Mom and Dad pull into the driveway.

"How as the movie?" I ask as we walk inside.

They provide a quick review and then I go upstairs. After a quick wash, I step into my room and, sure enough, there's the book lying on my bed.

I cross the hall and tap lightly on Debbie's door. "Good night. God bless. Love you, sis."

"Same to you," she replies.

A moment later, I'm on my knees in front of my bed. Placing my forehead on the book's cover, I wrap my around it and clasp my hands. I thank God for His many blessings, which include my family, my faith, my friends, and most of all His Son.

I must have faded off, because the next thing I know I'm back in that incredible realm of peace and love and calm. It swirls around me and fills me with perfect contentment.

"James," Michael calls.

"Yes."

"Do you know where you are?"

"I am in the Book of Life."

"That is correct. What do you see?"

I pay closer attention than ever to the hazy air surrounding me, trying to make out details. Sure enough, vague shapes and figures make themselves known to me. There are also indecipherable letters and symbols. It's so hard to interpret them, but the feeling they convey is pure bliss.

"I see shapes and figures," I say slowly. "I see peace and happiness. I see love and warmth. I see things that don't have a physical presence… but somehow I still see them. I see figures and letters, but none that I recognize. They don't seem to form words or carry any specific meaning. I see the beauty of all this! I feel like a newborn baby being held by its mother…"

"James, focus your mind even further."

It's so hard to do. My mind doesn't want to focus; it wants to further relax into this state of complete comfort.

Pressing hard, I urge my unconscious to narrow its concentration.

Those formless shapes and figures around me continue to swirl… but more slowly. As I watch, they become increasingly sharp and finite. I can make out the letters and symbols now, although I only recognizable a few of them. They seem to be arranged in groups, and perhaps they are words. But I still can't make any sense of them.

"Good, James."

"Are they words? If they're words, why can't I understand them?"

"These are the names written in the Book of Life. You have been allowed to see them, but you will not be allowed to know them. This knowledge is beyond the power of man to control or comprehend."

I'm struck by the awesome glimpse of eternity I've been given. It doesn't seem real.

"Look closer," Michael says. "What do you see?"

I focus again—although that seems like the wrong word for it. I'm not focusing with my eyes; this spiritual sight comes from somewhere deep inside.

"Some of the names seem to be larger and darker than the others," I say. "Like bold print in a book. Others are very light, almost faded out completely. Why is that?"

"The Lord has given you discernment. The names of those who have left the physical world appear in the boldest of print. When they left the world, their names were found in the Book of Life. Having taken their last breath while still in God's grace, their names will remain in the book until that day when the Lord Almighty opens it. As God's Word has told you, 'And I heard a loud voice from the throne saying, "Look! God's dwelling place is now among the people, and he will dwell with them. They will be his people, and God himself will be with them and be their God."'[16]

"The rest of the names are those who still live and breathe the air of your world. The state of their spiritual health is reflected in the boldness of their names. The bolder the print, the stronger their faith and commitment to follow the Son, for He is the key to those of the generations that live under the new covenant. The weaker the print, the greater the danger of having that name disappear from the Book of Life. A person can do much to change their own future.

"Our time is now over. You will awake to find yourself in bed and the Book of Life on the shelf in your closet. May your work be blessed and the Spirit give you strength as you go forward."

I wake up to find myself in bed and the light of the moon shining through the window. The moonlight is bright enough for me to make out the book on the shelf.

I'm shocked to see that it's only 1:30. Time doesn't pass logically when I have my dreams with Michael.

I lay my head back on the pillow and fall into a peaceful sleep.

Sunday

The sun brightening my room brings me back to the land of the living and I hop out of bed, feeling as refreshed as though I've slept for a week. I grab clothes and a towel and head for the shower.

Mom is in the kitchen, as expected.

"Good morning, James. A light breakfast today. Croissants or toast, jam or jelly, tea or coffee or juice. Those are the choices." She walks towards the stairs.

---

[16] Revelation 21:3.

"I'm going to wake up your sister. Your father has some things he needs to go over with Pastor Dave, so we need to leave for church a bit early today."

"No problem, Mom. And by the way, good morning to you too."

Dad soon joins me at the table. "How are you this morning, James?"

"Just great, Dad. How 'bout you?"

"I'm fine and thankful for this new day the Lord has blessed us with."

When Debbie walks into the kitchen, it doesn't take Sherlock Holmes to figure out she's not having a great morning. She plunks herself down into a chair, seeming a bit lost. I get up and get her a cup of coffee.

"Here, try that," I say, placing the cup in front of her. "Maybe it will help stimulate you."

"Thanks, James. I don't know why, but I just can't seem to wake up this morning."

"You should have had the dream I had last night!"

Her head comes up and her eyes brighten. "What kind of dream?" Then, realizing that Dad and Mom are nearby, she tries to cover. "Was she pretty and live close by?"

"Now, children, we don't have time for that kind of banter today," Mom says. "Your father would like to leave by 9:30, so let's get moving."

I finish my breakfast as Debbie starts hers and then head upstairs to put on my Sunday best and get my Bible. Once downstairs again, I head for the arm-chair in the living room and open my Bible to Job, the book of the month at church.

Debbie comes into the living room and sits on the couch and flips her own Bible open.

"So you had a good dream last night?" Debbie whispers.

"We'll talk later," I answer quietly. "Mom and Dad are going to be here any minute."

As the words leave my mouth, Mom calls from the front door. "You two ready? Time to go."

Off to church we go.

When we arrive, I look around hoping to run into Michael. He's nowhere to be seen.

It's getting close to time for Sunday school to start. As we meet up with Matt and Leah, we turn to the front just as Derrick asks us all to bow our heads. He's enthusiastic in the morning's lesson and the next forty minutes just fly by. Before we know it, we are closing in prayer.

"Have any of you seen Michael?" Leah asks as we head toward the worship hall.

"Not me," I say.

We take our seats at the back of the worship hall and scan the congregation, and that's when Debbie nudges me and nods to the left. Sure enough, there is Michael, sitting with Derrick and his wife Amanda.

It's a relief to see him, as I know we're all hoping to talk to him after the service. It's a terrible thing to say, but I think we're all so preoccupied that we miss the point of the morning message!

As we stand for the hymn of invitation, we keep our eyes trained on Michael so we'll see which way he goes after the closing prayer.

After the service, we track him down outside as he walks toward the flower garden and the swing set. We walk briskly to catch up.

"Michael," I call.

He turns and smiles. "Come, have a seat on the swing and we'll have a chat. Maybe I can answer some of your questions and put your minds at ease."

We take seats on the swings, each of us brimming with questions.

"Are we finished the scripture phase of our task?" I ask. "If we are, what's next?"

"Those are easy, James. Yes. Having said that, you also have to understand that the scriptures will continue to be an integral part of the task. As for what comes next, though, I cannot give you a definite answer. You must continue in faith and turn to the Lord your God for strength and direction, for only with Him will you succeed. There will be times of trouble and confusion. There will be fog and mist that distorts reality. Only with the Truth, the Light, and the Way will you be able to reach the goal. Do you understand?"

"I think so," Matt says. "There are some things happening that might change what we need to do. Am I right?"

"Indeed you are, young man."

Leah has been sitting with her head down. She lifts her chin and looks at Michael. "Will you be appearing in our dreams to keep us up to speed, telling us what's needed?"

"Not only will I be in contact in your sleep, but there may be times when I will contact you in your conscious state as well. Never fear when you hear from me. I am your friend. Or, as Debbie likes to refer to my kind, a guardian angel. As to what you need to do, you will be guided in many forms. You will receive guidance from me, but your faith will also help to keep your feet on the proper path. Walk with the Holy Spirit and you will never walk in danger."

"What about the book?" Debbie asks. "We've been given glimpses inside it. Are we going to see more? Are we going to understand it more clearly?"

"Talk to our brother, Debbie. He was given more information on that very subject last night. I will tell you that your knowledge of the Book of Life will grow, and with that growth will come great responsibility. I am not aware of just how much you will be privileged to understand, for the Lord has not made that known to me. Be assured that no man has ever been given this gift of insight into the Book of Life."

He stands up and turns to face us.

"We will talk further, but not at this time," he says. "There are times coming for which you must be prepared. I will prepare you to my greatest ability, but your faith and trust in the Lord Almighty will be your greatest protection—and at the same time, your greatest weapon. I will visit you soon, but for now I must go. May the peace of the Lord be always with you."

And with that, he vanishes into thin air.

PART THREE
THE TASK

EIGHTEEN

Sunday afternoon

We stand around the flower garden unable to speak. Even if we could speak, I'm not sure what we would say. He was there and then he wasn't. I guess we all know an angel can do things like that, but we've never experienced it—and I've got to say, it's a shock.

We don't have time to get over it, though.

"Leah, are you ready to go?" Mrs. Scanlon calls from the door of the church. "Your father is getting hungry."

"I'll be right there, Mom." Leah turns to us and almost gasps. "Can we get together tonight? We need to talk about this. And James, you've got to fill us in on what happened last night."

"I don't think there's any problem with meeting tonight," I say. "How about 6:30 again?"

Once everyone has agreed, Debbie and I walk off to find out parents. We find them talking with Pastor Dave and his wife Sue.

"Didn't I see you talking to Michael out by the swing set?" Mom asks.

"Yes," Debbie replies. "But he had to go."

The ride home is quiet, and through lunch we talk about the morning message. At least Mom and Dad do; Debbie and I have lots on our minds and don't contribute much.

"Is everything all right with you two?" Dad asks as we're getting up from the table. "You've been very quiet since church. You seem very preoccupied. Did something happen with Michael?"

Debbie shakes her head. "No, Dad, everything's fine. After Michael left, we were just talking about our project. We're facing some bumps in the road."

I nod in agreement.

"You do remember that your father and I have offered to help," Mom reminds us.

"And we're thankful for that," I say. "We really need to try to do this on our own. With God's help, of course."

Mom smiles. "I'm glad you added that last bit. With His help, I'm sure you'll overcome any obstacles in your way. The offer still stands, though. If you need help, all you have to do is ask."

"Thanks, Mom. We know we can always rely on you and Dad," Debbie says. "Do you want any help with the dishes or cleaning up?"

"No thanks. There's not that much. Your father and I are just going to spend a lazy afternoon, so it's every man for himself for supper. We'll have some tea, some sandwiches, some reading… and, knowing your father, probably some napping. He deserves a day of rest and God knows that. What are you two up to?"

"You just described a perfect afternoon," I say. "I think I'm going to follow your blueprint. What about you, sis?"

Debbie starts walking out of the kitchen. "Sounds like a good plan. I'm off to my room to put it into practice."

We go upstairs, but Debbie stops me before we go into our rooms.

"My head is spinning," she confides. "I think I need a rest."

"Just stay there a minute." I go into my room, get the book, and bring it out to her. "Here, have your nap in good company. Maybe you'll get the same message I got last night. And you'll wake up fresh as a daisy."

"I hope you're right."

With that, she closes her door.

As I lay down my head, I go over everything that's happened in the last day. Eventually I feel drowsy and begin to nod off…

"James?"

"Yes, Michael."

"James, I must apologize for my hasty departure at noon. Something required my urgent attention."

"Did it have to do with our task?"

"Yes, it did. I will visit all four of you tonight to inform you about what has transpired. The forces of the prince of darkness are becoming aware of the book. Their master wishes to possess it. There is… a stirring. It's important that all four of you spend time in the book in the coming hours. It will benefit you greatly. You will not be able to accomplish your task alone. God's plan is for the four of you to do it together, and the plan will only succeed if you follow His guidance and lean on Him for your strength. May God be with you."

I open my eyes and sit up, feeling somewhat alarmed. Before this latest visit, it was all scripture and talk. Knowing that Satan's forces are on their way, looking for something we have in our possession… well, it's a very hard fact to deal with. I feel afraid and wonder how the others will react.

• • •

In Debbie's room, all is quiet. She lies in the fetal position with the book clutched to her chest and a look of serenity on her face. That serenity comes from deep within, for she is having the same experience her brother had the night before.

"If we could only read these names with faded print," she says after Michael explains the meaning of the words that appear before her eyes. "If we knew who they were, we could seek them out and help them find their way."

"Each child of God has the opportunity to make their own choices," Michael says. "God has provided guidance in the form of His Word. In your world today, the Word of God is available to a great number. Whether they choose to accept it is their choice. Those who accept it have a responsibility to follow the Word on a daily basis. If you surround yourself with those who believe and live as Christlike as possible, there is only a small chance of slipping into the kind of lifestyle that will cause your name to fade from the Book of Life. On the other hand, if you follow the ways of the world, there are consequences. As 2 Timothy 4:3 says, 'For the time will come when people will not put up with sound doctrine. Instead, to suit their own desires, they will gather around them a great number of teachers to say what their itching ears want to hear.' Over the last few decades, the world has grown acclimatized to sin by a very patient prince of darkness. His influence has increased by leaps and bounds. To put this most bluntly, mankind cannot be trusted with the knowledge contained in the Book of Life. If man was given access, do you not think Satan would also have access? What do you think is happening now? Why do you think God has placed the book here at this time? You four are instruments of God and your task is to keep the book safe and secure from the evil that seeks it. The book cannot fall into the wrong hands."

In the stillness, all Debbie feels is an incredible sense of peace and joy.

"I must now depart," he finishes. "You will spend some more time experiencing the love of God, and then you will awaken. May God be with you!"

Debbie doesn't know how long she remains wrapped in the wonderful feelings that surround her in the Book of Life. What she does know is that when her eyes open, she finds herself in a state of perfect peace and calm. Her head is no longer spinning.

• • •

When I hear the sound of tapping on my door, I get up and find Debbie waiting for me. She has a big smile on her face as she hands me the book.

After returning the book to its place on the shelf, I follow Debbie downstairs. I notice her standing at the entrance to the living room, appreciating the scene of our parents snuggling together on the couch. They are snoozing.

Debbie turns to me and puts a finger to her lips.

"Let's go sit on the back deck and not interrupt," she says.

Once we settle in, Debbie tells me about her experience and then explain what happened in Michael's latest visitation.

"It makes me nervous to think of what could have been so urgent to make him leave like that," Debbie muses.

"So far we've had it pretty easy. This brings me back to reality. This isn't a game. It's serious."

"Sounds like we need to make sure Leah and Matt are able to spend some time with the book," she says. "I'll invite Leah for a sleepover. But what about Matt? Boys don't often have sleepovers, do they?"

I shrug. "Let's just leave it in God's hands."

"Debbie! James!" Mom's voice calls us from the back door. "Come on in for supper."

We enter the kitchen and find the table set with homemade bread and molasses. A large bowl of fruit salad awaits us on the sideboard.

"Come sit, you two," Dad says. "We'll say grace and enjoy the bounty we have been blessed with."

He asks a blessing on the food, the hands that have prepared it, and those who are about to enjoy it. With a final amen, we have a quiet supper.

We're just cleaning up when we hear a knock at the front door. I glance at the kitchen clock and confirm that it's only six o'clock. I figure it must be Matt.

When I go to the door, I'm shocked to find Leah there.

"He's coming up the road now," Leah says, gesturing behind her.

"Come on in. Debbie's in the kitchen."

Soon we're all gathered in the kitchen.

"You young people can use my den again, if you like," Dad says. "Winnie and I will watch some television in the living room."

"Thanks, Dad," I say. "You're sure?"

"Yes, James, I'm sure."

A few moments later, I close the door to the den and turn to the others, who are already settled into their usual seats. I put the book on the coffee table in the middle of the room.

"First I thought Debbie and I should fill you in on some recent experiences we've had," I say.

Our eyes all turn to Debbie, who takes a moment before she begins speaking.

"Do you remember seeing a bunch of figures sort of floating around while you were in the book?" Debbie asks. "Well, those are the names of people who are recorded in the Book of Life. When you look closely, it becomes apparent that some names have darker lettering than others..."

She goes on to explain the truth given to her by Michael. Leah and Matt absorb this new information with expressions of amazement.

"There's one more thing," she says. "It turns out there are many reasons we aren't allowed to read these names. The most important is that if those names were to be known, Satan would be able to gain access... and Satan must never be allowed to possess the Book of Life or know what's inside it."

By this time, Matt's mouth has opened wider than I'd ever seen it before.

"When Michael left us so abruptly this morning, it's because something required his urgent attention," I explain. "It sounds to me like things are getting a little more interesting. It also seems very important for all four of us to spend more time in the book."

"How are we gonna do this?" Matt asks. "We can't be taking turns going upstairs with the book. Even if your parents can't see it, that would look awful suspicious."

"And it's not like Matt and I can just move in," Leah points out.

"Leah and I can have a sleepover," Debbie suggests. "But that doesn't solve the Matt problem."

Matt grins. "The Matt problem? That's not exactly a confidence booster, guys."

"Well, you're not the problem," I say. "God will provide—"

"I have an idea," Matt interrupts. "Why don't we try putting our heads down as a group and focusing our prayer on the book?"

"You aren't just a pretty face, after all," Debbie remarks.

We all get down on our knees around the coffee table, joining hands and bowing our heads. With our eyes closed, we go to God in silent prayer.

Immediately time seems to lose all meaning and we're transported en masse to the now-familiar realm of peace, warmth, and tranquility. We see the names floating by like clouds on a summer day, but we can't read or understand them. We also can't see each other, but we can sense each other's presence.

"You have gathered here together to learn more of the Book of Life," Michael's voice intones. "As you come here today, each of you has been given the knowledge that the others possess. You are all on equal footing. I will lead you further into the Book of Life to more clearly understand the task before you.

"As you know, the Book of Life contains the names of all who find favor with the Lord our God, from creation to the present day. No new names will be added from His chosen people of the first covenant. The new covenant, the final covenant, was established by the Son of God when He was crucified, died, was buried, and rose on the third day. With that covenant came an offer of forgiveness not just for the chosen people but for all people. Only through the name of Jesus Christ have names been added to the Book of Life since that time. As it is written, the only way to the Father is through the Son.[17]

"You have been told that you would not be able to access this book unless your names were found within it. But this is not a guarantee that your names will remain there. That will depend on your choices. Rejoice that your names are presently found in the Book of Life, but be aware that they could be blotted out. That possibility exists for all who still live and breathe.

"As you look around at the names of the faithful, past and present, what do you feel? You feel the presence of peace and love that transcends all mortal understanding. As you've read in Revelation, in eternity there will be no death or mourning, no suffering or pain, and nothing impure, shameful, or deceitful. Such is the Book of Life.

"On the day of judgment, the book will be opened. This will be a day of great rejoicing for those who are found worthy to spend eternity in the presence of the Father, the Son, and the Holy Spirit. It will also be a day of wailing and gnashing of teeth for those whose names are not found in the Book of Life, for they will suffer the second death in the lake of fire.

"When you come to the book, I will be with you always, for I am the keeper of the book. You may come as one or as a group. You may come at day or night, for within the book there is no day or night. You may ask questions. However, you will only receive answers within the boundaries set by the Lord. You will now experience the peace the book offers. Feel it, absorb it, and find your rest in it. The Lord your God has blessed you with access to the Book of Life."

---

[17] John 14:6.

I don't know about the others, but I immerse myself in these powerful feelings. I want them to go on forever, which I guess is the reality for the many souls whose names are found there.

Sadly, it doesn't last forever. My time is cut short and my eyes open to see Debbie, Leah, and Matt opening their eyes too. We sit up, look at each other, and each start to smile.

"That was awesome!" exclaims Matt.

"I never thought I could feel so good," Leah says. "I can't think of a word to do justice to that experience."

"I totally understand," I say. "And I don't have a clue what we should do next. Anyone got any ideas?"

To our astonishment, Michael suddenly appears in physical form, standing in the middle of the den.

"I might have a few," he says.

Debbie and Leah gasp, which is probably better than if they had screamed. Matt and I just sit with our mouths hanging open.

"Where did you come from?" I manage.

"I could tell you, but you would not understand. It is enough to say that I told you I would see you tonight and I am here as promised. There are many things that must be said. It has been decided that as you each visit the book and gain knowledge of it, that knowledge will be shared with the others. Also, the euphoria you feel when you're inside the book will be lessened, and this is for your own benefit. Your mortal bodies and minds are not able to handle such intense sensations. Repeated exposure could lead to a debilitating addiction which affects your ability to perform your task.

"This house is protected by the grace of God, which is why the Book of Life is safe here. The prince of darkness roams the earth and his minions carry out his work in every corner of the world. But not in this house! It is shielded from the darkness which is not of the Lord's realm. All who remain under this roof enjoy that same protection. Satan and his spawn cannot invade. However, this will not stop them from their search. The prince of darkness has ordered that the Book of Life be found, for he knows it has left the heavenly realm. He is determined to possess it.

"The Lord has placed the Book of Life in your hands so as to avoid an attack on the heavenly realm, which would result in a war rivalling the last one, when Lucifer rebelled against the Lord God. The prince of darkness has charged his forces to find the book, and those who fail will face his wrath. This master of suffering and pain will stop at nothing to retrieve the Book of Life. He seeks to know the names of those whose names are written in its pages, those who still live and breathe, so he may focus his attention on them and attack their every weakness. He is patient in his efforts to erode a person's moral fiber. You have only to look at the world around you to see the decay that has crept into people's lives.

"When Satan discovers that you are the earthly guardians of the Book of Life, he will unleash all his power to get you to relinquish it to him. I have told you that the dangers of this task are great. I re-emphasize this now. Nothing will be beyond Satan's reach, including the minds, souls, and bodies of you, your friends, and your families. He will attack them all. You must be prepared for the worst and pray for the best. Do you have any questions?"

"You're not painting a very happy picture for us Michael," I say.

"My task is to prepare you for your task and help you protect the Book of Life, which has been mine to watch over for centuries. I take that responsibility very seriously and will not let you underestimate the dangers you face, James."

"What if one of us decides we don't want to do this?" Debbie asks.

"Search the Word of God for the story of a man named Jonah," Michael says. "You will find your answer. When the Lord gives you a task to perform, you must perform it, even if you make every effort to avoid it. The Lord has not asked whether you are willing participants because He knows your hearts. Your love and faith exceed that of many, including many who are well beyond your years. The Lord will provide you with everything you need, if only you ask. And I am here to assist you in every way possible."

"How will we know what to ask for, what we need?" Leah asks.

"I send you to the Word of God. The Lord Jesus told the twelve that they would be persecuted and arrested, but they were not to worry. They would be given the words to say; it would not be them speaking, but the Spirit of the Father speaking through them. When you have need, the Spirit of the Father will guide you.

"Have faith and trust in the Lord your God. You will find your strength through your faith, trust, and love. Do not dismiss the power of that strength. In the coming days, many things will unfold that you will not understand. My comings and goings will be more frequent. Be aware at all times that the prince of darkness will use deceptions and disguises to achieve his ends. Beware of things that seem too good to be true, for they probably are just that.

"Each time you enter the book, you will be strengthened by the Word and presence of God. You will feel it in your mind, body, and soul. Your ability to see evil will expand to a degree well beyond that of an average man. You will need that to unmask lies and deceptions and reveal the false paths on which he tries to lead you. The task will not be easy, but all things are possible with God."

His voice trails off, leaving us stunned.

"I will leave you now, but I will not be far," Michael adds in the ensuing silence. "May the hand of the Lord steady your path."

Just like in the flower garden at church, he suddenly vanishes. And no sooner has he left than we hear a knock at the door.

"I've got supper ready," Mom calls.

After that intense visit from the angel, we are more than ready to take a break. I place the book inside the backpack I brought down from my room earlier.

With that, I follow the others out into the kitchen where Mom has laid out a large spread of food on the table.

"How is your project progressing?" Dad asks as he walks in from the living room.

"Not too bad, Mr. Jeffries," Leah says.

Before anyone can speak, the phone rings. Mom gets up and answers it.

"It definitely is fine with us," she says into the receiver after listening for a bit. "Do you want to talk to him?"

She holds out the phone.

"Matt, your mom wants to talk to you."

Matt takes the phone and goes out into the hallway to take the call.

"What's up, Mom?" I whisper.

She puts her hand on my shoulder. "I'll let Matt tell you, James. But you'll probably find that it's good news."

"You've got our curiosity piqued," Debbie says.

When Matt comes back into the room, he's wearing an enormous grin.

"Stop looking like the cat that swallowed the canary," I tell him. "Spill, buddy. What's up?"

"Looks like you and Debbie have a new brother for the next two weeks. Dad has to go to Hawaii on business and Mom's going with him. Your mom says I can stay here. Isn't that great news?"

"Oh no!" Debbie whines. "Mom, we're going to be overrun with males in the house."

"I think it's divine providence," I say.

"Why would you say that, James?" Dad asks.

"I just feel it, that's all." I give Debbie and Leah a knowing look. "When does this all take place?"

"My mom says she's packing some clothes right now," Matt says. "I'll come over tomorrow afternoon."

Mom smiles. "That's right. I'll get the spare room ready for him in the morning. With Leah next door and Matt living here, you four should be able to make considerable headway on your project. Very opportune, I would say."

"Couldn't have planned it better myself," I agree.

Debbie, Matt, Leah, and I share a look. We're all thinking the same thing. We needed the Matt problem to be dealt with, and now here we are: problem solved.

"If you guys are done eating, we should get back at it," I say.

Debbie is the last one in the den and closes the door. She almost falls back against it.

"I thought I was going to pass out when your father asked what you meant by divine providence, James," Leah says. "Do you think they have any idea what's going on?"

"Not a chance. None of us has said a word. Have we?"

No one had.

"Matt, you've been awful quiet," Debbie says. "What's up?"

"I don't know," says Matt. "This whole thing is starting to take on a life of its own. Now my parents are part of it. Makes me a little nervous, that's all."

"I know what you mean, Matt," Leah says. "When Michael talks about Satan's tactics, and his complete disregard for everything and everyone, I worry about our families. James, Debbie... aren't you worried about your mom and dad?"

Debbie sighs. "I wasn't until now, thank you very much. Maybe we can ask Michael about whether there's a way to protect our families."

I take the book out of my backpack and put it back on its traditional spot on the coffee table.

"Dwelling on our fears only plays into the hands of Satan," I remind them. "Fear is a weapon of the enemy. It causes us to throw caution and common sense to the wind and rush foolishly into something harmful, or run from something we should embrace. Michael says that the more time we spend in the book, the stronger and more prepared we'll be to handle the evil that's coming. Sounds like we're going to need all the strength we can get! So let's kneel, join hands, and bow our heads as we go back to the Book of Life."

As we close our eyes and our heads lower to touch the Book, we are again met by Michael's distinctive voice.

"Welcome! The grace of God be with you always. Your troubles and fears will melt away within these pages of peace, tranquility, love, and salvation. Draw upon the power that comes from them. Your eyes will look upon the saved and see no evil or uncleanliness. When you leave the Book of Life, your eyes will discern the dark from the light, the cleansed from the stained, and the good from the evil in your midst. While the rest of the world seems to be like the first man, not knowing good from evil, you will be like that same man after having tasted of the tree of the knowledge of good and evil. You will be able to see the evil in your presence and guard against it. I will leave you in peace with the weightlessness of experiencing no worry, fear, stress, or pain, for these weigh down the body and soul and tire your resolve. As it will be in the new Jerusalem, so it is in the Book of Life. However, the Lord does not live here with His people as He will in the new Jerusalem. May the Lord's peace be with you."

And then he was gone—or at least we no longer detect the feeling of his presence.

We float in a weightless expanse, absorbing the powerful sensations of the Book of Life. As I dwell on these feelings, I notice that the euphoria isn't as intense as it was, just as Michael warned us. But it still feels heavenly. Someday I hope to know what heaven really feels like and for now I appreciate that this is closer than most ever get.

I open my eyes to find the others doing the same thing. I get off my knees, sit on the sofa, and let out a huge sigh.

"I could stay there forever," I murmur.

Leah looks up at the clock. "It's quarter to ten. Maybe we should call it quits for tonight?"

"She's right," Debbie agrees. "Time's up."

"I sure am glad the book gives us that intense feeling of peace," Leah adds. "I wouldn't be able to sleep at all if it wasn't for that."

"We're all probably in the same boat," I say.

We discuss the upcoming week and decide to rest for a day before hitting the work again full-force on Tuesday. That will allow us to work around Debbie's work schedule and give Matt a day to settle in at our place.

After stowing the book in my backpack, I leave the den. Mom and Dad aren't in the living room, so we look in the kitchen. They're sitting at the table with mugs of coffee.

"We were just getting ready to say good night," Mom says. "Are you all done? You certainly have been putting a lot of time and effort into this project."

"When you're doing the Lord's work, you don't worry much about time," I say.

Dad gets up and puts his mug in the sink. "To that I'll say amen! And also good night, God bless, and love you. In fact, that goes for all of you."

"I'll second that," Mom says. "Good night. God bless. Love you."

They head up the stairs together.

Debbie and I usher Matt and Leah to the front door.

"I'm really looking forward to the next couple of weeks," Matt says. "I've never had brothers or sisters around. Gonna be a new experience!"

"Look at it as a working holiday," Debbie remarks. "We need to get in as much book time as we can."

Matt nods. "But getting to do God's work and do it in the company of someone you really care about? That's a win-win situation. Right, James?"

"That's true, Matt," I say with a smile. "And on that note, I'm going to walk Leah home. That is, if no one has any objections. If you do, then keep them to yourselves."

"Ooh! James is the big protector," Matt crows. "Debbie, are you going to walk me home?"

"Get out of here, you big goof."

With that, Leah starts down the front steps. Matt and I catch up in a few quick strides, me on her right and Matt on her left. We walk to the end of her driveway.

"I know you're sorry to see me go, but this is where we part company," Matt says. "See you tomorrow, James. Good night."

Matt heads down the road and we call our good nights after him.

As we walk slowly up Leah's driveway, I suddenly get up the courage to slip my hand into hers—and she doesn't pull away. I'm relieved. She grips my hand tightly and then leans her head on my shoulder.

What used to be a fairly long driveway seems to be awfully short tonight. Before we know it, we're at the front steps.

"We're here," I say sadly.

Leah responds with that soft voice that excites and relaxes me all at the same time. "I know."

"Are you going to be all right, Leah?"

"What do you mean? With us, with the book, not knowing what's going to happen next… I don't know, James. I'm pretty sure you and me are okay, but the rest is so unsure. The only thing I do know is that I have to trust God. I believe He has chosen us in His wisdom. He knows we can do the task He's asked us to do. All we have to do is put every bit of faith we have in Him and everything will be okay. I just have to know that you're there with me too."

"You don't have to worry about that. I'm here for you and I always will be. Together the four of us will tackle this assignment and come out the other side stronger because of it. When you need a hand to hold, I'll be there. When you need a shoulder to lean on, I'll be there. If you need a hug, I'll be there. God has brought us together for a reason and I think it extends beyond the task He's given us. We'll have to wait and see what happens, but I pray that you and I can continue on this path together once it's done."

"I feel the same way," she says. "It makes me feel better to know how you feel. But I should be getting inside…"

She looks up at me and closes her eyes. I'm no ladies man. In fact, I have zero experience with the opposite sex. But I know right then and there that I want to kiss her, and I'm pretty sure she wants me to kiss her too.

Tilting my head, I lean down and put my lips softly on hers. As we kiss, it's like those movies where fireworks explode and music erupts—only better. It isn't a long kiss. It isn't a passionate kiss. It's a kiss that says "I love you" without the words.

As our lips disengage, we look into each other's eyes and both smile in happiness.

"Good night, Leah."

"Good night, James."

And with that, I float home and end up in my bedroom. When I see my backpack on the bed, my first thought is the book… is it still inside…?

I let out a sigh of relief when I look up and see it sitting on the closet shelf, exactly where it's supposed to be. How could I be so careless?

Leah and I both know that our personal relationship can't interfere with the task at hand. Yet here I am, having forgotten my responsibility. I realize that I left the book in my backpack by the front door. I assume Debbie saw it and brought it back to my room.

After getting undressed, I place the book on my bed, then kneel in prayer, close my eyes, and thank the Lord for all the blessings in my life. I humble myself before Him because He is the Creator, not just of man but of all things visible and invisible. I also ask for forgiveness for the mistake I made by leaving the book by the front door.

As I continue to pray for family and friends, I realize that by now I should have heard Michael's voice calling me into another session in the book. It hasn't happened. Why not?

Instead all is still. All is quiet.

I have to say, I'm worried. Have I messed up badly enough that I've been locked out of the book? I grip it more tightly and renew my prayers. I break into a sweat as I ask God to forgive me. I admit my mistake and ask for a second chance. I ask for guidance in going forward with the task, assuming He still wants me to continue.

I haven't felt this bad in my whole life. I've let God down and it hurts to know that.

Still on my knees, gripping the book, I become aware of a light. It's more than just the regular glow of the book; it's even brighter, and it soon fills the entire room.

I open my eyes to see Michael standing in the corner.

"How bad have I messed up, Michael?" I ask, almost in tears.

"You have committed an error, James. You have admitted making a mistake, but in reality you have made two mistakes. First you erred in your responsibility to guard the book, and second you erred in letting your emotions cloud your vision. You will not be granted access to the book tonight. Instead you will be visited by me again in your sleep. Leah will be there as well. The course of action to be taken will be laid out before the both of you. Now put the book back up on the shelf and go to bed. We will talk later."

Michael disappears, and the only light remaining is the glow of the book. I do as I'm told, but I feel terribly.

This is the first night in more than a week when sleep doesn't come easily. When I finally drift into a fitful slumber, Michael's voice calls me to awareness.

"James."

"Yes, Michael."

"I told you that Leah would be part of this conversation, but I have decided to include Debbie and Matt as well. This is a learning experience and you must all learn from it. James, you left the Book of Life unattended. The reason you did this is that your attention was focused on Leah. It has already been established that you have feelings for Leah and those feelings are mutual. It also has been established that Debbie and Matt have similar feelings for one another. These feelings must not interfere with the task the Lord Most High has given the four of you.

"Love is powerful. But what is the first great command? It is that you are to love the Lord your God with your whole heart, body, soul, and mind. To this end, you must put aside your love for one another and focus on the work of the Lord. At the same time, you must remain close to one another while not losing sight of the task at hand. Channel your feelings into the task. Use your love for each other to strengthen your bond in the work you do for the Lord.

"James, you have asked for forgiveness and forgiveness you have received. Part of repentance is resolving not to make the same mistake again. This has been a minor lesson and no harm has been done, but going forward you must all be careful, for the prince of darkness will use your mistakes to push his objective. Now rest in the peace of the Lord. When you awake, be prepared for the trials you will face in the coming days."

NINETEEN

The morning light is already brightening my room when I open my eyes. The worries of last night are gone. I feel forgiven, free of the guilt that usually goes with messing up. If God has forgiven me, who am I not to forgive myself? It's time to move on.

I get up, grab fresh clothes, and have a shower. Once I'm clean and fresh, I arrive in the kitchen to find Mom and Dad having breakfast.

"Good morning, James," Dad says. "You're up early."

"Surprised you're still here, Dad."

"I have a late start today, but that means I won't get home until ten o'clock tonight or even later."

"That's a long day."

"I know, but sometimes I make concessions. They're very understanding when it comes to not making me work Sundays. They understand my need and I understand theirs."

"Well, we'll miss you at supper."

"Me too. What do you have planned for today?"

"I was going to mow the lawn. It's overdue, but it's supposed to rain. I think I'll call Matt to see if he needs help getting his stuff together for his visit." I turn to Mom. "Do you need help getting the spare room ready?"

"No, but thank you for the offer."

Dad gets up, puts on his jacket, and waits for Mom to fall into his outstretched arms for a hug before he leaves for work. They exchange kisses and I-love-yous as he heads out the door.

I settle down for a breakfast of oatmeal and brown sugar, wondering about how the whole Leah situation will unfold. Michael has made it clear that we have to put our relationship on hold until the task at hand is over and done. I don't think it's going to be a problem for me, but I'm not as certain about Leah. She's so sensitive.

I'm washing the last of my oatmeal down with orange juice and reaching for some toast when Debbie steps into the room.

"Don't eat it all," she says. "There are others who haven't eaten yet."

I smile. "Early bird gets the worm. Late risers get to hunger and squirm."

"I suppose you think that's amusing. Well, it's not!" She gets her own bowl of oatmeal and sits down. "What are you up to today, James?"

"Other than checking in with Matt, nothing."

"Why don't you come with me to Leah's for a bit? We can discuss the project."

I look at her with a question on my face and see the look of concern on hers. "I can do that."

"I'm heading over right after breakfast. I'll tell her you're coming."

"I'll be about half an hour."

I head back up to my bedroom to change into my running gear. On my way, I grab the phone and call Matt. It turns out he doesn't need help. I should expect him after lunch.

"Are you okay?" he asks.

"What do you mean?"

"About everything that happened last night."

I hesitate. "Oh. I'm okay. Worried about Leah, though. I'm going to drop by to see her before I go for my run this morning. I guess we'll talk it over."

"Tell you what. Stop by afterward and I'll join you for the run."

"Thanks. See you in about an hour."

Mom is still in the kitchen as I get ready to leave.

"Do I detect some tension in the air?" she asks.

"Nothing gets by you, does it, Mom?"

"God made mothers to be special. Haven't I always told you that?" She laughs. "Is there anything I can help with?"

"No. It's just something we have to work out by ourselves. But thanks. Have you seen Debbie?"

"She left already."

I head out the door and do some stretches on the porch—not so much for the benefit of training but for the benefit of putting off something I want to avoid.

Biting the bullet, I head over to Leah's house and knock on the door.

"Come on in, James," Mrs. Scanlon calls.

I poke my head in and Leah's mom points me upstairs. "Go on up."

The door to Leah's room is open and she and Debbie are sitting on the bed. Before I can say anything, Leah looks me in the eyes.

"Oh, James, I'm so sorry! I knew we're supposed to keep our personal emotions at bay and I let things get too involved."

"Wait a minute. This isn't your fault. I'm supposed to be our group's leader. I knew exactly the same thing you did, so don't go taking the blame. The main thing is we've learned a lesson and won't let it happen again." I glance at Debbie. "Not for any of us. We've been forgiven and now it's time to move on."

Debbie nods. "That's right. Time to move on. Keep those emotions on hold for now. We have things to do."

I turn to Leah. "You're sure we're okay?"

"Yes! God's work comes first. We never should have lost sight of that. I guess I thought we could do both without them interfering with one another, but I guess that's not the case."

I give her my best smile. "What do you think of coming over after supper?"

"I'll ask my mom, but it should be fine."

Glad that wasn't as uncomfortable as I thought it might be, I head back outside and finish my stretches.

The air is damp when I get to Matt's house, but there's no rain yet.

"How did things go?" Matt asks as he jogs out to me.

I recount the conversation between me and Leah, explaining that everything between is good and we've learned a valuable lesson.

"I messed up, but that's ancient history now," I say. "We have a task to do and we're going to put everything into it. God first, us later."

"Amen to that, I guess. Debbie and I aren't as lovey-dovey as you and Leah, so it shouldn't be a problem for us."

"What d'ya mean, lovey-dovey?"

"Man, if you were on the outside looking in, you'd know what I mean. But hey, onward and upward."

We jog for the next half-hour without saying much. When we reach the turnaround point, we stop for a short break.

"Whatever's going to happen next, I don't think there's going to be much warning," I say. "Satan's not going to give us a head's up. Our part is going to be done with God as our strength. He's with us and we've got Michael too. Gonna be interesting."

"I'd say I can't wait, but I'm really not in any kind of hurry."

"Let's get going. You should help your mom get your stuff together."

"To tell you the truth, she was happy to get me out from underfoot," Matt says. "Said I was just getting in the way."

We both laugh as we head back.

"We're going to do a lot of running the next couple of weeks," I tell him.

"Why's that?"

"Mom says she's doing some extra cooking because of how much you like to eat. If we don't go running, no way will your clothes fit after two weeks. That and you'll be in no condition for football when school starts! You're the best linebacker we have. So get ready to be run off your feet, buddy."

Matt is smiling from ear to ear. "It'll be worth every step."

Eventually we get back to his place and part company.

Once I'm home, I have a shower before heading back into the kitchen. The smell of food makes my mouth water.

"Need an official taste-tester, Mom?"

"I don't need a taste-tester, but you can take on the job of quality control. A few of those cookies around the edge are darker than I like." She grins as I take a look at the cookie sheet for myself. "We're having a light lunch. Bread, molasses, or jam and cookies with tea or milk. So I won't bother telling you not to ruin your lunch."

"By the way, is it okay if Leah comes over after supper?"

"It most certainly is."

I grab the milk carton from the fridge and a tall glass from the cupboard, then plunk my backside down at the table.

"Let quality control begin!"

Am I ever going to have fun with Matt when I tell him how I spent the last part of the morning! I'm on my third peanut butter cookie when Debbie comes in.

"What are you up to?" she asks.

"I'm in charge of quality control."

"Sure you are."

I detect a definite note of sarcasm in her tone. "Ask Mom. She's the one who hired me."

Debbie looks at Mom, notes the smile on her face, and decides not to intervene.

"I asked Mom if it was okay for Leah to come over after supper," I add.

"And what did she say?"

"She said no. Leah is a terrible person and she won't have her in the house. What do you think she said?"

"James, there are times I could just... well, I don't know what, but you wouldn't like it!"

I laugh. "Aw, come on, sis. Can't you take a joke?"

"All right you two, enough of that," Mom says. "If your hands are washed, we'll sit and have lunch. Debbie, would you say grace please?"

Debbie does and we have a filling lunch, punctuated by good food and good conversation.

We're just finishing up when we hear a car pull up. Knowing it has to be Matt, I jump up to help him with his stuff.

"Hello, Mrs. Philips," I say. "What have you got there, something you found on the side of the road?"

Matt's mom sighs. "Now, James, be nice to my baby. He's very sensitive, you know."

"Well, when you put it that way... I guess we can cut him some slack."

"You two are just hilarious." Matt laughs. "But the comedy club is full up, so don't give up your day jobs."

While our moms have a private conversation, Matt and I carry his stuff up to the spare room at the end of the upstairs hall.

"I don't see a fishing rod, Matt."

"Darn! I knew I was forgetting something."

"No worries. We have a couple of extras. And we can go back for your bike if we need it."

"Good idea. We could go fishing this afternoon if the rain holds off."

"You shouldn't have said that. Look out the window."

Sure enough, the rain is starting to come down and it seems to get harder and harder by the second.

We go back downstairs just as Matt's mom is coming out of the kitchen.

"Give your mother a hug and a kiss," Mrs. Philips tells her son. "I'm going to miss my little boy for the next two weeks."

"Mom, would you stop? James and Debbie don't need any extra ammunition."

"Okay, but I still want that hug and kiss."

Debbie taunts him. "Give your mommy a huggie and a bye kissie, Mattie."

"See what I mean, Mom? Thanks!" Matt gives his mother the hug and kiss she asked for. "See you in two weeks. You and Dad have fun and send me a couple of postcards, okay?"

"I will. Bye now. You be a good boy."

Off she goes, running through the pouring rain to get to her car. She toots her horn as she backs down the driveway, waving one last time as she turns onto the road.

"What are you three up to this afternoon?" Mom asks.

"I don't know about the boys, but I'm going back over to Leah's," Debbie says. "We're in the middle of a video game and had to put it on hold for lunch. It's up to us to save the universe!"

I roll my eyes. "Matt and I don't have any plans yet, but we'll think of something."

"Sure thing," Matt says. "You mentioned your mom was doing a lot of baking. We could check that out."

"I'm going to hold you at bay until three o'clock. Then I'll let you loose in the pantry," Mom says. "Find something else to amuse yourselves with until then."

"If the rain lets up, we'll go get Matt's bike and have a ride."

Mom looks out the window. "Judging by the color of the sky, I doubt you'll get to it today."

The phone suddenly rings.

"Would you get that, James?" Mom asks.

I go to the hall phone and pick up the receiver. "Hello?"

It's my friend Gary from youth group. His parents have a cottage across the lake from the Sand Bed.

"We were sitting on the veranda watching the rain come down when out of nowhere a lightning bolt came down and hit the float we always dive off," he says, releasing pent-up excitement.

I put him on speaker so everyone else can hear.

"Go ahead, Gary. We're all listening."

"I've never seen a lightning strike before," Gary says. "The float just blew up! There was this bright flash and then the float was flying through the air in a thousand pieces. You could see the water boiling… and then we detected a smell almost like burning sulfur. You know, like in the chem lab at school. My dad says he's seen lightning strikes before but never anything like this. There was no thunder, just the lightning. Dad says it doesn't make sense. Guess we're gonna need a new float!"

"I want to come over and take a look," I say. "But not in this downpour."

I thank him for the call and assure him that I'll see him at youth on Wednesday. Then I hear the dial tone.

"Wish I had seen that!" Matt exclaims.

"Me too," I say. "That would have been awesome!"

"I'm going over to Leah's," Debbie adds as she puts on her rain jacket and heads out the door.

"Let's go up to my room, Matt. We can fire up the video game console and do some motocross racing. You up for it?"

"Promise not to cry when I beat you."

"You wish."

TWENTY

O nce we're up in my room, I power up the game console. But one look at Matt tells me that something's on his mind. I'm pretty sure I know what it is, because it's on my mind too.

"What's up?" I asked.

"You know. The book. It's sitting there on the shelf and we're right here. Can't we just get it down and maybe, you know, make some contact?"

"I was thinking the same thing."

After getting the book down, we sit on the bed with the book between us. As we put our hands on the cover, we close our eyes and immediately find ourselves transported to that place of peace and tranquility where we feel safe and wrapped in love.

"James. Matt."

"Yes."

"Welcome again to the Lamb's Book of Life," Michael tells us. "In your journey today, you will encounter more of the names you cannot read, but you will feel the souls of the saved and feel what they're experiencing as they wait upon the day of judgment. The experience will fill you with the strength to withstand the coming confrontation. Those who have left this world and have their names written in the Book of Life have overcome the power of the prince of darkness and rejoice in the Lord as they wait in a place where time has no meaning. You will draw upon their strength, which is of the Lord. You will feel how to face evil with the power of the cross in your hands, even as you are awed by the power which you stand against. Be aware that the power of the Lord will always overcome the power of darkness. Open your minds and your hearts. Let your souls come to a state of total peace. I leave you now to be enveloped by love, absorbed in hope, and given awareness of the Almighty who is with you always."

Michael is right when he talks about time having no meaning in the book. I feel so good! I know that when Revelation describes the new Jerusalem, it must be something like this. I can't imagine feeling any better than I feel right now, basking in the presence of God.

I don't know how much time goes by, but I soon hear Michael's voice again. "James. Matt."

We answer together: "Yes, Michael?"

"There is darkness in your community. The event at the lake was not a natural phenomenon. The demons of hell are trying to trace the Book of Life by the power of salvation that emanates from it. They followed it to the lake. When they found it no longer there, they erupted in anger. They will not leave the area until they are sure where the book has been taken. The nature of your task is becoming clearer.

"I warned you before and I will voice that warning again: be aware that not everything is as it seems. Those who are known to you may not be who you think they are. Some of the strength you gain from the book will help you discern the difference. Trust those gifts. Do not rely on your senses. The prince of darkness is a master of masquerade. His demons have invaded bodies and souls in the past and I warn you that they still do so in the present day. I will visit you again tonight. Be forewarned: danger is present and very near!"

I open my eyes and find myself looking into the very wide open eyes of Matt.

"Wow!" Matt says breathlessly. "Do you believe that? That whole thing at the lake was Satan's imps at work. I never thought I'd ever get this close to the devil. You know… we learn about him in Sunday school, and we're not that far removed from being kids. To be involved in something that has to do with the real thing! It just boggles my mind. How are we going to handle this, James?"

"With the grace of God, Matt. Just slow down a little. Sure, Satan's close and he's looking for something we have. But God is on our side. How can we lose? We have Michael in our corner too, and that has to count for something."

The sound of the rain on the window pulls me out of the moment.

"We have to get Debbie and Leah up to speed," I realize. "What time is it?"

"Just past four. What time did you say Leah was coming over?"

"We didn't set a time, but probably around 6:30." I stand up and stretch. "Want to go down and have some cookies and milk?"

"Is the pope Catholic? Let's go."

As we're heading down the stairs, we hear Mom on the phone. Not wanting to interrupt her, I make eating motions and point to the kitchen. Mom just nods her head and smiles.

Meanwhile, Matt is already at the table with a cookie jar open. He's on about his fifth cookie when Mom finally comes into the kitchen.

"These are just great, Mrs. Jeffries," he says.

"I'm glad you like them, Matt." She clears her throat. "I have some important news that will affect you both."

That gets our attention.

"What's up, Mom?" I ask.

"I just got off the phone with Leah's mom. Her parents are apparently in the same sort of predicament as Matt's parents. Her dad is being sent to the west coast on a work-related project and Mary wants to go with him. She called to see whether it would be too big of an imposition for Leah to stay with us. I told her that we'd love to have her stay. It would be good company all the way around, especially with Matt here as well. The four of you are best friends, after all, so it's no trouble."

Mom takes a cookie for herself and takes a nibble.

"What do you think of that?" she asks.

"As long as Leah doesn't eat too many cookies, I guess it's okay with me," Matt says.

"Always thinking about food, Matt." I give him a playful swat. "You know it's okay with me, Mom. Is she going to stay in Debbie's room?"

"Yes. She has lots of room."

"This is gonna be great," I say. "I get a new brother. Debbie gets a new sister. And Mom and Dad get two new kids to boss around."

"I'll have to sit down and make up a list of chores I want done over the next two weeks," Mom says. I can't tell whether she's serious for a moment. "Maybe I'll get Debbie and Leah to give me a hand with it."

I glance away. "All right, all right… maybe I shouldn't have said *boss around*. You know all you have to do is ask and we'll get it done."

"That's better." Mom puts down the rest of her uneaten cookie. "Time for me to get supper started. Just remember that your father is going to be late tonight. I thought we would have spaghetti and meatballs with garlic bread. How does that sound?"

"Sounds good to me," says Matt. "How 'bout it, James?"

"I'm in. Is there anything we can do to help?" I ask.

"It's raining cats and dogs outside. Why don't you give Leah a call and see if she and Debbie need any help getting Leah's things over here?" Mom suggests.

"I can do that."

I pick up the phone and call Leah's. Her mom answers and tells me all about her upcoming trip. She's excited. When she pauses for a breath, I ask if I can speak to Leah. She asks me to hold.

"Hi James," says Leah. "Are you as excited as I am? This is working out as though someone planned it."

"I think someone did, but we'll talk about that later. Right now, do you and Debbie need any help with your stuff? It's pouring outside and Matt and I can help carry things."

"That would be nice. It would take Debbie and me a couple of trips by ourselves."

"We'll be right over." While hanging up, I call over to Matt, who's still sitting at the table with the cookie jar. "Come on, cookie monster. Leah and Debbie need some help."

"Your wish is my command, son of the great cookie queen."

"Grab a raincoat. Let's go before I throw up, you joker."

We go over as soon as we've boots and rain gear on. The girls are ready and waiting, having gotten everything wrapped in plastic garbage bags. Debbie and Matt grab a suitcase each and head out while I wait for Leah to finish her emotional goodbye with her mother.

We head for my house, heads bent against the wind and monsoon rain. Debbie lets us in and takes the stuff Leah is carrying and heads upstairs with it.

I look around for Matt and find him—where else?—at the kitchen table. He looks a little lost and I soon see why. The cookie jar is missing.

"Mom cut you off?" I laughingly ask.

His head droops. "Yes."

"Your mother left behind a healthy young man," Mom says. "I don't want her coming home to a cookie with arms and legs. Do I?"

"I suppose not," Matt answers.

"I was figuring that we'd run a mile for every cookie you eat," I say. "I figure we're up to about twelve miles by now."

Matt scrunches up his forehead at my math. "I think you're a little low, but twelve's okay with me."

We head up the stairs with the last of Leah's things and find Debbie's door open. Matt and I stand in the doorway as the girls go about arranging Leah's wardrobe. With guys, unpacking is a totally different experience: open a drawer, shove it in. I guess that's too simple for the female mind.

"Looks like Mom's almost got dinner ready. You two going to be ready?"

"Sure," says Leah. "If not, we can come back and finish later. Right, Debbie?"

Debbie shrugs. "That's right. A place for everything and everything in its place. You guys wouldn't understand that."

"We sure wouldn't," Matt says. "In fact, we wouldn't even try."

"I think you should move closer to the trunk of the tree before you saw much more off that limb you've crawled out on," Debbie muses.

We all start to laugh.

Then I get serious. "Matt and I were in the book this afternoon and we learned something new."

"We know, James," Leah tells us. "Remember, every time one of us learns something from the book now, we all benefit."

"Anyway, we'd better go down," I say. "Mom will be calling us soon. You girls wash up here and Matt and I will wash up downstairs."

Matt and I head downstairs where Mom is in the kitchen. We wash our hands in the sink and go to the table.

"You boys just have a seat," Mom says. "Are the girls coming down? We're ready to eat."

"Here we are," Debbie announces as she and Leah come around the corner.

"Then if everyone wants to sit, I'll say grace."

We take our seats and bow our heads.

"Okay, ladies first," Mom announces after the prayer is done. "We'll get our spaghetti and sauce from the stove and the garlic bread is in the oven."

I raise a finger. "If ladies go first, when does Debbie get to go?"

"See what I have to put up with, Leah?" Debbie groans. "Be glad you don't have any brothers. He's just trying to show Matt how smart he is. And by the way, James, you're failing miserably."

Everyone laughs.

Once we're all back in our seats, we start to talk about the day. The biggest topic is about the float at the Sand Bed and the weather. We can still hear the rain coming down in buckets.

"Have you heard from Dad?" Debbie asks.

"He texted just before supper to tell me he's still going to be late," Mom says. "I told him to be careful. The driving conditions could be dangerous. I'd rather have him be late than get in an accident. I'll be glad when he's home safe and sound."

"We will too," Debbie says for both of us.

"Oh, by the way, he said you could use his den tonight." Mom pauses. "How is your project coming, if you don't mind me asking?"

"It's getting very exciting, Mrs. Jeffries," Leah says. "None of us ever thought we would be involved in anything like this."

"Be careful, Leah," Matt warns. "You don't want to give away too much…"

"Leah's right, Mom," Debbie says. "It is getting exciting, but we're not ready to reveal everything. We swore a pact of secrecy and plan to keep it. The four of us and God."

Mom smiles at us encouragingly. "Well, if you've made that type of commitment, I'm proud of you for sticking to your resolve. I'm sure that whatever it is will be wonderful."

"We are certain it will be," Matt adds. "Tell you what. James and I will clear the table while you ladies relax with your tea."

"Matt Philips, you are so obvious. You just want to see what Mom has for dessert." Debbie rolls her eyes. "Have you no shame?"

He shakes his head. "That's not true, Debbie. Your mother made this great meal and I thought James and I could show a little appreciation by helping out. We don't even need a dessert."

"We do have dessert, Matt," Mom says. "There's a cherry cheesecake in the fridge. Debbie, why don't you bring it to the table while the boys clear the table?"

"Okay, Mom, but we only need four plates. Matt doesn't want any dessert. He just said so."

Matt looks panicky for a moment. "Wait a minute, just wait a minute! I said we don't *need* a dessert. I never said anything about not *wanting* any. Big difference between need and want!"

"There you are out on that limb again, just sawing away," I say, teasing. "When are you going to learn?"

"Come on, buddy," Matt pleads. "Back me up a little."

I shrug. "Sometimes there's only room for one on that limb you're on."

And all start laughing.

Things settle down as the table is cleared and dessert is served. We're all having fun and I know Debbie's watching Matt to see whether he goes for seconds on the cheesecake. I happen to know that the only thing keeping Matt from that second helping is his knowledge that Debbie is watching him.

I look across the table at Leah, and from the smile on her face I can tell we're on the same page.

Supper is soon over and we all help Mom with the last of the dishes. With the dishwasher loaded and turned on, Mom tells us that she's going to her quilting room.

Off I go to get the book.

When I return and enter the den, I find the others seated. I place the book on the coffee table and sit down.

"Has Matt told you anything about this afternoon?" I ask as I close the door.

We collectively recap the latest news about Satan and his imps blowing up the float at the lake, to make sure we're all on the same page.

Debbie raises a finger. "Wait a minute. If they tracked the book to the lake, what's to say they won't track it here next?"

"Michael did say the book is safe in our house and can't be detected," I remind her. "But I'd really like to ask him how protected it really is."

In the next moment, my eyes widen. Michael suddenly appears right behind the seat where Leah is sitting.

"Now is the time to ask that question, James," says Micheal. "Your house is a sanctuary for the book and those under its roof. No evil will befall the book or any of you, or even your family members, while you remain inside these walls. Nothing evil or controlled by evil will be able to affect you here. The power of God the Almighty rests upon this house. Take comfort in that."

Leah turns around to make eye contact with the angel. "But what about when we go out?" she asks. "We can't stay here forever. We can't wait for Satan to just give up the search."

I have to say that she seems awfully calm about this whole thing.

"Your concern is valid and warranted," Michael replies. "The trail has been blurred and confused, to some degree, but nonetheless it will eventually lead here. That is a foregone conclusion. Because of your nearness to the book and the strength and power you have absorbed from it, the four of you will be able to withstand and overcome any powers of darkness that make themselves known to you. But Lucifer is treacherous and will prefer to use lies and deceit to overpower you, just as he did with the angels who fell with him in the great rebellion. Use the power of discernment that has been given you to distinguish between what is good and what is evil. We are approaching a time when your hearts and souls will be tested. Always remember that the Lord your God is with you, that the Holy Spirit is with you to guide and strengthen you, and that the love of Jesus your Lord and Savior is without limit and without end. Also remember that I am here, and I am not without means."

The next question comes from Matt.

"I know this is just a minor thing," he says, "but what about my parents and Leah's parents? They suddenly had to leave on trips. Is that a coincidence or a matter of divine intervention?"

"You know the answer even as you ask the question, Matt. The four of you needed to be together. At times the Lord works in mysterious ways. Other times, His ways are seen by the discerning." The angel speaks calmly and with force. "I will leave you now. It is important that you spend as much time in the book as possible to build yourselves up for what is to come."

Just like the other times Michael has appeared to us, he suddenly ceases to be there.

"You guys want to talk about what just happened or do you want to get right into the book?" I ask. "This is staggering, but talking about it won't change a thing."

The others all nod. With that, all four of us reach our hands toward the book as we close our eyes and go to God in prayer.

It isn't long before Michael's voice greets us and tells us that our time is precious, assuring us again that he will be watching. Deep we go into the enveloping peace and love that is the book. It still escapes our ability to describe it. I feel more connected to the book than ever, a feeling which has grown each time I've entered this heaven-like environment. The names, the souls, the peace, the love… it's like being cradled in the hand of God.

When I open my eyes, it feels like I'm stepping out of a timeless place. I'm greeted by three sets of eyes that are all doing the same thing.

"I don't know about you three, but every time we finish a session in the book I feel not just rested but like there's an energy there that wasn't there before," Leah says.

We all agree.

Mom knocks on the door. "James, Debbie… can I come in for a minute?"

"Sure, Mom. What's up?"

As Mom steps into the den, she stops in the doorway. "Your father just texted to say he won't be home tonight. The rain has washed out the bridges, meaning the only way back is through the backroads, and there's no telling what kind of flooding might be going on there. So he's going back to work to spend the night. The phone lines are out too."

"I'm glad Dad's going to be safe and we're all together, warm and dry," Debbie says. "Guess we have some additions to our prayers tonight."

"Yes, we do, Debbie," Mom says. "Anyone want a hot chocolate and maybe a cookie or two before bed?"

We all notice that she's looking at Matt as she says it. Laughing, we all agree to the snack.

As the others follow Mom out to the kitchen, I pick up the book, which has been sitting out in the open the whole time, and take it up to my room. We all trust what Michael said about the book being safe, even from Mom's eyes.

When I come back down, I look at the clock on the stove and can't believe that it's already 10:30. We have our hot chocolate and cookies—some had more than others, if you know what I mean—and then call it a night.

Mom gets additional hugs to go along with her usual impartations from me and Debbie: "Good night. God bless. Love you." We know she's going to miss Dad like crazy tonight. I think the hugs from Leah and Matt help too.

TWENTY—ONE

When we get upstairs, we all stop outside my room. I offer Debbie and Leah the opportunity to take the book tonight, since Matt and I had it in the afternoon. It'll give Leah some time to catch up, since she's had the least amount of time with it.

"Good night, ladies," I say as I hand over the book.

Matt echoes this sentiment and the girls reply in kind.

I watch Matt walk down the hall to the guest room, then turn and enter my room and close the door behind me.

I kneel beside my bed. I have so much to pray for. First I pray for all the blessings in my life, like my family, my friends, my church family, and my faith in the divine Creator. Next I pray for Debbie and Matt and Leah. I pray that we don't let God down in this task He's asking us to perform. I also request the strength of mind, spirit, and soul to meet that task. I pray that Dad gets home safe in the morning, and then I pray for Matt's and Leah's parents as they travel. To close, I pray for the souls whose names aren't found in the Book of Life; they are the lost who won't share in the eternity God has provided through His Son and our Savior, Jesus Christ.

Afterward I slide between the sheets and drop into a deep sleep.

"James, get up!"

For a second, I think that the voice belongs to Michael—but then it hits me. It's female and there is an urgency to it that Michael has never employed.

"James!"

I sit up. "What?"

"It's me, Leah." I realize she's calling from the hall. "Come here! You have to see this!"

I look at my watch and see that it's two in the morning. Feeling a bit groggy, I stumble up and open the door. Leah is standing there completely dressed.

"What's going on?" I ask.

"Come into Debbie's room, quick!"

I look through the door to Debbie's room and see Matt and my sister staring out the window toward the street.

"You've got to see this, James!" Matt says.

I join them and see that it's still pouring rain. But through the rain, I glimpse a source of light. In fact, it's not just a light; it's a flame... and it's probably four feet tall.

I brace myself as I realize that the flame is moving—it's coming closer to our house. How can a flame exist in a rainstorm like this? And how could it possibly be moving?

"What the heck is that?" I wonder.

"Leah and I have been watching it for about half an hour," Debbie says. "We have no idea what it is, but I get the feeling that I'm not going to like whatever it is. It's creepy."

As we watch, the flame seems to slow down when it gets to Leah's driveway. But then it picks up speed again and keeps moving down the street, coming towards us...

...and then it slows again, this time right in from of our house.

And then it stops.

"Look out!" I cry. "It's coming up our driveway..."

Instead of coming right to the front door, the flame shifts its trajectory and seems to head for the back yard.

"Let's go to my room." I'm already running across the hall.

From my window, we see the flame again. It seems to pause in the middle of the yard, then revolve in a complete circle a couple of times.

I gasp as it suddenly rushes over to the shed—but it stops before reaching it. For a couple of seconds, nothing happens.

The shed door flies off its hinges and lands about fifteen feet away. Leah stifles a scream.

"Wow!" Matt mutters to himself.

As for me and Debbie, we're rendered speechless.

The flame moves slowly into the shed and through the open doorway we can see the interior lit in red and orange. The reflection of the flame also pours out of the side window.

Again there's a pause.

We all jump back from the window when the roof of the shed rises about twenty feet straight in the air and just floats in place before bursting apart, millions of toothpicks flying off in every direction.

With the roof missing, it's easier to see now that the flame has engulfed the old dresser. The dresser begins to rise next, the flame consuming it as the drawers fly open one at a time.

As the last drawer explodes, we cover our ears. A terrible squealing sound rises as the rest of the dresser burns in midair. No flaming debris drops to the ground and no smoke curls upward. All that's left is ash.

Once the dresser is gone, the flame descends and settles back on the ground. The remains of the shed now go up in flames, instantly consumed in a powerful burst of fire.

"Should we try to put the fire out?" Matt asks.

"That thing seems to have a life of its own," Debbie says. "Let's just leave it alone."

We watch as the flame now travels around the ashes. I catch my breath when it moves toward the house, inching closer and closer.

"Get ready to evacuate if things start to go down like they did with the shed," I warn. "I'll wake Mom. You guys just get out as quick as you can if you need to. We can meet over at Leah's back porch."

As we keep our eye on the mysterious flame, it moves left… then right… then turns in a circle. It repeats this pattern a few times and starts to shake like a candleflame in a breeze, flickering violently…

Suddenly, the flame disappears. All the tension goes out of the room.

But is it really over?

I run down the hall to the master bedroom and ease the door open as quietly as I can. My heartrate triples when I see that the bed hasn't been slept in. Panic sets in. Where is Mom?

Noticing a glowing light behind me, I jump. Has the flame come back? Is it inside the house?

"James."

I breathe out in relief at the sound of that familiar voice. "Michael! Am I ever glad to see you! I've got to find Mom. She's not in her room… I don't know where she is…"

The panic in my voice must be obvious.

"Calm yourself, James," the angel instructs. "Your mother is sleeping in the den and is totally unaware of the events that have transpired. Come, let us go join the others in your room. We have much to discuss."

I follow him down the hall. When we enter my room, everyone's heads turn from the window where they had been focused on the yard, waiting for the flame to return.

"How's Mom?" Debbie asks. Her eyes widen when she sees Michael behind me. "Michael! What just happened?"

"Your mother is sleeping comfortably in the den, oblivious to what has transpired here tonight. As for your other question, you might as well sit on the bed as I explain."

All four of us perch, sitting on the very edge. That's how we feel—on edge.

"What you saw tonight was a servant of Satan. Appearing as a flame, he has been tracking the book since the episode at the lake. He followed the grace of God to your house—to the shed, specifically. You saw what happened. When the servant failed to find the book, he cast around, searching for the trail. But as I've told you, this house is protected from evil. He couldn't follow the trail here. He was diligent in his work for the prince of darkness, but he has failed. His pain and suffering will be multiplied tonight in consequence for his failure.

"But do not entertain any thought that this is over. Satan has thousands upon thousands of servants who can take his place. I am here to tell you that this is only the beginning. Much more will occur before this night is over. You must be vigilant. Do not leave the house. Above all, do not take the Book of Life beyond the doors of this house. Your senses will be attacked and you will struggle to discern what is real from what is not. Do not be overcome by your emotions. Stop to judge truth from falsehood. Always remember that when Lucifer lies, he is speaking his native tongue."

"What about Mom?" Debbie asks.

"She will sleep the sleep of the innocent. Do not worry about her."

"Should we stay together or go back to our rooms?" Matt asks.

"There is always strength in numbers. Your combined strength is far greater than you realize. Use it and trust in it. But your trust in the Lord your God will be the foundation of your success."

"How do we use the strength we've gained from the book?" I ask. "We didn't realize it existed until now."

"You will know when and how as the need arises. Trust in the Lord. As new situations emerge, so will your ability. It will feel natural, even though there is nothing natural about it."

Leah is concentrating on taking deep, calming breaths—in and out, in and out. "Okay… what's next for us?"

"I am afraid that is in the hands of the prince of darkness," Michael says. "It is no mystery why this is happening at night. He rules in darkness. That is where he is most comfortable. Much can be hidden in the dark that cannot hide in the light. For years, he has been turning daylight to darkness, but he is still more at ease in the dark. Although I am here to help you in this time of trouble, the task is yours. I will not interfere unless there is a need."

"How about right now?" Matt exclaims. "I think we need all the help we can get!"

I put my hand on my friend's shoulder. "Come on, Matt, we haven't really had to do anything but watch out a window. Michael says that we have the power in us to protect the book. We should trust God. We're going to have to step up! I know it's not going to be easy, but how can we fail with God on our side?"

Leah nods solemnly. "James is right, Matt. God gave us this task, and with Him we will do it! Remember—one for all, and all for God. We can't lose."

"That's right, Leah," Debbie cheers. "One for all, and all for God!"

"I am being called away, but I will return soon," Michael says. "Do not fear, for the Lord is with you."

And then he is gone.

"I think now would be a good time for prayer," I say.

Matt sighs loudly. "You've got that right, James!"

Bowing our heads and closing our eyes, we join hands.

"Heavenly Father, we come to You humbly in prayer," I begin. "We are Your servants and we know we have a task. We ask, dear Lord, that You give us the awareness to use that which You have given us to perform this task when the time is right. As in Your Word, dear Lord, each time You gave someone a task You also gave them the tools they needed to accomplish it. You have supplied us with everything we need. Lord, we now ask for Your help in using those gifts. We are Your children, but we are asked to stand against the prince of darkness and his evil. Give us the unwavering strength that only comes with true faith and love in You, Father. Guide us and protect us... and at last save us. We ask this in the name of Your Son, our Savior, Jesus Christ."

As I finish, we all open our eyes and lift our heads.

I feel a rumble—well, I hear it more than feel it—and it seems to get louder. We get up from the bed and crowd around the window. It's dark outside. And when I say dark, I mean it's darker than I've ever seen before.

In that darkness, leaves and branches fly by the window. As the rumble turns to a deep howl, the rain starts up again. It pelts the window mercilessly. From the groaning all around us, it feels as though the house might come apart.

Reaching out, I take Leah's hand. Without me saying anything, she takes Debbie's hand, and Debbie takes Matt's hand.

"Together now." I try to speak from the strength of my conviction, unifying us in common purpose. "Concentrate on the peace you felt in the book. Let it fill your mind and soul. Picture Jesus in the storm, calming the sea. Reach out and calm the storm as He did. God is with us. We can do this."

Not a word is said, but the overpowering noise around us lessens. The turbulent swirl of branches, leaves, and debris of all description falls off until the sky around the house is calm. A great peacefulness settles over us. Everything becomes quiet and still. No wind. No rain.

That's when I realize how tightly I have been gripping Leah's hand. I look down and loosen my hold a little. While I do, I notice her looking up at me. I smile and she returns it.

We both look over at Debbie and Matt and see that they are looking at us with odd expressions.

"Now we're sure why God wants you to lead, James," Matt says. "You acted when action was required. When you spoke, we listened. Then we all acted together. That was some of the power we received while we were in the book, the power to bring about peace and calm in the presence of turmoil. As a group, we turned back the storm!"

I nod to myself, but I also know we aren't done. What new calamity will soon make itself known?

"I guess we have to expect the unexpected," I say. "Satan must have a lot more in his bag of tricks. That wasn't even close to a test. I bet we won't have to wait very long either."

"I hope you're wrong, James," says Leah, "but I wouldn't bet against you."

Debbie is already pointing out the window. "You may be more right than you want to be..."

I perceive several sets of eyes looking in at us from the blackness. They seem to multiply by the second until our whole field of vision is nothing but staring eyes.

Leah squeaks but keeps herself from screaming. I tighten my grip on her hand and I'm pretty sure she does the same to Debbie, and Debbie to Matt.

"Nobody move," I say. "Let's just wait and see what they're up to. Stare back at them. They're just trying to shake us up and generate fear. Michael has said that evil feeds on fear. We have no reason to fear because God is with us and we are with Him."

"Let's pray as we stare them down," Matt suggests.

"It can't hurt," Debbie agrees. "I bet these things don't like prayer."

Matt begins a prayer. "Heavenly Father, give us the strength to stand up to these servants of Satan. Let us show them no fear. Give us the vision to see through their deceptions and lies."

As Matt continues in prayer, these myriad sets of eyes dart back and forth, seeming to get more agitated by the second. Suddenly, they stop moving and every one of them becomes intensely focused.

But they aren't focused on us.

I realize that they're staring straight towards the back of the room, up high, toward the top of the closet. They're focusing on the Book of Life, which is in plain view through the open closet door. If I can see its glow, I figure maybe they can too.

Letting go of Leah's hand, I jump up and lift the book down from its shelf. As soon as I have the book in my hands, though, I don't know what to do with it. Should I hide it? Should I take it out of the room, out of their sight?

Leah turns and watches me carefully.

"James, bring the book over here," she says in a very calm tone.

When I do, she pats the bed. I sit down beside her.

"Everyone, come and sit," she adds. "Now put the book here in the middle of us. Take my hand again. Matt, you take Debbie's hand. Now, James, put your free hand on the book—and Matt, you do the same. We'll form a circle with the book being part of it."

We all do what she says and suddenly feel a rush of tranquility settle over us.

At the same time, we hear a shriek outside, the same kind of sound as when the flame was consuming the dresser and finding it empty—only this time, the sound is a lot louder.

The eyes seem to press hard toward the window, but it looks as though they've already gotten as close as they can come. They aren't able to get any closer than six feet from the glass.

As I watch, the pupils of these eyes all turn to flame, growing brighter as the shriek grows louder. Ordinarily we'd have to cover our ears, but that would cause us to break the circle. And for some reason we seem to be protected from the horrendous clamor. We are enveloped in the tranquility of the book and the peace of God.

The noise reaches a peak and the eyes begin to vibrate. Then, without warning, they blink and disappear with a whoosh that sounds like a giant vacuum, sucking them away into another place.

Again, all is still. Nobody moves. Nobody speaks. We continue to hold each other's hands tightly, with the book sitting half on Leah's lap and half on Debbie's. I don't even know whether any of us are breathing.

I exhale, which brings me back to... what? Reality? But this isn't any reality I'm familiar with.

"That was intense," I say, looking around at the others. "Leah, what made you think of using the book as a link in the circle?"

"I don't know," she says. "It just came to me and felt like the right thing to do. Most of the time when we talk about divine providence, we're joking. But this was no joke."

"Do we dare break the circle now that those eyes are gone?" Matt asks. "Or should we stay here and wait for whatever comes next? Cuz you know there's gonna be a next."

"I'm in favor of just sitting here and waiting for a while," Debbie says. "I like this feeling anyway."

"While we wait, I think I'll go check on Mom," I say. "Michael said she's in the den. I know it breaks the circle, but I have to know that she's okay."

I take my hand off the book, let go of Leah's hand, and head downstairs.

As I get to the den, I find the door open a crack. Just as Michael said, Mom is lying on the couch sleeping like a baby all wrapped up in an afghan.

With a sigh of relief, I return to my bedroom.

"How is she?" Debbie asks.

"Just like Michael said. Sleeping like a baby. Anything happen here while I was gone?"

Matt is still staring out the window at the night sky. "Not a thing. Makes me a little nervous. It's too quiet."

"I almost wish something would happen," Leah whispers.

"I hope we don't regret those words," Debbie says. "You know that there's worse to come. James, why don't you sit back down and complete the circle again? I think it helped before... and it sure gives me a better sense of security."

"Okay, sis." I get back into position. "It would be a good time to go to God in prayer again, don't you think? Leah, you want to do the honors?"

We all bow our heads.

"Heavenly Father, we thank You for getting us through so much," Leah begins. "We know that the trials of this task are not over and we pray for the strength and wisdom to be successful in defeating the powers of darkness."

Before she can say another word, we hear a new sound—and this time, it's coming from inside the room. We all jump, startled, and turn towards the closet door, gripping each other's hands almost painfully.

There stands Michael.

"Don't do that," Matt almost shouts at him.

"My apologies. I am here to tell you that you are doing well in the eyes of the Lord. He has seen your efforts and is pleased. You are correct in your estimation that there is more to come and that what is to follow will be of increasing intensity as the prince of darkness attempts to instill fear in your hearts and division in your purpose. Remember above all things that the Book of Life must not be removed from this house or the results will be devastating for this and all generations to come. The Lord is with you and you are with the Lord. Continue with that faith, trust, and confidence and you will prevail. I will repeat that you must beware of deceptions, be they visual or spiritual or physical. Lucifer is committed to possessing the Book of Life and he does not consider four mere children as a threat to his objective. Trust in God. I must go once more."

"Couldn't you just stick—"

But Matt never gets to finish his sentence. Michael has already vanished and doesn't hear another word.

"I didn't think it would hurt to ask," Matt says.

I turn to Leah. "You want to continue in prayer?"

But her gaze is fixed on the window again, her eyes as big as hockey pucks. "Look at that!"

Outside the window, up in the darkness, I see a glowing ball of fire. It's spinning and growing. As it spins, smaller flames detach themselves and fly into the trees along the edge of the yard. Those trees burst into infernos, engulfed from top to bottom.

As the ball of fire grows, all we can see is fire. Then it splits into two fires, both continuing to grow and spit flames into the yard.

The main ball of fire splits again, creating a third spinning red and orange orb. All three of them rise higher into the sky and we have to lean forward to keep them all in sight of the window.

They stop high above where the shed used to stand. We hear the roar of the flames and feel the heat coming off these three suns hanging above the property. I sniff and detect the scent of sulfur and, I assume, brimstone. Even though I have no experience with brimstone, I associate it with Satan.

One of the balls suddenly breaks formation and plummets toward the ground, but not toward us. It passes over our house.

A second later, we hear an explosion.

"My house!" Leah gasps.

She tries to let go of my hand and get up, but I grip harder and won't let go.

"Nobody move!" I order. "The circle must not be broken. Leah, nobody's home there. Besides, there's nothing you can do. Take a deep breath and pray. Go to the book, God's Book of Life, and find peace and strength."

I feel the tension go out of Leah as she settles back onto the edge of the bed.

"Thank you, James," she whispers.

"Is everyone else okay?" I ask. "We still have two fireballs to deal with, so hang on. This isn't over yet."

We grip each other's hands and wait. The two remaining fireballs hang for a second and then separate, one moving to the north and the other to the south. Both remain within sight.

Without warning, they come crashing at the house. This time it's Debbie's turn to scream while the rest of us gasp. I'm glad Leah's not stronger than she is, or she probably would have broken the bones in my hand. We all brace for impact.

The fireballs strike simultaneously and erupt into a humungous shower of sparks. I don't think any of us breathe as we wait for the terrible effects of those fireballs to take hold. The following seconds feel like hours.

But nothing happens. And when we realize that we're safe, all four of us breathe in a lungful of air in synchrony.

"Did you see that?" Matt exclaims. "How are we not burnt to a crisp?"

"Have you forgotten who we serve and in whom we put our faith and trust?" Debbie speaks softly. "Come on, Matt, you know perfectly well how come we're still here. God is with us."

"I know, but you have to admit that was awesome," he says. "I know God is with us. I know that without Him we'd be toast right now. I know that we pray for His power, that He is the Almighty. We also know about the power of Satan, but did any of us ever think we'd see any of that power demonstrated right before our eyes? I know I never did. It makes me excited to see what's next!"

I give him a warning glance. "Be careful, Matt. You know that this isn't finished. In fact, it's probably gonna get worse, a lot worse, before it's over."

As though I've been in a daze, I shake myself and remember what just happened to Leah's house. Is it all right? There's only one way to find out, since we're not allowed to leave the house.

"Leah, why don't you come with me? The window in my parents' room looks out toward your place."

We both stand up, breaking the circle, and go out into the hall, hand in hand.

I open the door to my parents' bedroom and walk to the window. As we peer out into the darkness, Leah gasps and grips my hand hard.

Where her house once stood, there's nothing. When I say nothing, I mean nothing. Not even a single charred beam remains in the rubble… because there is no rubble. All that's left is a crater.

I feel her start to go limp and am forced to let go of her hand. I put my arm around her and ease her onto the bed to keep her from falling.

"Gone!" she cries out. "All gone!"

"I know…" I put my arm around her shoulder, trying to comfort her. "Be glad that your parents weren't home. Things could have been a lot worse."

She surprises me by quickly standing up straight, taking a deep breath, and looking me right in the eyes.

"Let's get back to the others," she says. "There's lots left to do."

With that she turns and leaves the room.

As I get up to follow her, I hear a scream: "James!"

Leah and I both rush back to my room, where Matt and Debbie are pointing out the window. As far as we can see, the ground in the back yard is turning to molten lava. The bubbling miasma is creeping toward the house slowly but steadily. I stare at the scene, transfixed. The earth is melting right before my eyes!

"What are we going to do?" Matt asks.

"Nothing," I tell him. "This isn't real. Do you feel the heat, like with the fireballs? This is different. It's meant to scare the daylights out of us—and it *is* scary—but remember what Michael said: Satan is the master of deception. This is a fake. Leah, let's complete the circle again and concentrate on prayer, the book, and the power of God."

Leah and I both join hands. As soon as we complete the circle, the volcanic scene outside the window disappears, replaced by a calm that makes us all nervous. We know something worse is coming.

Then it starts.

Outside I perceive a whirlwind, like a tornado, spin and kick up debris. It's as black as anything I've ever seen, and it's growing larger.

I squint. I can almost make out something solid at the center, but it's impossible to be certain with all the turbulent air swirling around it.

"Everyone remain sitting with your hands joined!" I say. "Keep the circle complete!"

As we watch the maelstrom grow more intense, I can't help but wonder: where this is going to take us?

The tornado stops growing and even seems to slow down. As it slows, I can make out a figure at its center. It looks like a person, dressed in a black cloak with a hood. It reminds me of an old vampire movie, with the villain rising out of the ground amid swirling mist with his head down, buried in a majestic collar that hides his appearance.

The tornado's rotation stops and it suddenly disappears, leaving behind the man standing in the midst of it. My gaze is riveted on him as his head rises and I get a look at his face, shrouded by the hood. I expect a gruesome, fear-inspiring visage meant to inspire fear and terror.

Instead I find myself looking into the kindly countenance of an elderly gentleman.

TWENTY-TWO

"James, Debbie, Matt, and Leah... I would like to introduce myself," the grandfatherly man begins. "I am the much-maligned Lucifer. Today we are at odds over what is known as the Book of Life. I would like to possess that book and I understand you have been given the task of preventing that from happening. I would like to reason with you and explain my purpose for the book when it is in my possession.

"As you know, when the Book of Life is opened everything as we know it will end and all whose names are not found in its the pages will begin an eternity of pain and suffering. Do you want to be responsible for countless millions, even billions, of people being put to suffering and pain for all of eternity? What if some of those people are your friends or relatives—or even worse, your parents? If I possess the book, I can guarantee that this will never take place. The world of mankind will continue. Although there will still be death, there will never be judgment! Why? Because the Word of God you studied says that judgment will not occur until the Book of Life is opened. If you give me the Book of Life, all that eternal pain and suffering can be avoided. Imagine the souls you will save from eternal torment.

"Turning over the book to me will also give those whose names are not in the Book of Life an opportunity to change their lives. The time is near for the book to be opened and there are so many whose names are not found in it. If I am in possession of the book, there will be ages yet to come with so much opportunity for change—change that you will have given them time to make.

"We must be quick with the decision, for the Lord will want His pound of flesh. The rewards for you will be great in this life, and life will be beyond all imagination if you comply with my wishes. Embrace life. Avoid eternal pain and suffering for multitudes. Show love for your fellow man. Give me the book!"

Leah is the first to respond.

"I just looked out at what used to be my home," she almost screams. "There's nothing left."

She lets go of my hand and releases her hold on the book and stands up. She steps up to the window and shakes her little fist as though in a threat to do violence to this epitome of evil.

"You're right when you say that we've been given the task of keeping the Book of Life out of your hands," she continues. "But you failed to mention that we have been given that task by God Almighty, the Creator of heaven and earth."

Leah pauses to catch her breath, but she's not done.

"We've studied the scriptures relating to the Book of Life and have come to a basic knowledge of what it is and appreciating its place in God's plan," she adds. "We have been inside the book and know how it feels there—peace and tranquility without any hint of pain or suffering. Your plea on behalf of those whose names are not found in the book is meant to melt our hearts, isn't it? Can we help those poor souls by giving the Book of Life to you? I think not! Who is responsible for those names not being in the book in the first place? Isn't it your fault that souls succumb to the temptations you put in their paths? You do it just to keep their names out of the Book of Life! The millions and billions who will suffer eternal pain and suffering falls on your shoulders, not ours—and certainly not God's.

"We have a saying: misery loves company. Well, you love to see souls in misery... because you are in misery. You, sir, are the definition of misery. Just because we're young doesn't mean we're gullible. Your attempt to convince us that judgment day is close at hand is lost on anyone who has read in God's Word what His Son Jesus Christ had to say. The end will come like a thief in the night. Not even the Son knows when it will happen, only the Father. I doubt that God the Father would take you into his confidence before His own Son. In fact, I know He wouldn't. Besides, prolonging the final judgment only gives you more time to steal more souls from their heavenly reward.

"We will embrace life, but it will be a life serving our heavenly Father and living as Christlike as we can. Your rewards and promises are nothing compared with what is offered to the children of God whose names are found in the Book of Life. We have felt the joy and peace of the book, and that's just a taste of what is to come after the book is opened. God offers this to all who live by His Word, all who accept His Son. You say that we should avoid pain and suffering. What is a little pain and suffering in this lifetime compared to an eternity of suffering on account of listening to you?"

With that, Leah throws her hands in the air and sits back down beside me, the whole time not breaking eye contact with the figure standing out in the yard.

"I will give you a short time to discuss my proposal and return for your answer," Lucifer says. "Do not dismiss what I have said. There will be dire consequences for refusal."

Just as we've seen Michael do, the prince of darkness vanishes from view.

"That was quite the speech, Leah," Matt says.

"Yeah!" Debbie cheers. "You go, girl!"

I smile at her. "I'm impressed, Leah. Talk about take no prisoners! He said he was going to give us some time to talk this over, but is there any need? Giving this proposal any thought at all just seems like a waste of time to me."

"A total nonstarter," Matt puts in. "Leah called him on all his lies."

"I think we better brace for the next round of whatever he throws at us," Debbie adds. "That was probably the last time we'll see any nicey-nice from Mr. Lucifer. Did you get a load of how he tried to deceive us? Grandfatherly! Phah, what a joke."

"You're right, sis," I say. "I think things are gonna turn ugly again. Most likely they'll get worse than ever. Anyone need to use the bathroom before we get busy?"

No one seems to need the break, although we do let go of each other's hands and allow ourselves to relax a little.

"I think a group hug is in order," Matt suggests.

Without a word being said, we all stand to do just that.

"Just a minute, something is missing," Debbie says.

She turns and lifts the Book of Life off the bed and places it where it belongs, in the middle of our embrace. Immediately we feel a change. The tension in the air and in our bodies and minds fades away. It's like we're drawing strength from the book. It feels good.

"I wonder where Michael has been through all this?" I ask.

As though on cue, Michael appears. "I have been observing, James."

His sudden arrival just about makes me jump out of my skin. Turning, I see Michael standing in front of the open closet again.

"I told you before, don't do that!" Matt says, raising his voice.

"With what the four of you have been through tonight, I did not think my appearance would startle you," Michael says. "I must say, I have been impressed with the way you handle yourselves. By the way, Leah, my condolences on the loss of your home."

"No one was hurt," she says. "That's the important thing. But thank you."

"Are you going to stay around for the next onslaught?" Matt asks.

Michael nods. "I am always 'around,' as you say. Even though you may not see me or feel my presence, I am there. I do not want to reveal myself to Satan, though. He would change his tactics if he knew I was here. The less he is aware, the better it is for all. Again I will stress that your opponent is the master of lies and deception. When he speaks to you, you must look beyond that which he reveals to determine the truth. Nothing is sacred to him. He will use against you any weakness he perceives. Continue to pray. The Lord hears your pleas. Remain strong in your faith and always trust in the Lord, for He is with you. I will leave you now. May God continue to bless you."

And then he's gone, just as quick as he came.

"It's nice to know that he's around, but I'd feel better if he was standing by my side." Matt says.

"I don't think any of us would disagree," Debbie adds. "But God gave this task to us. With His help, we can and will do what the Lord our God wants us to do."

Leah smiles at her friends. "We were tasked with this assignment and we will see it through to the end. I lost my home, but Satan can't take away my soul— that is, unless I give it to him. And I'm not going to let that happen."

"One for all, and all for God! Right, Leah?" I say. "You have our backs and we have yours. Let's get comfortable, join hands again, and go to our Father."

We take hands and reform the circle.

This time, Debbie takes the lead. "Heavenly Father, we are so thankful for the many blessings You have given us. Even this task we have been given is a blessing, Lord. Who else has been blessed with a personal task from God on high? We pray, dear Lord, that You continue to bless our efforts as evil tries to overcome us. Help us to bar the door and shutter the windows so the darkness will be kept out and Jesus Christ, the Truth, the Life, and the Way, will shine upon us through this time of trouble…"

The sound of turbulent wind causes her to trail off. We open our eyes to see that same tornado, the one that announced the first arrival of the prince of darkness.

The same ritual produces the same result. Within a moment, Lucifer stands before us, once again in the guise of an elderly man.

"I have returned for your decision," he says. "Be very careful with your answer. I have tried to give you all the positive reasons for why I should possess the Book of Life. I have warned you of the dire consequences of denying me. They are considerable. To say they are unpleasant would not do them justice. However, the advantages of accepting my offer will have wondrous, far-reaching rewards."

He turns to face me directly.

"I await your answer, James."

I stand and face him squarely. "I think Leah gave you our answer when we last parted company. We are servants of the Lord God and we do His work. We have been inside the Book of Life and have experienced the majesty, love, and peace that envelops the souls found there. We will not give up the book to you or any of the demons in your service. God will decide when the Book of Life is opened and the Word is accomplished. It will be then and only then. This is our decision. To put it in old English, 'Get thee gone, Satan!'"

As we watch, Lucifer's peaceful old grandfather countenance begins to transform. His skin brightens into a distinct shade of red and his eyes turn to fire. Smoke rises from the collar of his cloak and horns sprout from the top of his head. He is, indeed, evil incarnate.

A blast of dark and evil energy slams the house and shakes it to its foundation.

"You dare defy me?" roars Satan. "You have no idea of the wrath you have just called down upon your heads! Prepare to meet the horrors of hell and to meet the spawn of the damned! There will be no mercy. There will be only pain and suffering. I am Lucifer and no one stands against me. You are mere mortals, puny children, and you think you can say no to me?"

"We just did!" Matt shouts. "Now get lost!"

With another blast, the house shakes again. We watch with wide eyes as the tornado surrounds Satan and grows in power and intensity. The shrieks rise in volume—

—and then it all stops. No wind, no noise, no Satan. Quiet!

Too quiet. We all know something bad is coming.

I look down and notice Leah's white knuckles as she grips my hand.

"You can relax your grip a little." I'm trying to lighten the moment. "I'm starting to lose the feeling in my hand."

"That goes for you too, Debbie," Matt says.

"Well, let's just ease up," I say. "We don't want to let our guard down even for a second. We've been promised hell on earth and I'm sure that's what's coming. We won't leave this room for any reason. We have to keep the circle unbroken. Prayer wouldn't hurt, though…"

We're all in the process of closing our eyes when the world outside erupts into hideous howls and blood-curdling screams. To accompany those sounds, creatures appear out of the wind and fly at the window, creatures the likes of which we've never seen. Bolts of lightning shatter against the window as scene after scene of the suffering of mankind flashes in front of us. Obscenities are screamed, the filth and depravity of mankind exhibited before us.

I've never seen a horror movie with special effects that could match what's being thrown at us.

The grip on my hand resumes its circulation-interrupting pressure.

"Everybody, shut your eyes," I instruct. "Do your best to shut out the sound!"

"Heavenly Father, give us strength," Matt prays. "Give us endurance. Father, protect Your children from the assault on our souls from the prince of darkness and his hordes. Help us, dear Lord, to retreat into the Book of Life and remove ourselves from this onslaught of evil."

As he prays, we all drift to that exact place—inside the book, where there is no pain or suffering, no fear and certainly no evil.

"Thank You, Father, for the safety of the book. May it never fall into the wrong hands. Help us to protect it with our very lives if necessary. We are Yours, dear Lord. Please guide us and protect us, and at last save us. This we pray in the precious name of Your Son and our Savior, Jesus Christ. Amen."

I open my eyes to stare into the blackness. The demons and their opera have gone and Leah's grip has relaxed again. I turn to her and see nothing but peace glowing from her face. She is still in the book, as are Debbie and Matt. Not wanting to disturb their few moments of peace, I close my eyes and join them.

I don't know how long we remain in that state of peace, but I'm brought back by the tightening of Leah's grip again. Opening my eyes, I see what new tension has brought this on.

In the darkness, I perceive a finger reaching towards us, and not just any finger. It is a finger of flame. As we watch, it writes a message against the darkened sky as though it were chalk on a blackboard.

You have shown bravery. Let us test your love!

"What does that mean?" Debbie asks with concern.

"I don't know," I say. "But I don't like the sounds of it."

Leah points. "I don't think we're going to have to wait long to find out. Something is happening out there…"

I narrow my eyes and make out the early signs of a swirling mist. Like the tornado before it, the mist becomes a whirlwind with something at its center. Is it another figure?

As the mist settles, though, I am momentarily filled with horror. The figure is none other than my dad—and his face is twisted in pain.

Debbie gasps and Matt and Leah seem to be in shock. We can't help it. Debbie and I jump to our feet and go to the glass. Matt and Leah, understanding why, get up and join us so we can reestablish the circle.

"James and Debbie, your father is in my hands," the voice of Lucifer proclaims. "He has already received punishment for your failure to comply with my wishes. Do you wish to see him suffer more at the hands of my loyal followers? They enjoy inflicting pain and have had centuries of practice perfecting their craft. Let me demonstrate."

The voice of Satan booms in the darkness.

Suddenly, Dad doubles over. Then, some unseen force straightens him up and lifts his body off the ground. His head tips back and he screams as fire erupts from his eyes and mouth.

"Make it stop!" he pleads, sobbing.

Again he screams as the fire burns.

"James, we have to do something!" Debbie cries. "We can't let him suffer like that."

Before I can answer, Satan answers us—this time in a quiet, calm voice.

"You know what it is I want. It is the only thing that will stop the suffering you are causing your father. Bring me the Book of Life. Bring it to me now and the torture stops. For every second you make me wait, he will be subjected to increasingly agonizing pain."

"Debbie, I know it's Dad, but we can't give that evil creature the book," I insist. "Over and over we've been told that our task is to keep the Book of Life safe. Under no circumstances can it fall into Satan's grasp. I know Dad and you know Dad. What would he want us to do? You know what he would want! It's not fair to ask a couple of teenagers to make a decision like this, but we have to. The answer has to be no."

"I know." Debbie breaks into tears and shakes from sobbing.

I take a deep breath as I prepare myself to give Satan an answer. Dad is hanging in the air, his head down as blood pours from his eyes and mouth.

This is hard. I feel Leah tighten her grip on my hand as she leans a supportive shoulder against mine.

All right, here it goes.

"The Lord God Almighty gave us this book to protect and to keep out of your hands," I announce. "My father is a man of great faith and will understand that the will of God must triumph over anything else on earth or in heaven or hell. You will not receive the Book of Life from us."

With that, I close my eyes and pray that God in His mercy will intervene and save my dad. I know that Debbie, Matt, and Leah are doing the same thing.

"You have asked for this," Satan replies. "It falls upon your shoulders, James. Prepare to see the consequences of your refusal."

A flash of light forces me to slam my eyes shut—and when I open them again, I see all of our parents suspended in the air in the middle of the yard alongside Dad. They're hanging in front of us with expressions of pain etched on their faces. Demons appear out of thin air and begin to dance around them, prodding them with tridents tipped with flame. Each prod brings forth a scream. Fire erupts from their eyes and mouths.

Matt and Leah freeze in a state of terror. I know what's going through their minds. Debbie and I just went through it with Dad, and now Mom is out there too.

Wait a minute! The last time I saw Mom, she was sound asleep in the den.

"I have to go check something," I say in a rush. "It won't take long. I'll be right back. Just pray until I come back, okay?"

All I get are nods. Besides, I suspect that if any of them were to try to speak it would only come out as blubbering gibberish.

I let go of Leah's hand and place it on the book. "This will keep the circle intact. Be right back."

Getting up, I head downstairs and make my way in the dark to the den. I lean on the door casing and look toward the couch.

Tears well up in my eyes. My prayers have been answered.

Turning, I run back upstairs and retake my place beside Leah. I squeeze her hand.

"I think I've found the answer," I whisper just loud enough for Matt and Debbie to hear as well. "Don't say a word. There's something going on that doesn't make sense."

Keeping my voice at a whisper, I tell them about Mom—that she's sleeping like a baby in the den.

"How can that be? She's out there suffering at the hands of those demons," Debbie quietly sobs.

"Who is the master of deception and Illusion? How many times has Michael warned us about that?" I remind everyone.

I refocus my attention back on the tragedy playing out in the yard. The cries of pain are hard to make out and rest heavily on our hearts, even though we know that it's not really our parents out there. It's so hard to watch.

"Just play along," I whisper. "I have a plan."

I turn toward the window and raise my voice.

"Satan!"

"Yes, James. Have you finally come to your senses? What is it you want? Do you want your parents to continue suffering? You know my only condition. Bring me the book!"

"I have a condition of my own. Send my mother to us as a show of good faith and we will consider your request."

"My request is non-negotiable, James. Send me the book or the suffering continues. In fact, it will accelerate!"

"Hear me and hear me good. Unless my mom comes through the front door of this house, you will never see the Book of Life, let alone possess it. Do I make myself clear!"

Debbie looks frantic, but I just put a finger to my lips. She knows to trust me.

Satan holds up a hand. "I can see, James, that you are the voice of reason in your group. I will consider your request and stop the suffering while I do so."

The demons abruptly stop their torture. The bodies of our parents hang limply in midair, unmoving. At least they're no longer writhing and screaming.

"What's going on, James?" Leah asks.

"I know what I'm doing," I reply. "I think."

Matt's eyes bulge in frustration. "You think! What do you mean, you *think*!"

"Shush," I hiss at him. "Whispering only. I'm not sure how much he can hear, but I don't want to take any chances."

Leah turns and looks toward the closet. "Where is Michael? Please, God, help us! Send Michael and the angels to put an end to this."

There is a flash of light outside and Satan reappears.

"I will grant your condition, James. Your mother will come to you. Bring the Book of Life to your front door when you meet her."

"What are we doing, James?" Matt nervously asks. "Fill us in. What's the plan?"

"I know this might be a little nerve-wracking. Just have a little faith." I look towards the door and the hallway beyond. "Now, we'll all have to get down to the front door together, and we have to do it without breaking contact with the book. That's important. I don't know why. I just know that it is."

I stand up and the others do the same.

"Debbie, you and Leah keep the book between you. Keep one hand under it and the other hand overtop. Matt and I will place our hands with your hands, one on top and one under. Okay? Let's do this. God, give us strength."

In a smooth, fluid motion, we all get up and slowly make our way to the top of the stairs.

"We're going to pull a little deception of our own on Mr. Lucifer," I explain as we walk. "We're going to let him think he has us and then pull the rug out from under him. I know it might sound a little dangerous, but I think it's time we got back at him a little."

Everyone nods, but I've got to say they aren't very enthusiastic nods.

Step by step, we head down the stairs.

Once at the bottom, I lead them down the hall and through the living room. When we get to the den, I gently push the door open so they all can see the same thing I saw earlier—the image of Mom sleeping soundly on the couch, wrapped in an afghan and oblivious to all the chaos around us.

I place my index finger to my lips, calling for silence, and then point toward the front door.

"Here goes nothing," I say as I turn the handle and ease the door open.

Outside in the darkness we see the suspended bodies of our parents. Ever so slowly, Mom's body settles to the ground. Instead of collapsing, though, she takes a tentative and unsteady step in our direction, followed by another faltering step, and then another. Each step looks agonizing.

The other parents start to plead. "Take me instead! Take me, please…"

"What do we do?" whispers Leah.

"We stick with the plan," I tell her. "God is with us."

As Mom gets to the front steps, she stops. We can all see that she looks terrible.

"Don't you move a muscle," I command to the others. "We have to stick together. None of us can step outside this house. Understand?"

I look this apparition in the eyes. "Mom, come up on the steps. Come in so we can look after you."

The ghostly woman lifts her head and puts her foot on the first step. But as she takes that step, she stumbles and almost falls. I feel Debbie tense and know how much she wants to step out and help, even though she knows it's not really Mom. So do I. This feels so real.

But we hold our ground.

"Take another step, Mom."

She does… but then she stumbles again. A mixtures of tears and blood are streaming down her face, and it's incredibly hard to watch.

"Just one more step, Mom. We've got you."

She smiles a little as she tops the steps…

And then it happens. In a moment, she transforms from the mother Debbie and I love into a hideous creature that lunges at us. Its arms stretch forward to snatch the book from our hands, but it hits some sort of invisible wall and disintegrates into a puff of black mist, its shriek sucked into the void.

"Shut the door, Matt!" I yell.

Slamming the door, Matt turns to me along with the rest. "What in blazes was that?"

"Before I answer, let's go back upstairs. And remember, keep your hands on the book."

Making our way back to my room, we return to our positions on the bed and maintain the circle. Outside the window, we can't see anything but darkness.

"What just happened, James?" Leah demands.

For a moment, I just close my eyes and thank God for the discernment to tell truth from Satan's deceptions.

"Seeing our parents being tortured, I was in just as much agony as the rest of you," I say. "It was tearing me apart! But then I remembered what Michael said. Our house is a sanctuary. How could Satan have gotten his hand on Mom? She couldn't be in two places at the same time. Satan was pulling a scam—and he was desperate enough to take my bait. I proved he's a liar. I'm just glad I had the guidance of the Almighty. Prayers of thanks are in order."

We all bow our heads and go to God in prayer. We each express our own personal gratitude to the Father for getting us through such a time of horror. We can feel that the nightmare is finally behind us. We also ask for the continued grace to finish the task He has given us, for we are prepared to do what needs to be done to honor our Father in heaven.

"Amen," I say aloud when I finish. This is followed closely by a chorus of amens.

As we gaze at each other in the aftermath of our trial, I'm surprised that we don't look as though we've been through a battle. It would be an understatement to say it's been a night of stress. We work to settle ourselves, drawing deep, calming breaths.

"I can't think of anything Satan could throw at us that would be worse than what we just went through," Matt says. "If it hadn't been for your quick thinking, I don't know where we would have ended up."

Leah lowers in head. "I do, Matt. We would have had to sacrifice our parents in order to keep the Book of Life out of his hands. The love of God has to come first. We all knew that when we agreed to take on this task. Nothing has changed." She looks up and smiles. "All for one, but first and foremost, all for God."

"We knew what we had to do and were prepared to do it," I agree. "It sounds harsh, but so did God's request when He asked Abraham to sacrifice Isaac. God gave Abraham a way out when push came to shove, just like He gave us a way out tonight."

"Look out!" Matt interrupts. "Here we go again…"

I follow his gaze out the window, feeling Leah's grip tightening again. I brace myself for the unknown, feeling a measure of surprise that it isn't over.

Out of the darkness, the face of Satan fills the sky.

"You have won this battle, but by no means is this war over," Satan says. "My thirst for the Book of Life is stronger than ever and I will not relent until I have possession of it. Your days will not be days of rest, because I will seek your downfall until your time on the earth is done. I will not rest until your names are blotted out of the Book of Life and you are mine. In fact, you have given me a weapon I did not possess before. For that I am grateful. But that gratitude does not quench my hatred for being foiled and made a fool of this night. We will meet again, and it will not be a time for you to celebrate."

As before, he disappears.

"Does that mean we're done for tonight?" Matt asks tentatively.

"Sounds like it," Debbie says.

I purse my lips. "That's the way it seems to me. How is everyone?"

Leah doesn't say a word. She just leans against me, turns her head to my shoulder, and cries.

"It's okay, Leah. I think it's over." I put my hand on the back of her head to comfort her.

Leah wipes away her tears. "These aren't tears of sadness, James. They're tears of relief."

EPILOGUE

"What do we do now?" Matt asks as we grapple with everything we've just witnessed. "If it's over, how long do we wait before going back outside?"

"My my, Matt, you certainly are full of questions!" The voice has come from the corner of the room, nearest the closet.

We all turn and find Michael standing before us once again.

"It is over, first and foremost," Michael says. "Your task is complete as far as the Book of Life is concerned. There will be future concerns due to your relationship with the book, but I will enlighten you about those later. For now, I can assure you that nothing more will happen in the near future. You have done as the Lord your God has asked and kept the Book of Life safe. You performed that task much better than even I expected. Throughout the ordeal, I never had to get involved. For that, I am very thankful.

"Your parents were never in jeopardy. Angels were guarding their safety. When Lucifer tried to use them, his demons were repelled. Your faith and theirs made this possible. You see, their names are written in the Book of Life as well.

"You may not be aware, but you have stood against powers you have read about before. The numerous eyes staring through the window belonged to Legion, the demon our Lord Jesus Christ drove out of the demon-possessed man described in Mark 5. Legion, if you remember, was sent into a herd of swine that ran into a lake and drowned. That herd was about two thousand strong! Legion wasn't killed, though. He was sent back to where he came from to await his master's next command.

"As for the demons that tortured the images of your parents, these are the same seven demons that were driven from Mary Magdalene in Luke 8.

"But enough about what *has* happened. Let us instead focus on what *will* happen. The Book of Life is now returning to my protection. You have done what is right in the eyes of the Lord. Because of your faith, trust, and love of the

GREG MAHER

Lord, the consequences of your decision to stand against the prince of darkness were not severe. All will be reversed. Everything will be as it was before the events of this night."

"You mean my house wasn't destroyed?" Leah asks, sounding hopeful.

Michael shakes his head. "Although your house was destroyed, it has now been restored by the power of He who made the world, the sun, the moon, and the stars. You may see for yourself."

"Oh, thank you!" All the stress of the night drains from Leah's face. "Thank you, thank you, thank you!"

She runs from the room and crosses the hall to my parents' bedroom.

"It's there!" she calls back to us. "It looks just like it always has. Thank You, God!"

As I turn my attention back to the window, I see that the shed is intact again, without so much as a scorch mark on it. The trees and the grass don't look any the worse for wear either.

"Well, that's a couple more things to be thankful for Michael," I murmur.

Debbie is sitting very quietly, and it makes me nervous.

"What's up, big sister?" I ask. "You look deep in thought."

My sister turns to Michael. "You said you would enlighten us about some future concerns related to our relationship with the Book of Life. I'm curious what that means."

"It is time to tell you of the future," Michael says. "You have made a formidable enemy this night and he will never forget the humiliation of having been bested by four young people—children, in his eyes. But you stand head and shoulders above any children. For that matter, you stand head and shoulders over most adults, of this and any other age. Although these events will never be written about, you stand in the same category as David, who slew Goliath in the service of the Lord.

"Lucifer will turn his attention to your lives. You have told him that you have been inside the Book of Life, giving him another reason to focus on you. You saw the names, even if you didn't understand them. Satan values that information. He wants to identify these souls so he can target them while they still live. His only pleasure is in stealing souls from our heavenly Father. It's his only way to cause God sorrow. And he now thinks the four of you possess those names—if not in your conscious minds, then in your subconscious. In revenge he would be only too happy to rip your minds apart, both your conscious and subconscious. You must be ever-vigilant, for he is tireless, always looking for weakness. He will

210

place temptations before you the rest of your days. I fear the four of you will receive his special attention."

Matt grimaces. "Oh, you're just a bundle of good news."

"What should we do?" Debbie asks.

"We do what all people do," Leah says. "We love the Lord our God with everything we are, with everything we have, and we love our neighbor as we love ourselves."

Michael inclines his head toward her. "Well said, Leah. If you can do those two things, your walk with Christ will be complete."

We all smile at Leah.

"Previously, Debbie asked about guardian angels and I did not give an answer," Michael says. "All four of you will have guardian angels hovering nearby for the rest of your lives. The Lord God knows that your battle with Satan will take on a more intense flavor because of this task you have done for Him. For that reason, He is providing additional help as your lives unfold."

Our smiles grow even wider as we consider the implications of this announcement.

"I must leave you again," the angel continues. "This may be the last time our paths cross. It has been a pleasure and a privilege to have met you and to have seen your faith and obedience."

I get up off the bed and take a step toward him. "Before you go, I have a request."

"What is it, James?"

"Could we visit the book one last time?" I ask.

"Your request will be granted. Put your hands on its cover and close your eyes."

We do as Michael has asked and immediately are overwhelmed by that indescribable, all-consuming feeling once more. With no idea of how much time has passed, we eventually feel the reality of the world around us again. It comes far too soon.

Opening our eyes, we find that Michael is gone—and so is the Book of Life.

"Kids, come on down," Mom calls from downstairs. "Your father's home."

THE END

ABOUT THE AUTHOR

Greg Maher was born and grew up in Halifax, Nova Scotia. He moved to rural N.S. early in his married life. He is now retired and finds the time to commune with nature and God's Word. That time has also allowed him to return to the passion of his youth and that is writing. His writing reflects his upbringing, his faith, and the love he has and receives from God and family.

He is now an elder in the church and enjoys bringing inspirational messages to the small congregation. His poetry fills a need to express his faith and reach out to others. His first book, a book of poetry to sooth the soul, *I Sat Down With My Father* was published by Word Alive Press in 2022. This is his first novel. He has another book of poetry ready for publication and is currently working on a sequel to the novel *Few Are Chosen*.

ALSO BY GREG MAHER

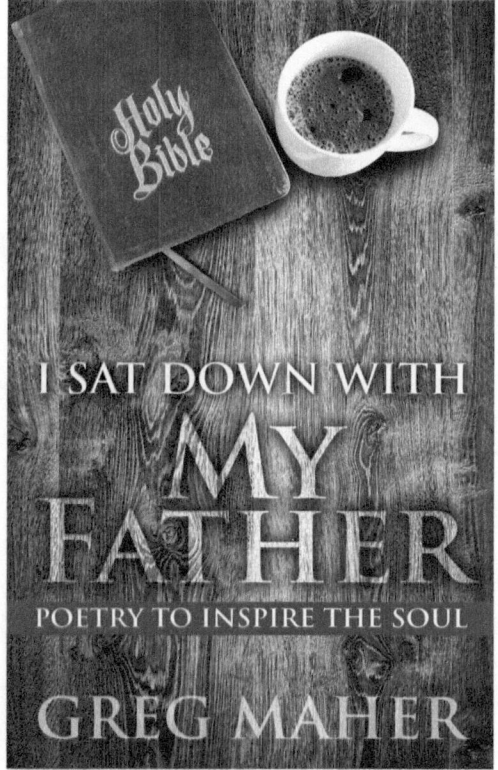

ISBN: 978-1-4866-2273-3

Poetry is the language of love, and God is the greatest author of love. The pages of this book are my heart's attempt to put God's love into words. In these words, I pray that you will find the love that I have felt throughout the years, that you will see and perhaps even feel the presence of our Heavenly Father, or that you will be intrigued to investigate beyond my words and delve into God's Word.

Seek Christ, and you will find Him, for He is seeking you.